DIVING UNDER

DIVING UNDER

A SPARK OF LIFE NOVEL, BOOK ONE

by

GINNA MORAN

ISBN 978-1-942073-74-1 (soft cover)
ISBN 978-1-942073-76-5 (epub ebooks)

Cover design by Silver Starlight Designs
Cover images copyright Depositphotos
Fonts: Ostrich Sans, Adobe Garamond Pro, Love Moon, and Linna

For Inquiries Contact:
Sunny Palms Press
9663 Santa Monica Blvd Suite 1158
Beverly Hills, CA 90210, USA
www.sunnypalmspress.com
www.GinnaMoran.com

WELCOME ABOARD THE OCEAN JEWEL

CRISP SEA AIR BLOWS STRANDS of my blond hair across my face, veiling the view of the Ocean Jewel, the luxury yacht I'll be calling home for the next week. The three decked, two hundred and fifty-seven foot monster of a boat waits at the end of a long dock in the middle of Azure Waters' harbor with dozens of other boats around it, none of which are comparable in size or extravagance. I'm the last one on the dock, standing in the dead center as the deep, blue-green ocean surrounds me only feet away.

From twenty feet ahead, my best friend, Giselle Nash,

waves a hand over her head, trying to grab my attention. When I don't move, she drops her bag in front of a man in a dark blue blazer and khakis—one of the crew members—and jogs my way without glancing at the dock beneath her. I tense, imagining her tripping on the wooden beams and falling into the sea, but she makes it to me without a problem.

She stops a foot away, placing her hands on my shoulders, and stares at me with her amber eyes. "You can't change your mind, Ava. We're already here, and if you turn around now, you'll regret it. Look at that thing." She points to the yacht. "We're not traveling to sea in a rowboat."

She's right. Yet I still can't suppress the fear that freezes me in place. You'd think that after all this time I wouldn't be so afraid of the ocean. It's been nearly eight years since the accident that swept my older sister away and left me almost drowned. I'll never forget the silent look of terror on Bailey's face as the ocean current broke us apart moments before she disappeared under.

"So, are you coming or not?" Giselle asks, shaking my shoulders, forcing me to draw my attention away from the yacht.

I open my mouth to say, "not" but instead, I say, "Yeah, just give me a minute."

With a deep sigh, my best friend spins on her heels. Her bronze hair flies behind her, and she skips down the dock and back to where our group of friends waits for what's supposed to be the best adventure of the year, thanks to Sapphire King's eighteenth birthday, an obnoxiously large trust fund from her grandma, and as a gift to all of us for graduation.

When the others climb the ramp to enter the deck, I finally find the nerve to start walking. My bag hangs heavy in my fingers, but before I make it halfway to the yacht, a boy my age, wearing the same blue blazer and khakis as the other crew members, jogs to my side to take it from me.

He meets my eyes with a smile that manages to ease my fear of the ocean enough to where my legs no longer tremble. I really needed this incredibly hot distraction. Scruff covers his handsome face, his skin bronzed with a deep tan gorgeous enough that someone like me, who doesn't get much sun, would pay a lot for.

"First time out to sea, huh?" he asks, amusement lining his eyes.

"That obvious? I haven't even been in the water since I was a kid," I say.

I expect him to ask why and get ready to tell him the same story everyone in Azure Waters already knows. But he doesn't say anything. Instead, the boy offers his free arm to me, and I take it, hooking my hand around the sinewy muscles of his forearm.

"I wasn't even going to come, but my best friend basically threatened me—mostly with a good time," I add to fill the silence.

His smile widens as he glances at me in the side of his vision. "I can promise she's right. The Ocean Jewel speaks true to her name. I even have fun, and I'm on the job."

As we reach the ramp that'll take us onto the Ocean Jewel, I slow down. Everyone has boarded, and no one waits for me. They're probably already heading to their staterooms or exploring the upper decks. Apparently, the sundeck contains a hot tub and pool, according to Sapphire.

This is my last chance to turn away and run when none of my friends are looking. I wouldn't even have to explain myself for a few days, and by then, they'll all have moved on.

As I start to turn away, the boy blocks my path. "Why don't you board before you make the decision to bail? We won't leave port for another twenty minutes or so. You can change your mind if you hate it. And if it makes you feel any better, I'm an excellent ocean swimmer and diver. We've never had a single person fall overboard, either."

"And I'm supposed to trust you? I don't even know your name." Crossing my arms over my chest, I hold myself, imagining being in the middle of the ocean with no signs of land. The thought unsettles me.

He holds out his hand, but I don't take it right away. "Carter Stevens, deckhand, steward, activities coordinator, cook—basically, I'm at your service..." His voice trails off, his eyes smiling though his mouth remains firm.

I meet his blue-green eyes that match the ocean around us and reluctantly shake his hand. "Ava Adair."

He cracks a smile, holding my fingers long enough to make me uncomfortable. Instead of releasing me, he pulls me forward onto the short ramp, the sudden movement causing it to shake under our feet. Using my free hand, I grip the single guardrail and shoot him a death glare that only makes him smile wider as he pulls me the short distance onto the yacht.

Without giving me a chance to glance at the calm ocean beneath us, he guides me up a set of stairs, and we cross the main deck and head into what he calls the saloon. The lavish room shines with metal, glass, and light wood, all gleaming to perfection. Two short, white leather sectionals face an eighty-inch television stationed in an entertainment center that also serves as a room divider to another sitting area with a few tables and chairs. The magnificence of the room is breathtaking. I almost feel like I'm in a swanky penthouse hotel room. Almost.

Instead of guiding me all the way around the main deck, he directs me to a small elevator past the sitting room and hits the call button. The door opens, and we step on and ride it to the upper deck where our staterooms are located.

Voices hum through another lounge area surrounded by a panoramic view of the harbor and the ocean that disappears into the blue horizon. Giselle waves her arms when she spots us, flicking her eyes to Carter before pursing her lips at me in a look that says I must've found the hottest crew member on the boat. I'd be lying if I didn't agree.

"I already picked out our room." She takes my hand and pulls me toward a short hallway where voices echo from within the opened doors of the staterooms. There are five rooms altogether, and another suite toward the bow of the yacht where

Sapphire's parents will be staying since they're the ones chaperoning our vacation.

Carter follows behind us, still holding my bag, and I grin at Matty and Logan, who each sit on the end of a twin bed next to each other in one room, and then to Sapphire, who talks to Daisy and Chloe in her own room with a queen bed and a view of the ocean through the porthole. I poke my head into two more staterooms, both with queen beds, which Giselle and I could've taken since Giselle is Sapphire's cousin, but we agreed to share a room because there was no way I was sleeping on the ocean in a room alone.

Our stateroom is the last door in the hall, and two beds, identical to the ones in the room where Matty and Logan are staying, sit against each wall of the white and blue room. A long window allows sunlight to shine across the white-carpeted floor, and along another wall is a flat screen TV and built-in drawers. It's simple yet chic, and my fear of coming aboard disappears the moment I perch on the edge of the comfy bed.

Carter sets my bag on the other bed and flashes another smile. I don't think I've ever had someone smile so much at me besides Giselle. It sends my heart beating faster, and not because I'm about to embark on a luxurious vacation on a yacht.

He places his hand on the doorframe. "This is your last chance to get off," he says.

Giselle swings her gaze to mine. "You're not going anywhere."

I lean back on the bed. "You're right. I'm not."

Carter hovers for a second longer. "Enjoy your stay aboard the Ocean Jewel, Ava."

Giselle smirks at me as she waves goodbye to Carter. Covering my face with my hands, I release a long sigh. This is less terrifying than I expected, and I'm glad I decided to come.

Giselle flops next to me, the bed small for two bodies. "He's cute. This is going to be a blast."

I grin. "Should we go explore the rest of the boat?"

"I bet we could get your hottie helper to show us around."

"That's exactly what I had in mind."

Without missing a beat, Giselle pulls me from the bed and we fly into the hallway. Voices hum from the other staterooms, and I grin at Giselle when I see Carter talking to a man outside the elevator.

The man looks over at us and smiles. "Welcome. It's a pleasure to have you aboard the Ocean Jewel. How do you like it?"

I politely turn my gaze from Carter to the man. "It's lovely, thanks. We were actually going to just ask Carter to give us a tour."

Carter offers a warm smile from next to the man, sending my heart racing.

Before he can respond, the man says, "I'd be happy to show you two and the rest of your friends around. I'm Hank, by the way."

I force my mouth to remain smiling though I want nothing more than to frown. "That would be great, thank you."

Giselle sighs next to me but just shrugs when I look at her.

"Perfect, I'll be waiting in the saloon for when you're ready. We'll leave port shortly thereafter." Hank nods once to Carter before heading to the stairs instead of the elevator.

"You two have fun," Carter says, still grinning at me. "You'll get a better tour with the first mate, anyway. But I'd be happy to take you out on the water when we anchor after lunch."

Giselle grins. "Definitely!"

I shrug, disappointment creeping into me. The last thing I'll do is go out into the water, no matter how cute Carter is or how much he smiles. *Oh well.*

Voices sound from behind us as the others leave their rooms, and Giselle hooks her arm through mine. "Come on, Aves. Let's get the stupid tour over with."

I glance up to Carter. "I guess I'll see you around."

The dining terrace overlooks the sprawling ocean on the stern of the yacht opposite to where our staterooms are located. It's enclosed with floor to ceiling windows, which pop open to allow in the salty sea air. The sturdy wood table with seating for twelve sits on top a navy blue and gray rug that matches the curtains that could be pulled down, like anyone ever does that with such a startling, vast view.

A buffet table displays hot trays filled with all sorts of food from the chef on board. Warm dinner rolls steam from a basket, and the scent of garlic wafts through the air. My mouth waters as I follow Giselle. She grabs a white and blue ceramic plate from the stack near the start of the buffet. The others trail around us, and we all greet Ruby and Carlton King, Sapphire's parents and Giselle's aunt and uncle.

A familiar face pops up from his position behind a small bar where he scoops ice into glasses. Carter greets me with a dazzling smile, his ocean eyes quickly trailing from my face to the rest of me, taking in my strapless swimsuit cover. I won't be riding jet skis with the others, but my fear of the ocean won't stop me from hanging at the pool on the sundeck.

After a woman in her mid-twenties fills my plate with seared salmon on baby spinach, a side of garlic pasta, and one of the rolls, I set my plate down and head to the bar.

"What can I get you, miss?" Carter asks, taking on a more formal approach with Sapphire's parents behind me.

"Lemonade," I say, resting my elbows on the shiny counter. "And it's Ava."

As Carter stands in front of me, glass in hand, all I can think about is how good he looks in his dark blue polo since he's no longer wearing the blazer. He rubs a lemon wedge on the rim of the glass before dipping it onto a small tray of sugar. "Okay, *Ava*," he says as he sets the glass in front of me. "Any-thing else?"

"A Coke for Giselle."

He tips a glass of ice against the soda fountain and then hands it to me. "Enjoy your meal."

I try to think of something more to say, but Matty pushes

up next to me, forcing my conversation to end with Carter. As much as I want him to ignore my friend, I don't want him getting in trouble on my behalf. We'll be on this yacht for a week, so I'm sure there will be plenty more chances.

I smile once more at Carter before turning my back and heading to where Giselle sits across from Sapphire on the opposite side of the table from her parents. I set the glasses down and take a seat next to my best friend.

"The bartender is checking you out," Sapphire says, leaning over her plate of salmon. "God, he's hot."

A warm blush blossoms up my neck. "His name is Carter."

Her eyes widen. "That was fast."

"What was?" Matty says, plopping down next to Sapphire before giving her a kiss on the cheek.

I shake my head, letting my hair veil in front of my face. "Nothing."

"The bartender," Sapphire says, causing me to blush even more.

"Oh, shit. Sorry, Ava. I totally messed that up, huh?" Matty wags his eyebrows before tearing into his roll. With his mouth full, he says, "I can go back and put in a good word."

"Oh, my God, you guys!" Giselle exclaims, throwing her hands up. "Shut up about it. Ava's got it under control."

Whatever *it* is, Giselle's right. I can handle it. I pick up my roll and chuck it at Matty, who catches it and takes a bite. "What she said."

Logan, Daisy, and Chloe join the rest of us, and I lose myself in my thoughts as Logan and Matty talk about the jet skis and share stories from last summer—stories I've heard a dozen times since I was the only one who stayed out of the water. My friends, while sometimes clueless, never make fun of me about my fear, but it also leaves me out of a lot of plans since we live in a beach community. They probably all took bets on whether or not I'd actually come.

"So, you're sure you'll be okay if we all go out riding?" Giselle asks. Even if I wasn't okay, I wouldn't say so. The way to guarantee people don't bother you about your weird quirks is to make sure it doesn't interrupt their own lives.

"Yeah, totally cool with it. Look at this place. I'm sure I can find some sort of entertainment." Leaning back in my chair, I gaze around the dining terrace, trying not to stare at Carter as he helps his coworker clean up the empty food trays.

Giselle bounces in her seat. "Perfect. You'll tell me if you're not okay, right?"

I exaggerate a long exhale. "Yes, Mom. Don't worry about me."

She hugs me before joining the others. They leave the table to head to the jet ski garage. Carter glances at me once, before following behind them, probably to help. I'd follow, but I want nowhere near the swimming platform that leads directly into the water.

Instead, I head to the elevator and ride it up to the sundeck and find a few padded lounge chairs surrounding a pristine, rectangular swimming pool with swimmer jets and a round spa on a raised platform. I scoop a towel from the cabinet under a covered lounge area and head to the lounge chair closest to the railing to get a better view of my friends. Carter helps them launch the jet skis into the ocean, and my heart sinks into my stomach when Giselle and Chloe take off at an unsettling speed. *They're wearing life jackets. They're excellent swimmers. It'll be okay.*

As much as I want to turn away, I can't. As Carter helps the rest of my friends onto the other two jet skis, I find that I'm gripping my knees for dear life. Laughter and playful screams echo through the salty air. The jet skis fly over the water, leaving glittering bubble trails in their wakes.

Giselle navigates the jet ski in figure eights before turning in a circle and jetting off again with Matty and Sapphire hot on her trail. I'm so afraid that if I look away from them for even a second, the ocean will swallow them whole like my sister.

A shadow falls over my shoulder, but still, I don't turn away. "I can take you for a ride if you want when they're finished." Carter's voice causes me to jump, and I spin around and bump into his chest.

Ignoring his offer, I say, "Shouldn't you be down there watching them?"

His brows furrow when he catches the fear cross my face. "I asked Keith to take over. They're fi—" He snaps his mouth closed for a second before adding, "Ouch."

Spinning back to the railing, horror sweeps over me. I spot Giselle and Chloe bobbing in the water a few feet from their jet ski. Logan and Daisy are closest, but neither of them does anything except laugh.

"Oh, God. Come on, Giselle. Get back on," I whisper under my breath.

It must've not been low enough, because Carter makes a point to say, "They're fine, Ava. If they were in danger, Keith would get them."

"But how do you know they're not?" I watch Giselle struggle to climb back on with Chloe in the water next to her. I imagine a hundred horrible things that could possibly happen before Keith could even have the boat in the water. We're not in some lake. This is the same ocean that took my sister.

My hands grip the guardrail so hard my arms shake. Carter reaches out and touches my shoulder. "Hey, whoa. It's okay. Look." He points at Giselle as she helps Chloe back on the jet ski, proving my fear to be unwarranted.

Blinking away embarrassing tears, I pull myself from the guardrail, watching Giselle speed away again. I'm so mortified I can't even meet Carter's eyes. His silence speaks volumes, and all I can think about is getting away from him. Coming on this trip was a terrible idea.

"Excuse me," I say, nudging past Carter before he can block my way. "I need to lie down."

"Ava, wait up," he says from behind me as I stride toward the elevator.

I don't wait, though. Instead of getting on the elevator that could trap me and force me to explain myself to a boy I've just met, I fly down the stairs and head to my room, locking the door behind me.

I should've stayed home. If only I could magically transport myself to dry land.

2

DIVING UNDER

AFTER PULLING MYSELF TOGETHER, I force myself to leave my room to join the others. They regroup on the sundeck after showering off the saltwater. The sun sets on the horizon, casting an orange glow over everything. The water no longer looks blue-green but murky gray, and I shiver, imagining what hides in its depths.

Giselle sprawls out on a lounge chair, soaking up the last rays of sunlight, the air cool around us, causing goosebumps to prickle across my arms. Sapphire and Matty are nowhere in sight, probably sneaking around in Sapphire's room. Logan and Daisy come from the elevator holding plates of food, and behind them, Chloe chats with Carter as he helps her with an extra plate, which I assume is for Giselle.

"Oh, hey Ava. I'd have brought you a plate had I known you were up here," Daisy says, setting her food on a small table near her lounge chair. "We decided to eat up here to get the best view of the sunset."

"It's okay. I'll go ahead and grab something myself," I say as Carter starts to open his mouth, like he's going to offer to get something for me.

Strolling past him, he hesitates for a moment to make sure everyone else is happy, and then he rushes up behind me and puts his hand on my shoulder to slow me down. When I spin to face him, he crosses his arms though a smile plays on his lips.

It stops me from snapping at him. Instead, I say, "I apologize for earlier. I'm a little on edge being here. You don't need to worry or check on me, though. I'm fine."

He nods even though he clearly doesn't believe me with how intently he stares into my eyes. I don't know how to convince him otherwise. It's been so long since someone has looked at me this way, with eyes of curious pity, and it crawls under my skin. No one truly understands what I go through among my friends. I doubt Carter would either. He loves the ocean enough to work on a yacht.

"Really, I am," I add for good measure.

His eyes, now the same murky gray of the ocean in the sunset's golden light, don't waver until I force myself to look away. Turning toward the elevator, I glance once over my shoulder to watch both Giselle and Chloe peering at me. Neither comes to my rescue. They learned long ago that nothing can save me from myself.

Carter presses the call button for me when I don't move. Imagining being in such a confined space with him does nothing for my anxiety. The scent of the salty ocean and sunscreen clings to him, a constant reminder of the sea, but I can't help sucking in a breath. He stands close enough for me to feel the heat radiating from his bronze skin.

Just as the silence of the short trip to the dining terrace starts to unnerve me, the door to the elevator slides open, and I take in the view of the sitting area near the staterooms. I stride off the elevator, readying to dash away to save myself from the boy who leaves me confused and anxious.

"Ava," he says, nearly whispering.

It's enough to freeze me in place. The sound of my name on his lips sends my heart racing in a good way, like his voice alone can strip my fears away from me. His tone is neither sympathetic nor curious, and when I shift to look at him, a smile plays on his lips. Who knew a boy could smile so much.

I can't help myself and smile back. "You probably think I'm ridiculous."

"No, I think you're intriguing is all, but that's not what I was going to say." He actually looks nervous, rubbing the back of his neck, his arm muscles flexing with the gesture. It's enough to make me nervous, too.

"What is it then?" I ask when he doesn't continue right

away.

He breathes a small sigh from his lips. "I know this is your vacation, and you and your friends are here for a good time, but I was wondering if maybe later tonight you'd hang out with me."

"You make it sound like hanging out with you won't be fun. Is this a line you use on every girl who catches your attention on one of these trips?" I don't know why I ask, but it did cross my mind.

"I—what? No." Just when I think he's going to abandon me due to my lack of tact, he shifts on his feet and stares at the floor.

Reaching out, I brush my fingers on his forearm. Giselle would probably laugh so hard at how embarrassingly awkward I am when I'm trying to figure out what to say to a cute boy. She says I have a problem with pushing them away before they even have a chance with me. Maybe I do.

"So, do you want to?" he asks again.

I consider saying no, because after everything, Carter seems so different from me and a week on this boat could end up feeling extremely long if things turn weird. On the other hand, it could also fly by and leave me hurt because the reality of my life will come crashing back to me. *It's summer. You deserve a little fun.*

"I'd like that," I finally agree.

He grins. "Cool."

Carter strolls next to me, and we walk toward the dining

terrace where another buffet awaits on hot trays. Ruby and Carlton sit in the same seats at the table, enjoying a quiet candlelit dinner, and I wave, heading to the unmanned buffet table. Before I can reach to fill my plate myself, Carter takes his place on the other side and serves me a plate of crab legs, mashed potatoes, and mixed veggies.

If Ruby and Carlton weren't talking softly behind me, I'd insist on serving myself. If I did that now, Ruby would chide me for not letting Carter do his job and to enjoy being taken care of, as though I'm incapable of doing things for myself. It's one of those things Sapphire has complained about for years—especially after the disaster last year where she tried to bake Matty a birthday cake and discovered she didn't even know how to turn on her oven. Luckily for her, baking is one of my favorite pastimes.

"Will you grab a few water bottles and a can of Coke to take up?" I ask, taking my plate from Carter before he carries it for me. I can see in his eyes that he would carry everything in an instant and not only because he thinks it's his job.

With his hands full, he leads the way back to the sundeck with me, walking so close that my arm brushes against his every so often. We're met with grins and crinkly eyes from my friends, and Giselle hops up and steals the Coke from Carter's hand that I had him bring especially for her.

Before my friends can make a scene, Carter whispers, "I'll come find you tonight." He offers me a warm smile and strides away, looking back twice.

As I find my place on an empty lounge chair next to Giselle, placing my plate of food on the table between us, I turn my gaze up to meet my friends. They'll never let me hear the end of this if I don't say something now. I'm the only one out of the four of us girls who hasn't had a serious boyfriend—though I have been on a few terrible dates.

"Did I just hear what I think I did?" Chloe asks as Carter disappears down the stairs.

I hope he's out of earshot. "You did."

"Oh, my God. It's a miracle," Daisy says, laughing. "Ava has a date."

I blush, thankful for the darkening sky so no one can see. "It's not a date. We're just hanging out."

"It's definitely a date," Logan says, chiming in.

Giselle reaches over and smacks his arm. "You're going to make her nervous. Can't we all just celebrate that Ava came along and now she's going on a date with a really hot guy?"

I cover my face in my hands, shaking my head. "You guys. Stop. It's not a big deal."

"Hey, it is," Logan says. "I lost fifty bucks the moment you stepped on board and another twenty when you stayed." How did I even know they'd be placing bets? It doesn't bother me, though. Matty and Logan bet on everything.

It's Daisy's turn to smack his other arm. "Seriously?"

"It's fine," I say, interjecting. "Matty deserves the seventy bucks for having faith in me."

"Harsh, Ava-babe. I have plenty of faith in you. I'm willing to bet Carter will kiss you by the end of the night."

"Not helping your case, Lo," Giselle says, throwing a cloth napkin at him.

"I'll take that bet," Matty calls out, trailing next to Sapphire as they stand near the elevator.

I sink lower into the lounge chair. Thank God Carter is probably on another deck out of earshot, because I'd probably die from embarrassment, especially because I kind of want Logan to win that bet, despite his quips.

Sapphire holds up a green glass bottle in one hand and an opaque white bottle in the other, drawing everyone's attention away from me.

"The wardens have retreated to their suite for the night. Who wants to join us for some festivities in the saloon?" she asks.

I sigh a relieved breath, knowing that all conversations about Carter are now completely off everyone's minds. Giselle pulls me to my feet, and we trail behind the others. They take the elevator while Giselle follows me to the stairs.

She stops halfway down and turns to me. "You're having fun, right?"

"Starting to," I say, nudging her to keep moving.

Grinning over her shoulder, she laughs as she says, "It'll keep getting better. I'm sure Logan will win that bet."

"You think?"

"Totally."

Carter hovers just outside of the saloon on the pathway that circles the perimeter of the yacht. The nearly full moon casts white light over him, sending streaks of silver-blue through his honey brown, sun-kissed hair.

Gulping the rest of my flute of champagne, I push to my feet and shuffle across the vast space ignoring my friends as they shout overly friendly greetings at Carter from their places at the table where they play card games while finishing off the alcohol Sapphire got her hands on.

Without his uniform, Carter looks even better, his sinewy muscles on display without the sleeves of his polo. His light blue tank top and dark board shorts bring out the blue color of his eyes. When I close the distance between us, he offers me the hoodie he clutches in his hand.

The scent of the sea and sunscreen clings to the worn fabric as I slide it over my head. A cool breeze blows my pale hair over my shoulder, and I stop myself from drawing my eyes to the black ocean around us. Only the sprinkle of lights in the distance reminds me that we're not hovering in some empty void where my deepest fears linger in waiting.

He guides me toward the back of the yacht where a barred railing surrounds the open deck where we get a clear view of the bubbling tracks left behind the yacht as we head north in the night. Built-in seats line one side, while a table with an umbrella sits in the center of the space. Without the light pollution of the sprawling city, the stars blaze brightly overhead like millions of shiny pearls sewn into endless black silk.

He motions me to the table, lit with dim, flameless candles. A silver tray of miniature desserts rests on top, and I turn to Carter with wide eyes. It's easy to ignore the fear of the vast expanse of dark, churning water behind me when he pulls the chair out for me to sit down.

"I know this might not be as fun as—"

I press my finger to his lips. "It's perfect, Carter. If you haven't noticed, I'm the outsider in my group of friends. They're used to me bailing on them."

"Why is that?" he asks.

Shrugging, I say, "We have different interests is all. Kinda like me and you." There. I said it. I had to get the words off my mind and put them in the open so Carter doesn't think he's going to magically change me and give me the courage to do things I'm afraid of. Just because he convinced me to come aboard, doesn't mean I'll be hopping on the back of a jet ski or going for an open ocean swim any time soon.

He smiles at me like I've said the silliest thing. "You say that like you know me."

"You love the ocean. I don't."

He leans closer to me, close enough to where I catch the coconut scent of his damp hair, fresh from a shower. "That's where you're wrong. I love the land more."

Frowning, I tilt my head to meet his gaze to see if he's joking with me. When he doesn't smile, I say, "You're not joking."

"No."

"But you work on a yacht."

"It pays well, and I have a place to live."

Wind gusts around us, the yacht rising and falling over a swell big enough to make my stomach drop. I grip the sides of the chair, fear pulsing through me, making me lose my train of thought. Carter's intense gaze studies me for a moment before he reaches out his hand and laces his fingers through mine.

My knees tremble, but I suck in a deep breath of the briny air. "So, you don't have a place near Azure Waters?"

"Only when we dock there."

Before I realize it, my lip pouts out and disappointment washes over me. What's the point of getting to know Carter when the moment we return home, he'll return back to sea, and I'll go back to staying far from any large bodies of water?

"Oh." It's all I can say to hide my disappointment.

He smiles, despite my reaction. "I'm not gone as often as it would seem. We charter a lot of weekend getaways and day long excursions up and down the coast, but anything more than a week or two only happens two or three times a year. Plus, I have most nights off."

Hmm. Maybe this could work after all. *Aren't you getting a little ahead of yourself?*

"That's a pretty adventurous life, Carter. You probably think I'm so boring. I mostly split my time between home and Giselle's and Sapphire's houses. I do volunteer at the Surf and Swim Museum downtown two weekends of the month."

He smirks. "Sounds fun."

"Liar. Just so you know, there's not a lot to do that doesn't involve the ocean in our town."

Instead of disagreeing with me, he only nods. "You know, I'm a great swim instructor."

Here we go. I knew it wouldn't be long before I'd have to explain why I am the way I am. I was hoping it could wait until I knew Carter liked me for sure. It's easier to play off when someone already likes me. But now, he'll probably find some way to let me down.

"I know how to swim," I respond to him after a moment.

"I can protect you from all the ocean animals, too."

I roll my eyes. I can't help it. "It's not that either."

"Something happened to you." It's not a question. My silence is enough of an answer. Carter doesn't pry though. He doesn't ask me to bare my soul to see if there's anything he can do to save me from my fears. The usual words of encouragement I get from people never come. Instead, he says, "I'm sorry."

I open my mouth to tell him not to be sorry, but a loud voice cuts through the quiet air as Matty, Sapphire, and Giselle stumble in our direction. Sapphire laughs when Matty kisses her, and Giselle jogs forward, nearly tripping on her flip flops.

I jump from my chair to grab her, my worst fears playing out in my mind as they stroll next to the guardrail. Carter is on his feet in a flash, pulling Sapphire to sit at the table next to Giselle, but Matty brushes him off.

"Ava-babe!" he yells, even though I'm standing only two feet away. "How's your date? You guys kiss yet?"

I cringe, heat rushing up my neck. Matty reaches out and grabs my hand, pulling me toward him in one of his infamous drunken bear hugs. He squeezes me, rocking back and forth, causing me to laugh. When he pulls away, he grins, wagging his eyebrows. His sloppy movements make me nervous. All I want him to do is to sit down with the others.

The yacht rises and lowers on another swell, causing me to freeze and scream. Warm hands grip my waist, stopping me from stumbling, and I exhale a breath of relief when I meet Carter's gaze.

"Hey, Aves. Come here! Look into the water," Matty says.

"Don't be a jerk, Matty," Giselle snaps from her place at the table.

When I turn to glance at Matty, my heart nearly explodes from my chest. He stands on the first rung of the guardrail, his arms spread out wide like the wings of a bird. He rocks as another swell lifts and drops us against the dark ocean. My stomach rolls but not from seasickness. I'm terrified Matty will slip and fall into the ocean.

"Matty, get over here before you fall over," I say, inching closer to him and pulling away from Carter.

He laughs for a split second and starts spinning his arms, twirling them like windmills, and he yells out. Without thinking, I rush forward, stretching out my arms to grab the back of his shirt. A million horrible images flash through my mind.

"Matty!" I scream, the world slowing with the swell of another wave.

While spinning to face me, Matty starts to say, "Hey, cool it. I was only mes—" But before he can finish his words, his outstretched arm clocks me in my back.

The force is enough to send me reeling forward toward the guardrail. The world kicks into motion, too fast for me to do anything. The barrier hits my stomach, and I flip over, staring at the dark ocean below. My friends' screams reverberate through my bones. I don't even have time to scream myself or take a breath as my head splits through the water. I dive under, the ocean swallowing me in a merciless swell.

This is it. I always knew the ocean would kill me.

I'm about to die.

LOST

I NEVER THOUGHT THE OCEAN was peaceful. But in this moment, as my body twists and turns in the swells of the night water, all I can think about is how quiet and comforting the dark sea is. Though my throat burns, I kick my legs, hoping to break through the surface. The pain of going without oxygen only squeezes my heart a little. It's because I've given up. I'm lost at sea, crashing among the black waters. Maybe I'll see my sister soon.

No longer able to hold my breath, my mouth automatically opens, and I gasp for air that isn't there. Salty water fills my throat and as much as I fight to swim to the surface, it's like it's no longer there.

Then I feel nothing.

My body numbs, my consciousness fading in and out. With a quick jolt, I swim apart from my own body, floating on the underwater current, watching my body get lost in the sea. Regret rushes through me. I should've never gotten on the yacht. I should've stayed home and lived my life in utter safe boringness. This is all Carter's fault. I'm dead because I liked the way a boy smiled. I'm so stupid.

A flash of light, like an orange spark beneath the water, draws my attention to it. But the image is impossible. Fire and water don't mix. The ocean is an indestructible force to be reckoned with. But alas, the spark remains, a burst of light in the darkness, and it pulls me to it.

I swim forward in my ethereal form, unaffected by the current or the darkness. The spark leads the way. Swimming faster, I glide through the murky depths until the spark is inches away from my fingers, its heat pulsing into my hands unlike anything I've ever experienced. It's mesmerizing and perfect—and in this moment, I know it's mine.

My fingers caress the spark. It sinks into the palm of my hand, the orange glow traveling through my arm and over my shoulder, lighting me in a soft glow as it consumes me. I gasp, not water but air. The spark lights my lungs and splits to travel from my head to my toes. And then the dark ocean lights up like someone flicked on the sun. It shines above me, lighting my way to the surface.

"Ava, please. You can do it. Follow the light." The familiar voice calms my nerves. I do exactly what it says, hoping to find something brilliant and eternal as I kick up to the blinding blue light shimmering above me.

When I break the surface, the light clicks off, leaving my vision hazy and my thoughts cloudy. The now freezing water sends my teeth chattering, but as quick as I feel the rush of ice, it's dulled by the heat of something—another body much hotter than my own. Hands grip under my arms, forcing my head to stay above the water, and I spit and cough up what tastes like gallons of the sea.

"Ava, you're okay. You're alive. Just keep breathing. Stay with me." Carter's voice rings in my ears, and I realize I'm no longer alone in the dark waters.

"I—I died," I whisper, my throat burning, another round of coughs seizing my chest. "But now I'm alive."

He laughs, holding me tighter. Another swell lifts us higher in the water before lowering down again. "You're very much alive," Carter confirms. "But I have to tell you something."

Before the words can escape his mouth, a bright light shines over us, coming from an inflatable motorized boat. I blink, shock and relief coursing through me as crew members from the Ocean Jewel come to pluck us from the sea.

"Ava," Carter says again. The sound of my name coming from him sends a million butterflies racing from my stomach to my chest. "Ava, listen."

But I can't focus. My head swims, exhaustion taking its toll on me.

"Ava, please. Look at me," Carter says.

Forcing my eyes to open, I peer into Carter's deep, green-blue eyes lit by the flashlight from one of the crew members as their boat cuts through the water. Something looks different about him, but I can't put my finger on it.

Then I see them. Along each of his forearms are short, thick ridges that look similar to small fins. As quickly as I see them, they disappear, and Carter wraps his arms around me.

"I'm truly sorry for this," he whispers into my hair.

But I can't wrap my mind around what he's saying.

"I didn't have a choice," he continues. "I couldn't let you die."

Shaking my head, I try to understand his words, but all I can think about is the bright light from the boat, the faint memory of another light—a spark—tickling the back of my mind. But the spark is gone, and now I'm so tired. I don't want to think any longer.

"Ava?" Carter says again. "Ava, please. Listen to me."

But I can't.

Listening to the sound of Carter breathing, I succumb to my exhaustion. The last thing I see before I close my eyes are Carter's eyes, but for once they're not smiling at me.

Carter sits on the cot across from me as the onboard medic examines me. The last thing I remember is opening my eyes to a team of people rushing to pull me from the inflatable motorboat to take me to the lower deck to what I heard someone call the sickbay, which is a small room with a few medical supplies near the crew's cabins.

Ruby hovers in the doorway, anxiously wringing her hands together. She watches as the medic, who I recall someone call Sasha, checks my vitals, shines a light in my eyes, and asks a series of questions about where I am, how old I am, the date, and if anything hurts.

"I'm fine," I manage to say. "Can I please just go back to my room?"

"You're very lucky, Ms. Adair," Sasha says. "You're temperature is slightly lower than it should be, but I think with some rest and some warm liquids, you should feel fine in a few hours."

"So, we don't have to cut the trip short?" I ask. Out of everything I've been through, the thing I was most worried about was having to go to a hospital, cutting Sapphire's eighteenth birthday/graduation vacation short.

Sasha shrugs. "That's up to Mrs. King."

Ruby frowns from the door. "Are you sure you feel all right, Avie?" Very few people still call me by my childhood name, Ruby being one of them. I've been friends with Giselle and Sapphire since our diaper days because all our moms went to college together. "Your health is more important than this vacation. Maybe I should call your mom—"

I raise my hand out. "No! You'll freak her out for nothing. I'm not hurt or anything. She doesn't need to know. Please,

Ruby. You remember how she was after—" The words stick in my throat. I can't even say them. Our town's small, and the whole place mourned after Bailey was swept out to sea. They even kept the search up long after it would have been possible to find her alive.

Ruby solemnly nods. "I suppose you're right. I want you to come back here and check in with Sasha in the morning, okay?" Turning to Carter for the first time through this whole ordeal, she says, "You were very brave for jumping in to save Ava, young man. You don't know how grateful we are, and after speaking to my husband and Captain Briggs, we'd like to reward you."

Carter rubs his hands over his knees. "I don't need a reward, ma'am. I'm just thankful I was there to help."

"As are we, and that's why the captain agreed to grant you time off for the remainder of the trip, and we're providing you with a bonus," Ruby says, smiling.

Carter doesn't smile like I expect him to. He shakes his head, his wet hair sticking to his cheeks. It takes a long moment for him to bring his gaze from the floor to meet Ruby's eyes. "That's very generous, ma'am—"

"Ruby. Call me Ruby."

"Ruby," he says, like the name feels funny on his tongue. "But I can't take you up on the offer. It's not fair for the others who'd have to pick up my slack."

Sasha scoffs. "Carter, we'll survive. Captain Briggs wouldn't have agreed if he didn't think we could handle it. I'm sure the others will agree with me."

"Then it's settled," Ruby says. "And tomorrow, we'll see you at breakfast."

With that, Ruby draws her attention to me, and I slide off the cot and follow her out to head to the stairs that'll take us up since the elevator doesn't come down to the lower deck. She wraps an arm around my shoulders, hugging me to her, and I breathe in her floral scent.

"I like that boy," Ruby says instead of asking me how I'm feeling for the millionth time.

She watches my face, and I can't resist smiling. "Me too."

As we ascend into a small hallway that leads to the saloon, I'm greeted by all my friends, Carlton, and a few crew members. Giselle is the first one to her feet, flying across the vast space. She throws her arms around me, yanking me from Ruby, and starts bawling her eyes out into my already salty hair.

"You scared the hell out of me, Aves," she whispers.

Matty shuffles up next to her. "Next time you can push me in instead, okay? I'm at your service the rest of vacation. You need something, I'll get it."

"It was an accident," I say. Matty had no idea I was going to try to save him from his fake stumble. It's the last thing I remember apart from opening my eyes, soaking wet, before being taken to the lower deck for medical attention. Everything else is a blank, like my mind pushed everything away to save me.

"I was an idiot," he says.

I smirk. "We already knew that."

After enduring hugs from the rest of my friends, I mention how tired I am, forcing them to let me retreat back to my stateroom. I take my time in the hot shower, sending away the chill that still clings to my bones.

Giselle joins me a bit later, chattering about all the craziness of the day and how happy Sapphire is that I refused to end the trip. We put on a cheesy, romantic comedy, and within ten minutes, Giselle is fast asleep, breathing deeply from her bed.

My gaze flicks to the almost full moon shining soft light through the window. The mesmerizing glow lights my skin in a pearlescent radiance, like someone painted a makeup highlighter over my skin. It tingles, warmth breaking through the coolness in my bones, and I find myself shifting off my bed to stare out the window.

Unlike earlier, the ocean radiates in a light blue color, the dark waters glittering like being lit from within. It ignites a memory of a spark in the water and how I followed the sun to the surface though the night was pitch-black.

And I remember Carter and his ocean eyes. How safe I felt with him. I remember...

A soft knock sounds on the door, pushing my faint memory away. Padding across the carpet, I make my way to the wooden door and crack it open to find Carter standing on the other side. He holds his finger to my lips to stop me from talking and pulls me from my cabin and into the small hall that leads to the sitting area.

We don't stop there, though.

Grabbing a throw blanket off the back of one of the leather sectionals, he wraps it around my bare shoulders. I'm only wearing a tank top and pajama shorts because I didn't bring anything warmer.

We take the elevator up to the sundeck, and he guides me to the farthest lounge chair, one that has a clear view of the glowing sea. It matches his sad eyes as he gazes at me for a long moment without saying anything.

Reaching out, I run my fingers along his cheek. I can't stop myself. Something about Carter in this moment captivates me. Maybe it was my fall into the ocean, or the memory of him saving me, wrapping his arms around me—something tonight brought me closer to the boy I just met this morning, and I can't put my finger on it. The thought excites and scares me.

"You look awfully sad for being my hero," I say, leaning closer to him.

His hand cups over mine and presses it firmly to his cheek, like he needs to feel the weight of my fingers against him. "I'm not a hero, Ava."

"You saved my life," I whisper, my smile melting into a frown. His gloomy gaze cuts into me, stirring the grief that has always lingered in my soul.

"Do you remember anything?" He ignores my statement, his voice deepening with his question.

I miss the easy smile he had for me all day, now long gone. He nearly leaves me speechless, and I find myself pulling away from him. I can't explain it, but the longer he holds my gaze, the more painful memories surface. I'm no longer remembering the fall into the ocean or the warmth of his skin and the relief of being pulled from the water. I remember all the other stuff—the fear and pain of losing my breath, of getting lost on the current. The pitch-darkness that made me feel trapped in a void.

"I died," I whisper, shivering against the memory. "I know it. But you—you saved me."

"Yes," he confirms. "But do you remember how?"

Closing my eyes, I try to recall everything again—the shifting color of the ocean, the fire underwater, the voice whispering to me. But none of it makes sense. Those are probably not even memories at all but hallucinations.

Taking a deep breath, I say, "This is going to sound crazy, but I touched an underwater flame. The spark..." My voice trails off, my head swimming with thoughts of the ocean. I wobble on the chair, my eyes training on the glowing ocean. "Everything looks weird, Carter. Something's wrong with me. Maybe you should take me back to Sasha."

Instead of helping me to my feet, he cups my face, looking deep into my eyes. He leans in, pressing his lips against mine, kissing me ever so softly. My heart pounds against my ribcage as I taste the salt on his lips, and then through my closed eyelids, I see the spark. The flame underwater.

Memories rush back to me, more clear than ever, and I envision my body floating before me, a large figure—an animal—circling me. It's unlike anything I've ever seen, with a glittering tail and muscular torso, two finned arms, a ridge across a muscular back like a dorsal fin. And beautiful—the creature radiates with life—and then I watch as it wraps my lifeless body in its arms.

The memory shifts, and I no longer watch from the outside, but from a different perspective. It takes me a moment, but I realize this new memory isn't mine. It's about me, though. I stare at my hair floating around my face, my eyes wide and afraid and empty. My mouth hangs slightly open and one last bubble erupts from my lips. Fear courses through me as the last of my breath travels upward, leaving me at the mercy of the sea.

A moment later, my perspective changes again, and now I stare through hazy waters at a blurry image of someone familiar—Carter. Deep in my heart, I know it's him. I can finally see past the spark glowing from where his heart would be. The light travels up his throat and to his lips, and he pulls me closer and kisses me like he kisses me now. Somehow, the memory comes to life, playing like a movie in my mind, blending and merging with the present.

I gasp as the spark engulfs me, setting me aglow, and I pull away from Carter, pushing the memory of us—one I'm not even sure is real—from my mind. When I snap my eyes open, my hand flies to my lips, electricity tingling from them, an energy sparked from Carter's kiss.

His sad eyes lock on me again. "Ava, I'm so sorry."

Why he's apologizing for kissing me, I do not know. The weight of the world hangs between us, Carter holding the majority of it on his muscular, bronzed shoulders. A thousand thoughts swirl through his eyes as he holds my gaze.

"I'm so sorry," he repeats again, bringing his hand up to brush the stray blond hairs from my face.

"Stop apologizing for saving me." My voice barely comes out a whisper. "Everything is fine. I'm fine."

"Ava, what did you see when I kissed you just now?"

My mouth suddenly dries. Saying the words out loud would make me sound insane. The boy who sits before me now isn't the same boy who saved me in the water as much as I want to deny it.

"You're a merman." The moment the words escape my mouth, they become utterly real—there's no denying the truth to them. "And you breathed life back into me—the spark, it still lingers in my heart. I can feel it with every beat." It matches the same rhythm as Carter's, because now, when I look at his chest, I can see the spark within him, too.

Silence falls between us—the silence confirming every last one of my words. The world shifts as shadows edge my vision. I fall back, lying on the lounge chair, trying my best to pull myself together—to think things through. The brilliant moon hangs in the sky, calming my nerves, and then I feel Carter's warm fingers twine with mine.

"I'm like you now," I whisper. "That's why you're apologizing. You didn't save me. You changed me."

But I still have my legs. I still feel like me.

"You'll transform under the full moon," he whispers, answering my silent question.

Panic trembles through me, imagining what's about to happen to me, how I'm now cursed to enter the one place I fear the most. The place that stole my sister from me—that killed me.

"But it's not forever, right?" The thought is the only thing that keeps me from breaking. Carter sits before me, legs and all. He's not confined to the ocean. He still has a life.

He tugs a chain hiding beneath his shirt with a silver ring encrusted with an unfamiliar turquoise stone. I realize he's wearing one on his hand, too. "This is an enchanted stone infused with the ocean."

I catch the swirling water within the tiny stone. "It's beautiful."

"It allows me to transform at will...except for the full moon."

"What happens otherwise? Will I be trapped in the ocean? Oh, God. My parents—I can't put them through this. You have to fix me." My voice cracks, the words flying from my mouth. Tears pour from my eyes, blurring my vision. "I can't be like you, Carter. Please, fix this."

Sobs heave in my chest when he doesn't say anything. He can't fix this. It's already too late. But why even let the crew members find us? Why put me through the torture of knowing my hours are limited before I must succumb to the ocean?

Strong arms wrap around me. "I can't stop the transformation, but I'm not going to force you into a life you clearly don't want, Ava."

"How?" Pulling away, I meet his sad eyes.

He unclasps his necklace and pulls the ring from it. "With this. It was intended for the one I choose for a mate, but I want you to have it."

My eyes widen. "I barely know you."

"I'm not asking you to be my mate. I'm offering you a chance to continue to live your life the best you can. This is all my fault."

But it's not his fault at all. It's mine. I'm lucky to even be alive. "Carter..." My eyes draw to the ocean. "Are you sure you want to give that to me? I'm thankful to even be alive. It's just—why?"

He uncurls my fingers for me and slips the cool ring into my palm. "I couldn't let you die," is all he says. "I've never met someone who loves the land more than I do. I couldn't just let the ocean have you."

"But it does have me."

He shakes his head. "No, Ava. You now have the ocean."

PULL OF THE MOON

I SNEAK BACK INTO MY stateroom minutes after the sun rises. If I didn't have to worry about meeting the others for breakfast, I'd have stayed with Carter even longer. A few hours of talking wasn't nearly enough time to take in what's going to become of my life. And come sundown, when the full moon rises into the sky, I'll transform into a mermaid. I barely even believe it.

Born in the ocean, Carter has spent his entire life traveling from land to sea with his parents who had also chosen a life on land. Every merperson has the choice to decide, but it's rare for them to choose land over their beloved waters with the danger of discovery. And somewhere far beneath the waves hide several colonies of merpeople, all under the protection of King Attilonious, though Carter says I'll probably never meet him.

So many questions still swim through my mind. But first things first, I have to survive the day and figure out how to get away with leaving after dark when the moon rises. If someone discovers we're missing, there's no coming back aboard. There's no going home at all.

I flop back on my bed, turning to face Giselle as she remains asleep. Her bronzy brown hair hangs around her pillow like she neatly arranged it before falling asleep. I'd give anything to wake her up and confide in her, tell her what's going to happen to me—even ask her to join me too, but that's impossible. According to Carter, since I'm human-born, I can't turn a human. As for Carter, I was his one and only chance. He still can't really explain why he did it, why he chose to save me, but it is what it is, and there's no going back.

The thing that concerns me the most above anything is that one day, Carter could decide I'm too much to deal with, and I'll be left alone and confused and incapable of dealing with this curse on my own. What if it turns out we don't actually like each other? What if he resents wasting his one chance to transform someone on me? What if I start despising him?

Pushing all the what-if questions away, I close my eyes, trying my best to sleep for the short period of time I'll have until breakfast is served. Carter's image dances on the inside of my eyelids, and I watch as the spark in his heart thrums to the sound of my own heartbeat. The change in my vision, seeing light where there is nothing but dark, is a side effect of the transformation. I'll never have to fear the black waters under the moon again, because now, they'll always be light.

Just as I doze off to sleep, the bed shifts under me. "Ava? Aves, wake up." Raising my arm, I smack Giselle away when she starts to shake my shoulders.

I groan. "Leave me alone."

"Not after last night."

Oh, jeez. I hope she's not serious, because I'll never get away tonight if she is. "So, I can't sleep in because of it?"

She laughs. "Exactly, now get up. I want to swim before breakfast."

After the five minutes it takes to slip into our bathing suits, I stroll next to Giselle, and we head up to the sundeck together. Bright sunshine bathes my skin in its warm rays. Giselle pulls me to a stop, and I notice a figure on the last lounge chair, the one I shared with Carter last night.

With a towel shading his eyes, Carter sleeps sprawled out with his hands hooked behind his head. He must've come back here after he took me to my room, probably because he mentioned he shares a cabin with three other people.

Giselle grins, holding a finger to her lips, and then tiptoes to the edge of the pool. She motions for me to follow her lead, and we stand on the other side of the shallow, rectangular pool, facing Carter. I know exactly what she wants to do.

Without warning, she grabs my hand and pulls me forward

with her, and we splash into the water, shooting up a small wave which lands right on top of Carter. He bolts upright, the towel falling onto the wet deck. When he sees us in the pool in front of him, he smiles. It's the first one since he revealed what he had done to me last night. It's bright enough to leave me weak in the knees.

"You're swimming," he says, trailing his eyes from my half damp hair to my halter bikini top before meeting my gaze.

"More like wading," Giselle quips. The water barely goes above our torsos.

Pools have never scared me. In fact, I swim all the time at home in my own pool. It's the deep, ever moving water that scares me—even lakes. Anything deep enough to lose myself in.

I lick my bottom lip as he continues to stare at me. "So, are you going to just watch us or are you coming in?"

He leans back on the lounge, and Giselle laughs, splashing him with water. A moment later, he tugs his tank top over his head, showing off his ripped stomach in all its golden goodness, and it's my turn to take in the drool-worthy view. Giselle nudges my shoulder with hers, having the same thought as I am. *Wow.*

Carter sits on the edge of the pool and swings his legs into the water before slipping under. I half expect his legs to turn into a tail the moment he gets wet, but after a lot of explaining, it turns out that would only happen without his sea stone, and it would be triggered regardless of touching the water or not.

He sinks lower into the pool, the water rising to his neck,

and then he swims in my direction faster than I expect. Without warning, he grips my waist and lifts me into the air before dunking me under water completely. When I break the surface, I laugh, half squealing, and swim away before he can toss me again.

Giselle jumps on his back, pushing him under, but he straightens up to his full height, tossing her in my direction. We all laugh, the heaviness of unspoken words and worries no longer weighing us down.

Giselle joins me on the edge of the pool, water dripping from her dark bronze hair, and she touches my knee. We watch Carter swim a small lap. "So, will there be a second date with the bronzed god?"

I wish I could tell her that there will be one at least once a month, but instead I say, "Tonight. I really like him, Gi."

"I can tell." She trains her gaze to Carter as he swims toward us but doesn't surface before he heads back to the opposite side of the pool. "He likes you, too."

I smirk. "If only we wouldn't be interrupted again, maybe Logan could finally win a bet." I don't tell her that he already did win, that Carter kissed me last night, but it wasn't exactly the kind of kiss I was expecting. It was his way to help me remember. I try not to put too much meaning behind it because everything is just so out of control and confusing.

She bounces next to me. "Oh, I know! I'll sleep in Matty and Logan's room, since neither of them has slept in there. You know Logan went straight to Daisy's and Matty slept in Sapphire's last night?"

Of course they did. Why wouldn't they? Ruby and Carlton haven't checked on any of us because we're all almost adults, and this is Sapphire's trip. They came along to be with each other in the romantic owner's suite. They haven't even been on the sundeck because they have their own hot tub and balcony. Giselle's plan is pretty perfect.

I hug her. "You sure you don't mind?"

"No way. It's not often I see you all smiles for a boy."

When Carter stops swimming, I hop from the edge of the pool and cross the water to him to tell him that I have it all figured out. His cheeks darken, and I almost think he's blushing when I explain how Giselle is letting us have the room for the night, despite the fact that we won't be anywhere near it.

"It might just work," he finally says, twining his fingers through mine underwater.

I suck in my bottom lip. "It has to. I'm really counting on it."

The fiery hue of the setting sun warms the entire saloon, making the white leather couches golden. Sapphire rests her head on the arm of the couch with her legs sprawled over Matty. Chloe and Giselle play a game of cards while blasting music through the surround sound. Logan and Daisy sit together in a recliner, staring at the screen of Daisy's laptop.

Across the room from everyone, I sit with Carter in the window seat, constantly glancing between my friends and my future, as the sun threatens to disappear, bringing night. Up until now, we haven't had a moment to talk about what happens next—and honestly, I'm absolutely terrified.

Carter leans in close, brushing his lips against my ear. "We're going to wait as long as possible after sundown to hit the water. I can resist the transformation for a few hours, which makes it a lot easier to slip away unnoticed, but you won't be able to. Not yet. You'll also start to feel what I can only describe as an uncomfortable pull at any moment. Don't let it scare you. Your transformation will take a bit since it's your first."

My heartbeat pounds in my head. "Is it going to hurt?" The idea of suddenly growing scales and having my legs fuse together just seems so unpleasant.

"It'll be an adjustment for you. But pain? No, I don't think so." Thinking is far from being certain. His words do nothing to settle my nerves.

I feel like I'm going to vomit at any second. It's like the time I waited in line with Giselle to ride the new Death Spiral rollercoaster at Sailor's Bay Amusement Park. All I could think the whole time in line was how terrifying the first drop would feel, sending my stomach into my throat and then crashing it to my feet—the thought alone was enough to make me almost back out, but by the time I realized I didn't want to ride, I was already harnessed in, and it was too late.

Now feels like the anticipation of that first drop. Like then, I can't back out now either.

"I'm going to be sick," I say, wringing my hands together

in my lap. "I can't do this. Maybe I'll just lock myself in the bathroom."

He gently pinches my chin. "That's the pull of the moon you're experiencing. Resistance will make you feel like you're dying until you do. You're a mermaid now. Without the sea, you won't survive the night."

Tears threaten to spill on my cheeks, my heart heavy in my chest. "Please," I whisper. "There has to be a way."

The muscles in my legs spasm, and it takes everything in me not to cry out and draw attention to us. The last thing I need is for someone to think I'm sick and send me to Sasha for an exam.

Carter rises to his feet, pulling me up from the window seat. His brows furrow, lowering over his blue-green eyes. My legs shake, but with the help of his arm around my waist, I stroll next to him, resting my head on his shoulder.

Giselle catches my gaze, her eyes crinkling in the corners for a second, before I offer her my best smile. I wink at her for good measure, just hoping she doesn't come to our stateroom to check on us. She already moved whatever she needed into the boy's room after lunch. She blows me a kiss, and Logan yells out that he's going to finally win a bet. The nausea rolling through me is enough to stop me from being embarrassed.

Carter guides me onto the elevator, and we head to my room first where I grab the waterproof bag he'd given me and lock the door so no one can barge in to find it empty. When we make it out on the empty sundeck, the crisp ocean air pushes my sickness away as I stare at the darkening purple sky.

Gripping the guardrail, I peer over the vast ocean. Fear trickles down my spine, and I imagine the unsettling fall last night. This one is a much taller drop, but it's the best place at this time of day since I can't stop the transformation like Carter. If he were alone, he'd wait until much later when his cabin mates were asleep to slip away. Now, most of the staff should be cleaning up or eating in the galley. Sapphire's parents have already retreated to their cabin at the front of the boat, and all my friends are hanging out in the saloon.

A tingling sensation crawls down my back along my spine, shooting cramps into my legs. Bending over, clutching my knees, I know it won't be much longer. The wind whistles around me, blowing my blond hair from my face. But still, I can't find the courage to straighten my back—to face the water and the moon as it feels like it's pulling my insides out.

The boat rocks on a small swell, and I groan, holding myself. The yacht glides over the current at a much slower pace than last night, and as long as I jump far enough, I won't have to worry about getting hurt.

The purple sky fades to dark blue. I can feel the pull of the ocean deep in my bones, the moon shining in the sky. If I don't jump soon, I'll surely die.

"Get ready to jump, Ava," Carter says, circling the small deck once for signs of anyone strolling the pathway that winds around the lower deck. It's dark enough now that it'll be harder to spot us. And I'm counting on the fact that everyone is busy and Carter knows the crews' habits from working on the yacht for a while. This isn't the first time he's been on the Ocean Jewel during a full moon. He promised it'll all work out as long as my friends stay away.

Swallowing my fear, I shimmy out of my dress and fold it neatly into the waterproof bag. My toes tingle like I've sat with my legs curled under me for too long. It's more annoying than painful, but the newfound sickness swirling in my stomach threatens to send me reeling.

When I glance up, Carter stands a foot away, his shirt and board shorts dangling in his hands in front of his naked body. Blush blossoms up my face as he takes the bag from me and shoves them in, and I look everywhere else but at him.

If the call of the ocean doesn't kill me, my racing heart just might.

"You can undress. I promise I won't look," he says.

Keeping my head up, I shift my eyes to stare at him. "What? I'm not getting naked here."

"You might rip your bikini."

"I have more."

He doesn't argue, though I do loosen the ties on my bottoms. I really, really love this bikini, but I don't know Carter well, and I didn't imagine the first time I'd be getting naked in front of a boy I liked would be because I'm about to sprout a tail. What is wrong with my life?

Another wave of cramps rushes through me, and I suck in a deep breath while gripping the guardrail. I'm afraid if it happens again, I'll fall instead of jump and end up a bruised and half broken mess splattered across the sea.

"Come on. It's time to go," he says, taking the lead. Climbing up a rung, he swings his leg over the guardrail. He helps me over, his muscled arms rippling, and I try my best not to look at the view of him as I find my footing. He smirks at my obvious averting eyes but doesn't say anything.

"What if I don't jump far enough?"

"I'll make sure you do."

"What if someone sees us?"

"They won't."

"What if—"

He reaches out and takes my hand, silencing the millions of what-if questions clouding my thoughts. "The moment we hit the water, we're going to dive, okay?"

I nod without answering.

"Are you ready?"

I inhale a shuddering breath. "No."

"Ava, look at me," he says, his voice deep and smooth and calm enough to quiet my screaming fear. When I meet his blue-green eyes, he says, "I won't let go of you until you're ready. If you want me to hold your hand until morning, I will."

Oh, God. I have to jump. The moon pulls at my very essence, forcing me to inch my bare feet forward toward the ledge.

Closing my eyes, I squeeze Carter's hand, imagining I'm a million other places than standing at the edge of the sundeck ready to plummet into the churning ocean. "Okay, count to three. Let's get this over with."

"Remember, jump out and then when we hit the water, dive."

Another shaky breath releases from my mouth. "Okay."

Carter shifts the waterproof bag on his shoulder before saying, "One. Two. Three."

Bending my knees at the same moment Carter does, we propel out and away from the yacht. The sea air whooshes around me, and my stomach rises into my throat. As my feet touch the water, ice swallows me, sinking into my bones. The last thing I see before my head goes under is the bright, round moon taunting me from the sky.

Then all I see is the glowing water.

✿ 5 ✿

JUST BREATHE

CARTER YANKS ME DEEPER INTO the ocean, not giving me the chance to even think. He swims with a grace I'll never manage to have, his body shimmering and morphing into a form more fitted for the sea. Through hazy eyes, I watch the spark in his chest pulse through him, binding his legs together until a shimmering, teal tail appears, matching the color of his eyes. The scales gleam as if they're made of gemstones. My fingers reach down without my mind's consent and brush along their smooth and slippery texture, like a fishtail but with the strength and toughness of the skin of a dolphin.

My vision shadows the longer we're underwater, my lungs threatening to burst from the lack of oxygen. Fear laces around my heart, squeezing me in its icy grip when I realize I'm far too deep in the water to ever make it back to the surface for another gasp of air. I kick my legs, still unchanged, and I know I'll die if the transformation doesn't happen soon. I'll be the only mermaid ever to drown.

Thrashing, I struggle to break the grip Carter has on me. As I pull away, he only holds me tighter, his handsome face too blurry to tell what expression he's giving me.

My heart hammers against my ribs, threatening to explode from my chest. Something is wrong. Nothing is happening. No more tingling sensation, no cramps, nothing. And no air to breathe. What if Carter was wrong, and he didn't use his one chance to transform me into a mermaid?

Just when I'm about to lose myself to the panic consuming me, Carter releases my hand to only cup my face between his palms. His face lingers so close to mine that his eyes shine clearly in the strangely glowing water.

"Just breathe, Ava. You must breathe." He mouths through the water, though his voice doesn't reach me.

Everything tells me not to breathe. Because if I breathe in, water will fill my lungs and I'll drown.

"Breathe," he mouths again.

At this point, my lungs are about to explode, and I automatically open my mouth, sucking in a gallon of ocean water. But unlike when I drowned, the water doesn't burn. It's a relief. The ocean fills me with life, and my lungs—gills—pull precious oxygen from the water allowing me to breathe among the fish.

Closing my eyes, I allow the water into my mouth and out the gills that have formed on my neck just under my ears, following my jaw line. Dull cramps seize the muscles in my legs, traveling from my toes to my thighs. Heat expands from my heart and circulates through my veins, pushing the chill of the ocean away.

I turn my gaze away to stare down as the shimmer from my own spark crawls along my body. The strings of my bikini dance in the sea, and while swallowing my embarrassment, I tug them until my bottoms float away. Carter doesn't take his eyes off my face. His eyes sparkle like two jewels, holding me in their precious gaze.

Another series of cramps rush through me, forcing me to arch my back. Scales burst from my skin, a cerulean blue with a metallic sheen, and I wish I had a mirror to check myself out. The muscles on my arms spasm and smooth, bone-like ridges press against the skin of my forearms. Even my fingers change slightly. My nails grow sharp and thin webbing connects my fingers together up to my knuckles.

"That's it, Ava. You're almost done." Carter's smooth voice echoes in my mind, sending my heart racing. His hand moves from my shoulder to my fingers, and he clasps his fingers around mine, swimming back a foot to take in the full view of my transformation.

The expanse of my caudal fin is wider than Carter's, glittering like jewels are encrusted in every blue scale. A small ridge protrudes from where my tail meets my torso, wrapping around my waist like a belt, and when I reach behind me, I feel a firm yet versatile small dorsal fin. The rest of my once human skin takes on a shimmer like a pearl, my pectoral fins on my arms nearly unnoticeable.

My blond hair flows in the water, twirling and swirling with the current, and I wish I had something to tie it out of the way with. A smile creeps along my face, my fear of the ocean, the transformation, the end of my old life, drifting away in the water.

Floating in the current, all I can do is watch Carter smile at me. A soft glow pulsates from where his heart is in his chest, and without having to look, I know mine mirrors his. Something flashes in his turquoise jeweled eyes—an emotion I can't decipher—but it's just for me. He drinks in my appearance, and I find myself leaning closer.

With a flick of his tail, he closes the distance between us, slides his arms over my shoulders and around my neck. Tiny bubbles escape his nose, oxygen still clinging to us through the water, and he studies my lips like they're the most fascinating thing he's ever seen.

"You're beautiful, Ava." His voice wraps around my mind, drawing me closer.

His lips brush softly against mine, just enough to tease me, test me—to see if I'll kiss him back. It's the complete opposite of the kiss we shared when he brought back my memories. This one's different. The images that flicker through my mind aren't my own. They're his.

An image of me in my mermaid state—my sparkling blue, metallic-like tail, my pearlescent skin, my cerulean eyes clearer than the brightest sky on a sunny day—settles in my head as I see what Carter sees. I kiss him more deeply, slipping my tongue into his mouth, clinging to him like the current will sweep me away. His fingers tangle in my flowing hair, and we hover in the middle of the glowing ocean for a long moment.

"Whoa," I say, realizing that my own voice falls flat as it projects telepathically to Carter.

The intensity of his gaze sinks deep in my soul. He blinks a few times, his face relaxing, and then he jerks his head before motioning me to swim.

In this moment, I realize that the swimming skills Carter possesses don't come from him simply being a merman. When I flick my tail, I shoot sideways, dragging Carter with me as I cut through the water like a drunken fish.

Embarrassment washes over me, and I try to compose myself. If I can't manage to swim in my new form, we won't get very far. Carter laughs out bubbles, wrapping his hands around my waist and gently tips me forward so I'm parallel with the surface looming overhead. A school of silver fish with black spotted tails swims over us, dancing with the water. It isn't until this moment that I take in the vastness of the ocean.

Beneath us, kelp stretches toward us like giant green ropes reaching for the surface. A menagerie of fish dart through the kelp forest like the tall plants cage them in. Yellowtails, some almost half my size, swim with powerful fins.

A shadow crosses over us, sending fear into me, as a boat floats on the surface above us. Carter glances up but doesn't give it more than a single thought. In the dark water, no one can see us from the surface.

As the thoughts of fishing equipment and radar whirl through my mind, Carter presses his fingers into the skin between my bikini-covered chest over my heart. "No human device can detect us. The light you see, our life force, protects us. It causes interference. It also disguises us from above. No one can see us as we are when we're underwater. It's surfacing that's dangerous."

He doesn't lessen the pressure of his fingers, my heartbeat drumming against his palm. His other hand settles on my lower back, rubbing gently across the short dorsal fin that runs from the top of my tail to the string of my bikini top.

Ever so gently, he guides the motion of my body like the ripples of a wave, showing me how to control my swim without stroking my arms out like I usually would in a crawl stroke, the most comfortable swim stroke for me.

After a few minutes, he nods his head, smiling at me. The motion feels more natural the more I do it. His hands release me, the heat of his touch still lingering on my skin. I jet forward, cutting through the water of the current that pushes me along.

Carter never leaves my side, holding my pinkie finger with his. We swim with our arms at our sides, propelled by the strength of our glittering tails. He guides me deeper into the kelp forest, and we navigate our way through like Carter has swum these waters a million times. I wouldn't doubt that he has.

Fish dart away, clearing a path, and I catch sight of a bat ray swimming like an expansive butterfly along the bottom of the ocean floor. Tugging Carter toward it, we descend until I can nearly brush my fingers along its back. The only time I've been so close to a creature of this beauty was at the local aquarium, which doesn't compare to the greatness hidden beneath the place I've feared most.

As we weave in and out of the kelp, my every movement matches Carter's. I thought I was aware of his body before, but it doesn't compare to this moment. Every glance he sneaks at me, every smile, every squeeze of my fingers. My attraction to him consumes my thoughts. I just hope he doesn't hear the thoughts I want to keep privately to myself.

When we reach a clearing in the water, I slow down. He circles me, creating a small whirlpool that twirls my hair in front of my face. I peek at him through my hair, letting myself float up a few feet toward the moonlit surface. The exertion of keeping his pace wears me down, but I don't want him to notice. I have the sudden need to prove that I can live in this new underwater world he's shared with me.

But even my hair can't hide my fatigue when a current catches me, pulling me away from Carter. He doesn't allow it to take me though, just like he promised. Instead, he motions for me to hold onto his broad, muscular shoulders. With my stomach pressed against his back, his short dorsal fin slightly digging into my skin, he takes off, pulling me along to more shallow waters. His skin radiates with warmth, and it's like energy pulsates between us, charged by the closeness of our bodies as we move as one through the water. He swims so fast, I can't even catch sight of our surroundings and any sense of direction is lost to me.

With a flick of his tail, we ascend, shooting up to the surface. A jolt of surprise leaves me breathless when we break through. Cold air wraps around me, the ocean air blowing against my wet hair. We bob through the waves, Carter sweeping his tail in the water to keep us in control.

I rest my chin on the crook of his neck, and he shivers when I release a breath of air near his ear. My body instinctually adjusts from breathing water to air, the action effortless. Ahead of us, lights sparkle from an island in the close distance. The moon casts a brilliant light over the ocean, creating a silvery trail to the waves crashing against the shore.

Boats pepper the harbor in the distance, sleepily floating on the water. Jetting rocks sprout from the waves ahead of us, and Carter swims in their direction. The muscles in his arms tighten as he uses only his upper body to pull himself from the water to perch on the edge of the rocks with his tail smacking the waves. Reaching down, he grips me under my arms and lifts me next like I weigh nothing at all.

My tail rests across his lap, my caudal fin lightly tapping the black surface of the rock. He removes the bag that was strapped to his side and sets it beside us. Through the clear plastic, I spot my bikini bottoms, relieved he thought to grab them, though now our clothes lie in a damp heap.

He absently trails his fingers along the side of my tail. We sit quietly, watching the waves crash into the shore from a far enough distance away that no one will spot us. I never thought I could be so at peace in the water that stole my sister away, but as long as I suppress the memory, I can see the ocean as a bright new world.

"For someone who was terrified of the ocean, you're doing surprisingly well," Carter says, his voice cutting through the air. Hearing the words out loud makes me miss the sound of his voice in my head.

"You're as surprised as I am. I never thought I'd ever go back in the water, let alone explore its depths."

"Why is that?" I knew the question would come up eventually. I was hoping I could avoid it, but what's the point? I share a new bond with a boy I never imagined I would. The ocean and this unbelievable secret binds me to him—at least for now. It's all so new.

Taking a deep breath of salty air, I hang my head to veil my face with my hair. "When I was a kid, my sister and I were playing in the waves late in the day. We got caught in a riptide, and she drowned. The ocean swept her away. It was a miracle that a neighbor managed to even save me."

He doesn't respond with words of sympathy or apologies like I expect. All he says is, "And now the ocean finally got another girl it wanted." The tone of his voice surprises me, like he's angry. Yet, his gentle touch says something else completely.

"You hate that I'm here now." It's not a question but a statement. I was angry and scared and confused until the moment I took my first breath of the ocean. But sitting here with Carter takes all those negative emotions away. It'll be strange come dawn when I'll return back to my normal life like none of this ever happened. A secret that'll weigh on me with every interaction with my friends, every step I take—even every time I suck in a breath of air.

"I hate that you never had the choice—I hate that I'm selfishly enjoying your presence, how I got so lucky to have such a beautiful, smart, caring girl with me now, sharing my world. I hate that I don't regret anything." Without meeting my gaze, he brushes his hand through his copper streaked hair, lit with a silvery glow from the moon.

I reach out and take both his hands in mine. The gesture relaxes his shoulders, and he brings my cool fingers up to his mouth and blows on them. Even though the air chills me, it doesn't bother me.

"I'm not going to lie. Everything about this terrified me. I'm still terrified. You wasted your one chance at transforming someone on me. You gave me, a girl you've known for so little time, the ring that was intended for your mate so I could return to my life back in Azure Waters." The words rush so quickly from my mouth, I feel like I'm bearing my soul. "And I don't even know what will happen when I get back." Tears threaten to fall onto my cheeks, but I blink them away.

"I didn't waste anything on you, Ava," he whispers, staring up at the stars.

He says it now, but what about in a few months? A year? Things can change in a split second. What if I realize I don't even really, truly like him? I can't imagine the thought, but what if my crush is temporary like the one I had for Chase Gibbons my freshman year of high school? It lasted all of two months, and then suddenly, I didn't like him anymore.

"The sea air might be getting to your head," I say, because it sure feels like it's making me crazy.

Instead of frowning like I expect, he tilts his head back and laughs. "It clears my mind if anything. You make me think past the day that's ahead of us."

I don't respond. How can I tell him the only thoughts of our future end badly in my mind?

He wraps his arms around me. "Please, don't look so sad."

Leaning over, I rest my head against his shoulder. His arms slide around me, pulling me close, and I listen to the sound of his heartbeat that thrums in perfect sync with my own. I can't think about my future when I don't even know how I'll slip back into my life as a human.

"It's just—I can't envision my future, Carter."

"Then just be with me in the now."

I nod. "Okay. I can do that. Why don't you show me more of your world?"

He smiles, giving me the look that I know is only for me.

"You mean *our* world."

Our world. It has a nice ring to it.

Shifting me off his lap, he adjusts the bag across his side and jumps back into the water. I dive in after him, wrapping my arms around his shoulders. In one quick motion, he takes off, diving us back into the ocean's glowing depths.

6

SPARK OF LIFE

IT'S NOT UNTIL ALMOST DAWN that we make our way back to the yacht, now docked in a harbor in a cove off Catalina Island. It's one of the first stops on the way up the coast to San Francisco, which happens to be where Carter has spent most of his life. I had no clue we'd be stopping, but I guess Ruby and Carlton wanted to surprise Sapphire as a birthday treat.

The moon will set any moment, the sky lightening with the rise of the sun. Sneaking back on the boat will be the ultimate test. There's no way I—the girl who's terrified of the ocean— could ever explain an early morning swim in the sea. According to Carter, Captain Briggs is probably already up with a few other crew members, but all their work will keep them inside and out of sight for now.

"We'll enter on the swim platform," Carter says, his voice echoing through my mind. A seal darts by us as we float just feet below the yacht.

"What if I can't transform back?" It wasn't until this moment that the thought crossed my mind.

"You will, I promise."

A second later, Carter closes his eyes, still holding my hands, and the spark of his life force flows from all over his body to enter his heart, making the spot on his chest glow brighter than ever. The intensity of his jewel-like eyes fades and his scales vanish, retreating back beneath his tanned skin. When his transformation is complete, he treads under the water in front of me, blowing out small air bubbles as he now relies on his lungs to breathe in the oxygen he needs to live on land.

But he doesn't surface. He remains at my side, completely naked, waiting for me to transition back to my human self.

Closing my eyes, I try to will my body to transform but nothing happens. I can no longer hear Carter's voice in my mind either. I motion for him to rise to the surface, but all he does is shake his head.

Come on, body. Don't be stubborn. As soon as the words enter my mind, a jolt of ice shoots up my legs and cramps grip my stomach, traveling down my tail to my caudal fin. My body convulses, the transformation taking hold, splitting my tail down the middle. I bend down, jerking away from Carter and hug myself. Another round of cramps travels to my arms, and then I'm forced to arch my back, a glimmer of pain seizing my spine. It's much worse turning back to human, my skin freezing in the cold water and my legs aching.

And then my lungs burn as my gills disappear.

I thrash, suddenly terrified that I can't breathe. Carter hooks his arm around my waist, yanking me toward the surface. As we break through the water to air, I cough, choking and spitting out the now disgusting saltwater. Carter rubs my back, patting me gently, and I rid my lungs of the sea to take a gasping breath.

I shudder, feeling weak. All the swimming of the night now hits me hard. I bob back underwater, this time holding my breath. Carter doesn't let me stay under long, the strength of his arms wrapping around me.

It takes me a moment to orient myself when I realize that like Carter, I'm naked from my torso down, and I'm pressed against his hips as he holds onto me and the swim platform.

Before I have a chance to blush, Carter tugs the other half of my bikini from the bag on his other side and hands it to me, keeping his eyes on my face. Awkwardly shifting away while his hand remains firmly on my waist to keep my head above the water, I tie my bottoms in place.

"Okay," I say when I'm ready.

He pushes me onto the swim platform with one arm, and I roll onto my back and stare at the pink sky of early dawn. Goosebumps prickle over my skin, my chest heaving. I catch my breath, getting used to the feeling of solid wood beneath me. With a small splash, Carter pulls himself next to me, tugging his clothes from his bag to get dressed.

I groan, sitting up on my elbows. I ache everywhere like I've hit the gym with my mom's personal trainer. I only went with her once, and my legs burned for a week. This is worse though. Much worse. I'm not even sure I can get back to my feet to make it to my stateroom.

Carter stretches his arms over his head before reaching for his toes. Water drips from his hair into his eyes, and then he shakes his head, spraying me with saltwater. My gaze lingers on how the rising sun shines golden on his skin. His eyes smile when they meet mine, though his lips press into a thin line.

He holds out his hand for me to take, but instead of letting him help me up, I fall back to stare at the sky. "I can't. My body's on fire, which means you lied to me, you know."

A dimple flashes through the scruff on his cheeks. "You asked if the transformation hurt. I find it uncomfortable, so technically I didn't lie from my experience."

Sighing, I wiggle my toes in front of me to make sure they still work. "You're just going to have to leave me here. I really don't think I can get up."

"I guess I'll have to carry you then." He laughs, grinning, and he bends over to scoop me into his arms.

I playfully slap his chest. "Carter, put me down."

Instead of setting me on my feet, he moves to put me on the row of seats lining the guardrail on the deck and off the swimming platform. He slips me my dress from the waterproof bag. I slide it over my head, the damp material clinging to me, and I run my fingers over the skirt to try to press the wrinkles from it.

I catch my reflection in the shiny metal trim along the wall of the yacht. My wet hair hangs limply and the pearlescent sheen of my skin is nowhere in sight. I just look like I've been thrown in the ocean. The only reminder of the night is the faint glow in my chest, the one only Carter and I can see.

Voices echo from above us as the crew starts to set up breakfast on the dining terrace. If we don't hurry, we'll get caught out here in the same clothes we wore last night, soaking wet, with a lot of lying to do.

Carter holds out his hand to me. "Come on."

With shaking legs, I manage to push to my feet. He half carries me into the empty saloon. We quietly cross the room. Each step gets easier the more I remind myself that I've been walking since I was eleven months old, according to my mom.

Carter calls for the elevator, and another two voices echo from upstairs. It's Giselle and Sapphire. They mention my name. When the elevator door opens, we don't get on. Carter pushes me toward the stairs and nudges me up, stopping just for a second to make sure no one spots us climbing to the sundeck.

Thankfully, it's empty. Carter runs to the cabinets near the closest lounge chair and grabs two towels. He strips off his shirt and wraps the towel around his shoulders. Following his lead, I tug my dress from last night over my head and wrap the dry towel around my cold body.

The elevator slides open and Giselle and Sapphire stand in front of us in their bikinis. Sapphire raises her eyebrows while Giselle blinks a few times, confusion crossing her face.

"I was just at our room trying to wake your ass up, but the door was locked," Giselle says, glancing from me to Carter.

I frown, squeezing my eyes shut. "Crap. I must've accidentally locked it."

Carter touches my shoulder. "Hey, don't worry. I can get the spare key." His fingers brush over my shoulder as he abandons me to the curious gazes of my friends. I'm tempted to run after him, but my legs still ache, and I might trip and fall flat on my face.

"So," Giselle says, a smile lighting her entire face.

Heat claws up my neck. "So."

"You look tired."

I lean against the cabinet of towels. "Been up for a while."

Sapphire snickers from next to Giselle. If I could throw myself over the guardrail and back into the ocean, I would. My friends won't give up unless I give them something to talk about. It's sort of a tradition. We've all definitely kissed and told—but only to each other. And out of everyone, I haven't had much to tell.

"Spill, Ava," Giselle says, pulling me away from the elevator and the stairs.

"It's not a big deal." It's a huge deal, though. And one I can never share as much as I want to. Giselle would flip if she knew my secret. She'd beg me to figure out a way to turn her into a mermaid. She'd beg Carter for a friend. She still has the pretend mermaid fin she got for her birthday a few years ago locked away in her pool shed.

As tempting as it would be to have my best friend going through the same thing I am, Carter would never go for it. Plus, Giselle would have to drown, and Carter said there was no guarantee. A lie will have to do.

Giselle hits a button to start the jets in the hot tub and cranks the heat up a bit. I slip on the small step, nearly falling in. My legs still tremble from the transformation. Knocking her knee into mine, Giselle meets my gaze with another brilliant smile. Her warm skin glows in the early morning light. As the jets kick on and the water warms, I sink lower until I'm covered to my neck. After swimming all night, it's a strange relief to just sit in the hot tub and relax.

"If you think we had sex, think again," I finally say. Because honestly, that's the first thing I would think if I knew Giselle spent the night with a boy. And it's definitely what happens when Sapphire and Matty share her cabin, though they've been together since sophomore year and friends since he moved to Azure Waters in the sixth grade.

"Hey, I wasn't thinking that," Giselle says. *Sure thing, BFF.*

"But we did kiss...and I saw him naked." I cover my face with my hands as I say the words. Because they're true. I technically did see Carter in all his muscular goodness, but I didn't exactly see all of him, though he clearly doesn't care whether or not I do.

"Oh, my God," Sapphire squeals. "I bet he's so damn sexy."

My cheeks heat so much that it feels like I'm getting a sunburn. "You have no idea."

"Oh, but I think I do," Giselle says.

Her eyes flick away from me and toward the elevator where Carter stands, holding a tray of breakfast foods. He's still in his board shorts without a shirt. A smile plays on his lips as he sets the food down on a nearby table. There's no way he didn't just hear our conversation.

The three of us girls start laughing—not only from embarrassment but because of how funny the situation is. My heart flutters, and I imagine what a night alone in a room with Carter would be like instead of under the sea. It's enough to send me under the bubbling water to pull myself together. If only I could still breathe.

The water rocks me when another body enters the hot tub and slides next to me. Carter's hand nudges my head up until I break the surface. His dazzling eyes smile at me, and I sigh, releasing the breath I was holding.

"You heard it all, didn't you?" I ask, darting my gaze to my friends as they hold back laughter.

Before he can respond, Giselle splashes water at us. "Look, Carter. Just so you know. If you want to hang out with Ava, you have to know that I'm her BFF, and we talk. Actually, all of us talk, and you're new, so we're going to talk about you."

"Only good stuff," I say quietly, nearly dying of embarrassment. Jumping into the ocean is looking better than ever, though fear still lingers in the back of my mind. I'm probably the only mermaid with an unhealthy fear of the sea.

"Especially the good stuff," Sapphire says.

I skim my hand across the water, splashing her in the face. Her laughter echoes through the air followed by Giselle's. Carter laughs as well, but I think he's only doing it to be nice. I, on the other hand, sink lower into the water. Carter slides his arm over my shoulders, and I tilt my head toward his chest.

"And another thing," Giselle says.

Oh, great. There's always more with her.

"If I start to hear anything bad, you better watch out. I know people."

I groan. "She doesn't know people."

"Oh, you know I know people, Aves," she says, her voice staying serious though she's really joking.

"Got it," Carter says.

"Good."

Sapphire giggles across from us. "Now that everything's settled, are you joining us for a day of adventures?"

Her mention of plans leaves a sinking feeling in my stomach. Today of all days had to be the one where we're not going to relax on the yacht. We just had to dock at an island where I'll be forced to do stuff. All I want to do is crawl into bed and sleep. Thank God it's summer or I'd die if the next full moon fell on a day I had to wake up early. *But you start college in the fall.* I guess night classes are out.

"Whatever Ava wants to do," Carter says, drawing my attention back to my friends' conversation. "I'm pretty sure all ocean activities are out, right?" He eyes me.

"Just because Ava doesn't go in the ocean, doesn't mean you can't," Sapphire says.

I shrug. "She's right."

His eyes turn serious. "I live most of my time on the ocean, but hanging with you is something I haven't had much time to do."

The hot tub is about to turn into a mess of melted girls as we all swoon at his words. Sapphire audibly sighs, and I lock my fingers with Carter's under the water.

"Okay, you're definitely not invited to go snorkeling with us," Giselle says. "Ava, he's all yours."

Even though my heart pounds and butterflies swarm in my stomach, all I can do is laugh. I never imagined meeting someone who can fit so easily with my friends, especially one who happens to be a really hot merman.

"I expect him to show you a good time, too," Giselle adds.

As I look at Carter, I know he will.

7

BREATHLESS

AFTER RETURNING TO MY STATEROOM and sleeping for a few hours, I shower and get ready. My light blue sundress with a sweetheart neckline clings in all the right places. My hair, now clean and free of chlorine and saltwater, sits in a ballerina bun on top of my head. My cheeks and lips are the perfect pink from my lip and cheek stain, but I don't wear much more makeup.

Stepping into my sandals, I stare at myself in the full length mirror on the back of the door. I expect to look as different as I feel, but I look like I always have.

A knock sounds on the door, and I step forward and swing

it open to find Carter standing on the other side. He smiles, his shaven face revealing his sexy dimples. The scent of coconut shampoo, sunscreen, and the ever present hint of the salty ocean wafts from him, sending my heart fluttering. Just his presence alone stirs something deep within me, almost like the pull the ocean had on me, but this pull is different—it embodies everything good in me and drags it to the surface.

Carter sucks in a small breath, drinking me in with his blue-green eyes. It's enough to send heat from my heart to my feet. I never knew how much a look could speak to me, but after last night, I can almost see my own reflection in his mind, and I love what I do to him. It makes today a lot less daunting, because in this moment, I don't doubt Carter wants to spend time with me and not only because he transformed me into a mermaid on a whim. How long that that look will last? God, I hope forever.

I twirl once, allowing the airy fabric to twist around my thighs before settling when I stop. He rubs his lips together, his eyes trailing to my mouth. I force myself to smile even though I'm suddenly feeling awkward, unsure if I should kiss him, if he's waiting for me to make the first move.

"You look beautiful," he finally says. He hovers in the hallway outside my room.

"Thank you. I wasn't sure what to wear. I didn't really pack for hiking or anything." On the island, there's not much to do outside of water activities except hiking, biking, shopping, and dining.

"You're perfect the way you are," he says, nudging a basket at his feet. I didn't notice it until now. "Come on. Keith's waiting to take us to the dock."

I should be more afraid than I feel about having to ride in the inflatable boat to the dock that leads to land, but I'm not. I suppose being a mermaid has its benefits.

As he takes my hand, I pull him closer. "Do you think I should tell my friends that my fear of the ocean isn't what it used to be?"

His forehead crinkles for a split second. Pulling my hand up, he rubs his finger across the sea stone in the ring on my ring finger. "This stops you from a forced change, but it doesn't stop the transformation all together. Once it starts, you can't just stop it either."

"Oh."

"I'm not saying stay out of the ocean, but you have to be careful. You've only transformed once..." His voice trails off.

"And I wasn't exactly that great at it," I finish for him.

He reaches up and brushes his fingers along my cheek. "You did perfect, but something as little as a thought could trigger you to change. It's better to just stay out of the water for now unless you're going in to transform. The ocean will be more alluring than ever, and you might actually never want to return to shore."

I frown, tilting my head to the side. "Doubt it but okay. I don't want to risk messing things up."

It's almost a blessing that I've spent my life away from the water. It won't be anything new to my friends. I couldn't imagine surviving this trip if I did love the ocean and did all the things my friends like to do. I've hated myself for fearing the ocean, and now it's finally saving me from more than my morbid thoughts.

I can't help being sad, though. I've missed so much over the years.

"It won't be like this forever, Aves."

I smile at the nickname Giselle sometimes calls me. "You hope."

He chuckles. "I know so. Now, come on. We only have a few hours to enjoy the land."

Then I remember what he told me the first day I met him, and how he prefers the land over the sea. It's why he's here and not at some hidden merpeople oasis.

I just wonder if I'll still feel the same about land as he does. What if one day I don't? Pushing the thought away, I lace my fingers through Carter's. I can't think about all the stuff that doesn't concern me in this moment. Right now, I'm here with Carter, and he's who I want to be with regardless of the land or sea.

Palm trees stretch toward the bright blue sky, decorated with puffs of white clouds. The sea breeze lifts the stray blond hairs on my neck, pulling them from my bun. I tilt my head toward the sky, absorbing the golden sunlight.

On the blanket next to me, Carter leans back on his elbows, his bare chest too irresistible not to touch. I'm starting to think that apart from his work uniform that he won't have to wear for the rest of the trip for being a hero—*my* hero—that all Carter owns are board shorts. I can't complain about the lack of shirts though. My friends were right. He's incredibly sexy.

We sit alone on the long stretch of pebbly beach. Being early summer, the water is still quite cold to swim in without a wetsuit, and the waves where we are aren't worth surfing if you could call them waves at all. Two kayakers took off from a spot just down the way, but apart from them, we've been alone, unless you count the fishermen in their boats in the distance. Most of the tourists hang out on the beach near the marina where the sand is powdery soft.

"Favorite color?" I ask, running my toes over the smooth rocks at my feet.

He rubs his chin for a moment. "Green."

"Mine's gray."

"Gray?"

I nod. "I know. Did I mention I'm boring?"

He laughs. "Far from it. Favorite food?" We've been shooting questions back and forth for a few hours now, like we're trying to catch up with everything else that has tied us together with a pretty, knotted bow.

"Mexican. Cheese enchiladas in a red sauce to be more specific. Maybe tacos. Yours is seafood, isn't it?" Apparently, I'll start to really enjoy sushi. Giselle will be ecstatic that I might eventually go with her to Sushi Days, but even then, there's a huge difference between nibbling on a California roll that barely counts as sushi and taking a bite straight from a still moving fish. Yuck. Nope, I'd rather starve.

"You'd think, since I eat a whole lot of it but no. It's any type of dessert. I could eat it for every meal no matter what it is. I might even trade my tail for some if given the option."

Laughing, I playfully smack his arm. "Well, it's a good thing I bake."

"Don't mess with me."

I laugh. "I'm not. You get permission from the chef, and I'll make dessert tonight."

His eyes light up, causing me to laugh. It's the same look all my friends give me when I tell them I've been busy in the kitchen. I was the one who ended up baking the triple fudge brownie batter cake for Matty's birthday to save Sapphire after her failed attempt at using an oven.

"I'm holding you to it," he says, brushing his fingers along my arm.

Leaning in, he rests his head against mine. We sit together, our bodies touching, as small waves lap at the pebbly shore. With anyone else, the sudden quiet would force me to make small talk, but with Carter, I can just sit and enjoy our peaceful surroundings without a single word.

I draw my gaze to the stretch of clear water before us. The crystalline sky meets the turquoise water in the horizon in a gradient of mesmerizing blues. In the distance, a pod of dolphins swim just offshore, a few jumping and diving, splitting the far off waves as they play in the water that whispers for me to step in.

A strange feeling washes over me. I watch another dolphin propel from the sea, barely splashing as it dives back under. Jealousy sneaks through my mind, causing me to shrug away from Carter to push to my feet. All I want to do is get a closer look at the creatures that I now share the sea with. In this moment, being on land doesn't feel right like it used to.

Before Carter has a chance to react, I stride to the lapping waves, allowing them to wash over my bare feet. My mind screams to back away, warning me of the dangers of the ocean, but my heart—the spark of my mermaid essence—begs me to stroll in a little farther.

"Ava, what are you doing?" Carter asks from behind me.

I point my finger at the dolphins. "Aren't they beaut—" As the words escape my lips, a tingling sensation crawls from my heart and down my torso to my legs. Cramps grip at my toes, sending me stumbling to the pebbly shore. A small wave laps over my legs, soaking my dress.

Terror washes over me as I realize what's happening.

"Carter!" My voice echoes through the air. "It's happening! I can't stop."

My back arches, cramps seizing my spine. Fear shoots through me, the struggle between wanting to dive into the ocean and the more dominant part of me not wanting anything to do with it, threatening to tear me apart.

I'm not even in a foot of water, but it doesn't make a difference. My body craves to transform, *needs* to transform. Resisting only makes me nauseated. The problem with transforming among the lapping waves is that if I sprout my tail in this spot, I won't be able to drag myself into the water. My arms already feel weak from last night's swim.

Cerulean scales sprout from my skin, sending tears into my eyes. Each scale glitters with a metallic sheen in the sunlight like they have a mirrored surface. I blink a few dozen times, wishing them away. But wishing doesn't work. There won't be a miracle to stop me from changing now.

My breathing quickens, full blown panic consuming me. The ridges of my pectoral fins emerge on my forearms, and my now sharp nails scratch lines into the pebbles. In just a few moments, I'll be a mermaid for anyone to stumble upon.

This can't be happening. Why is this happening? Carter had warned of the risk, but I didn't think it was that big of a possibility. I didn't think I'd end up in this form again for another month.

Carter sweeps one of his arms under my transforming legs while cradling my back in his other. He charges into the ocean, the cool, salty water muting the silent screams echoing through my mind. Relief courses through me, my body reacting to the ocean the deeper Carter takes me. He doesn't stop holding me until he's waist deep, and then he lets me go only to tug me by my arms, forcing me under.

My blurry vision clears, my sight adjusting to the water. Carter tugs my dress over my head in a quick motion, stopping my dorsal fin from ripping the fabric. I try to shimmy out of my bikini bottoms, but another series of cramps rush through me. The side strap starts to rip, and Carter helps me take them off as quickly as he did my dress before shoving them in our bag. I have no time for embarrassment, because a second later, my legs fuse together, a numbness rushing over them, and then I flick my tail, diving deeper and away from Carter in his human form.

My mouth fills with water, and I breathe my first breath of the ocean, the burning in my lungs dissipating. My heart hangs heavy behind my ribcage, my mind clouding with terror just thinking about how close I was to becoming a mermaid on land. It was easy to treat last night's transformation as a dream, more of an inconvenience. Now that I triggered it in broad daylight, on a beach that could've been full of people, I realize how awful this whole situation really is. How quickly my normal life is slipping from my fingers to be dragged out to sea by the unforgiving waves of the ocean that just refuses to let me go, even all these years later after taking my sister when it was unable to steal me away, too.

I spin around in the clear water with no idea of what to do next. I'm too afraid to break through the surface, but Carter isn't here with me. What if he's waiting for me to transform back? I don't think I have enough energy to do so in this moment. But if I don't, someone could see me. It'd end badly.

Swimming in a quick circle, I assess my surroundings. The water is shallow enough that if I stretch upright, my tail will sweep the sandy bottom. I'm unnervingly close to the shore. Someone snorkeling could swim up on me and then I'd have no idea what to do. Stop them and beg them to keep my secret? Maybe they wouldn't see me at all. Carter wasn't specific. He said we were safe in the ocean, but what if a person was in the ocean, too?

"Ava, calm down. There's no one around, and if they were, they can't see us. We're safe." Carter's voice rings in my mind. He swims up next to me in his merman form, taking me into his arms.

"But I can't change back," I say, panic lining the thoughts I project to him. Pushing a bubble through my lips to calm myself down, I peer around us again like I'll suddenly spot a bunch of people. But the ocean only holds aquatic life.

Bright green sea grass drifts back and forth with the waves like it's blowing in a breeze. Starfish cling to the rocky bottom while small fish jet around. Sunlight dances across the rippling water overhead close enough that if Carter flicked his tail, we could feel the fresh air on our skin.

"Then why don't we go for a swim? I could tell how much you wanted to see the dolphins," he says, lacing his fingers with mine to pull me deeper into the surf.

It takes me a moment to orient myself with the water, flipping my tail to propel myself alongside Carter as he speeds off faster than any fish I've ever seen. He navigates the bottom of the shallows, staying deep enough and forcing us to move fast enough past the boats that fish the kelp paddies.

When we reach the end of the kelp forest, Carter slows, spiraling around me. His tail slips against mine as he swims below me, barely an inch away. His fingers cling to my waist, guiding me to spin with him through the water. My blond hair floats around us, half pulled from my bun, veiling the view of the underwater world.

Grazing his lips against mine, he kisses me softly, half-smiling against my mouth. It's playful, teasing me, testing me for a reaction. An image of my sparkling eyes appears in my head as Carter's mind collides with mine. It's a side effect of his kiss, of who we are, and it makes me want to kiss him more deeply, to know him on a level no one could ever experience.

He grins at my reaction, and I hold him closely. The ridge across my waist rubs against his, sending tingles through me. Carter picks up speed, swimming without looking where we're going, and I can't stop thinking about the feeling of his stomach against mine.

He pulls away, a strange look crossing his face. Something holds him back from letting his emotions take control, and without words, I can see that I'm driving him a little crazy in a good way. The intensity of his gaze burns through me, and he tugs me along even faster. With him, I don't even have to really swim. I just float along with him, saving my energy.

A high-pitched, melodious sound unlike anything I've ever heard cuts through the water, drawing my attention away from Carter's pouty lips. I can't see where the noise is coming from, and I don't ask Carter what it is. I'm afraid that if I speak, this surreal moment will end.

He concentrates on weaving in out of a school of bright orange fish sparkling in the water like a sunset when they catch the light from above that beams rays around us. On the sand not far below, leopard sharks glide over the bottom, hunting for their next meal. There's at least a dozen, all on the smaller side, and Carter dips us down and swims right over them so I can study the beautiful pattern of spots on their backs. They don't bother us, just swimming along like we're not even there.

"We have no predators in the sea," he explains, his voice cutting through my mind, clearing the daze that holds me in a rainbow bubble. Reaching down, he runs his fingers gently above the animal without touching it. He flips to swim under me, facing upward to look at me. Holding out his hand, he presses two fingers gently against my chest, over my heart. "Our essence protects us."

I didn't even think about the possibility of being hunted by greater predators—everything too mesmerizing to even put those thoughts in my mind. The only fear I have is the silhouette of a boat crossing overhead. It's strange for me to fear what's above the water and not below for once.

Carter wraps his arms around my waist and propels us far from the shallows into the open water of the blue sea. I cling onto him, pressing against him so no water cuts between us. His heartbeat races against my chest, and I bury my face in his neck as the underwater world blurs around us.

Another high-pitched sound pulses through the water. It's

like a bell ringing, bouncing through the current, playing an underwater melody just for me. It isn't until I see the dolphins that I realize it's the pod that creates the magical sound. I'm hearing them with new ears, because they sound nothing like the squeaks and shrill calls I've heard a dozen times on TV.

Carter slows, trailing along next to the pod with over two dozen dolphins as they coast along the surface above us. A female dolphin and her pup dive down and swim alongside us. Another one, a much larger male, chatters from our other side, and I reach out and run my hand along its smooth, gray side. Breaking away from Carter, I keep pace with the dolphin, its tinkering calls bouncing around me in a harmonious song.

A smile crosses my face, and I dance through the water, the pod surrounding me, nudging me toward the surface. As the water warms slightly, and I can see the sun overhead, the large male nudges my side, pushing me up. If he continues his playful gesture, I'll be forced to break the surface.

"Ava!" Carter calls. "Dive. There's a boat up ahead."

But I'm trapped. The dolphins swim and bump against me, trapping me within their formation. A few ascend the short distance to the surface and pop out, flying through the air. It's enough to draw the attention of any nearby boaters.

"They think this is a game," I call through my mind.

Two dolphins flank each of my sides, their flippers slapping against me. They swim close enough that their smooth bodies graze mine, forcing me to keep their pace as they prepare to launch from the water.

Closing my eyes, I cover my face with my hands. I flick my tail, trying to gently push the dolphins away. It's a matter of seconds before my face will break the surface. The boaters are about to get the show of their lives. And with everyone having cameras, I'll be captured on film for the world to see.

I bet Carter will regret saving me now.

A moment before the dolphins can push me up, forcing me to jump out of the water, something grips my caudal fin, yanking me away from the pod. They launch up and out of the water without me and then dive back under, continuing their peek-a-boo show. Pain sears through me, the sheer force enough to make me scream underwater. Carter drags me down deep enough that it'd be impossible to catch sight of us even if they'd just assume we are some sort of fish. Our bodies blend well enough with our surroundings that it'd be hard to see us at all though.

My tears mix with the water, and I curl my tail up to stroke my fingers along the base where Carter grabbed me to pull me free from the pod. It hurts to move, like I've dislocated whatever new bones lie under my scales.

Carter treads next to me, gently fanning his tail back and forth. He lowers himself so I don't have to move much while he inspects my tail. His warm fingers brush along my scales, a tingling sensation coursing through me. The pain eases some under his fingers, but it's not because of anything he's done.

His shadowed teal eyes meet mine as a series of cramps rushes through me. The sudden pain radiating through my tail

is no longer caused by being jerked down but because I'm transforming again. The shock of the pain must've set me off.

"Carter!" My words shout from my mind.

We're at least two-hundred feet below the surface, and there's nothing I can do as my human form threatens to take control, leaving me breathless.

8

HEAD ABOVE WATER

WITH LIGHTNING SPEED, CARTER SCOOPS me into his arms and zooms toward the surface. Without air in my lungs, the pressure change doesn't affect me like it would've had I breathed in air to dive. Carter pushes me to the surface, my transformation back into my human form completing when I break through to air. Ocean water sprays from my nose and mouth as my lungs jump into action.

Kicking my legs, I tread water, my head bobbing up and down. Pain radiates in my ankle, and I push past it. If I want to continue to breathe in the salty air, I don't have a choice. I blink through my blurry vision until my eyes clear and search the area for the boat Carter had mentioned, but it's already en route toward the island miles away.

My muscles ache, exhaustion hitting me hard like it did after my transformation this morning. It'd be easy to reach the shore within minutes if I still had a tail, but now, I can hardly manage to keep my head above water.

The chill of the water makes me shiver. "Carter? Carter, no one's around," I say, waving my arms under the water. I'm not even sure he can hear me, but I know it's the reason he didn't surface with me. Had the boat been here, I could've claimed to have been swept away or something.

He surfaces next to me an instant later.

"I'm too tired to swim. I'll never make it." My voice is barely audible over the roar of the sea.

"Try to transform back. The distance might be too far for me to swim you back in my human form, and it's not safe for me to coast the surface." He cups my face in his hands. "You can do this."

Closing my eyes, I wait for the cramps to seize my muscles but nothing happens. No tingling sensation. Nothing but the ache in my ankle to remind me that in this form, I'm no match for the ocean.

"I can't concentrate. My ankle hurts pretty badly," I say. "It's what triggered the transformation back."

His brows lower over his blue-green eyes. He bobs under, sending a small wave over me. I can't see him clearly, but his warm fingers touch my ankle. It makes me highly aware that

I'm not exactly dressed.

A second later, he pops up next to me. "It's bruised, but I don't think it's broken. You're still moving it well. You'll probably heal within an hour or so—one of the benefits of being a mermaid."

"Think we should wait it out and see if I can transform in a bit?" An hour is an awfully long time to tread in place, though I know Carter would help me.

His jaw twitches. "We might be missed."

"Then they'll have to miss us, because I can't swim or transform." Annoyance washes through me. "This whole situation is ridiculous. I probably deserve to be found out here floating half-naked."

Carter doesn't smile like I expect him to. "Don't blame yourself. I should've been more careful. If I hadn't grabbed you the way I did—"

"Those dolphins would have forced me out of the water. This isn't your fault," I say, interrupting him.

He brushes his wet hair from his face. "But I—"

I interrupt his words with a kiss, his tense muscles relaxing when I slide my arms around his neck. Slowly pulling away, I say, "Stop. Blame isn't going to help me get back to the shore."

"You're right. But I will. I have an idea." He tugs the strap of our bag over his shoulder and pulls out my half ripped bikini bottoms before handing them to me. I guess I won't be trying to transform back into a mermaid after all.

After a few embarrassing failed attempts, I manage to slide

my legs through my bottoms. Carter smirks when I huff out a breath and meet his eyes. Slapping my hand against the water, I splash him in the face, and he sinks under the surface before circling me a few times. His tail brushes my torso, and I can't stop the excitement forcing my annoyance and fear away.

He stops in front of me and bobs his head back up from the water. I suck in a small breath at his sudden closeness, and he reaches out and pushes wet hair from my face. "You have to stop looking at me like that."

"Like what?" I know well enough what he's talking about. I can't hide the desire to kiss him, to trail my fingers along his muscular shoulders, the desire to stay near him.

"Like you don't want me to take you back to the shore."

"Maybe I don't."

He sinks back under and swims around me again before popping up. "Ava," he says, the sound of my name sending my heart racing. "Be careful what you suggest. You have friends—you have family—all waiting for you on land."

It's enough to force my lingering thoughts away. I could never just give them all up for the sea. They'd be devastated if I disappeared without warning. I couldn't put my parents through that. Not again.

"You're right," I say, even though a part of me wants him to be wrong. "I guess we should try to get back." Back to the secrets, to the pretending. "You said you had an idea?"

"I'm going to need you to hold your breath for a bit, okay? It's not safe to swim the surface with you, but I can take you under. It'll be slow going, but unless you transform back, I don't know of a better way."

I pout my lip. "I'm sorry for being so much trouble, Carter."

Water splashes between us as he stares intently into my eyes like he can peer into my very essence. Wrapping my arms around him, I run my fingers along the short dorsal fin that travels his spine. He shudders, leaning forward to kiss me. I catch a glimpse of what I look like in his eyes, our kiss letting me peek into his head.

When he pulls away, he says, "You're worth the trouble, you know. Like I said before, I don't regret anything."

I smile. "How did I get so lucky?"

"Lucky? I—"

"You saved my life. Given me so much more than I ever thought possible." I trace my finger along his jaw. "I don't know how I'll ever repay you."

"You don't owe me anything," he says.

I kiss him again, imagining what it would be like to trail my hands along his ripped body. I must've projected my own thoughts through our kiss, because he releases a low moan into my lips. He eases away and dips back under the cool water. With the heat of him near me constantly, I'm no longer even cold.

He surfaces again, turning his back toward me, and motions for me to slide my hands around his neck. My chest presses against his broad shoulders, and I breathe heavily in his ear as nerves tighten my chest.

"Ready, Ava?" he asks lowly, his voice sounding as breathless as I feel.

"As ready as I'll ever be."

"Okay, take a deep breath and hold on."

Sucking a long breath into my lungs, I tighten my hold on Carter, wrapping my legs around his waist while pressing my cheek into his shoulder blade. In a quick motion, he dives under, taking me with him.

My ears pop the deeper we descend, but I can't see anything with my normal sight. Carter swims too quickly, the world zooming by as we head toward the shore. To calm my racing heart, I count the seconds ticking by the longer I hold my breath. My lungs burn by the time I count to fifty-eight, just under a minute. Squeezing his shoulder, I alert him that I need air, and he ascends to the surface, and I release him and break through the water. He never surfaces and tugs me back under the moment I suck more air into my lungs.

We continue on in this stop and go motion for what feels like eternity. My head swims with dizziness from having to hold my breath with only moments to refill my lungs. Just when I feel my hold loosen on Carter, he slows down and pushes me back to the surface.

My chest heaves, and I gasp a few burning, salty breaths. Carter circles around me a few more times but doesn't pull me back under to my relief. The shore lingers in front of me but still quite a bit of distance away. A few boats leisurely float in the distant harbor, but luckily, we have a clear path to the shore from here.

After a few minutes, Carter bursts to the surface next to me. He spits out ocean water before inhaling a long breath. Rubbing a hand over his face, he clears the water from his eyes before smiling at me like this is the most fun he's had in a while.

"And you thought you were trouble," he says, treading the water next to me. "It's not every day I get to have a beautiful girl cling to my back."

Heat crawls up my neck to blossom in my cheeks. I can't think of a response, so I don't say anything at all. His smile widens as he closes the distance. Wrapping his arms around me, he stops me from bobbing under. His soft board shorts graze my thigh, his legs brushing against mine.

Without saying another word, he swims forward, pulling me with him toward the shore. The waves push us along, and I nearly fall over when my feet touch solid ground. Carter takes most of my weight, and I limp toward the pebbly beach right where we left our blanket and basket. I pull Carter to the ground, resting my back on the smooth rocks, and he lies next to me, catching his breath.

"Please, tell me it's not always going to be like this. I don't think I can handle being so out of control all the time. I thought this ring was supposed to help." I wave my hand over my half ripped bottoms and bruised ankle.

Carter leans up on his elbows. "It does, believe me. If you

weren't wearing it, you'd never change back. Your body's adjusting, Ava. It'll take a while to figure it all out."

I sigh. "I don't have time, though. You saw how fast I ran into the ocean. What if that would've happened while we were on the yacht?"

"Then we'd figure it out."

Sitting up, he leans over me. He blocks the sun from my view as he grazes his lips against mine, kissing all my worries away. I react to his touch, my back arching up to him, and he slides his warm fingers around my bare lower back before pulling me into his lap. My fingers trace up his firm chest, it rising and falling under my hands. He moans when I wrap my legs around his waist and kiss him more deeply, imagining what it would be like for him to explore my body with his gentle touch.

He breaks away from me, a smile on his lips. The adrenaline from our near disastrous swim runs hot through me, and I realize that I projected my desires into his mind.

But I don't care. I hope it drives him crazy. I want nothing more than to tempt him back into the ocean where we can find privacy from the world.

"Ava," he whispers. "Ava look at me."

I slowly open my eyes to meet his intense, startling gaze. His ocean eyes travel from my mouth down to my heaving chest to my ripped bikini bottoms. His desire mirrors my own but something holds him back.

"Ava, your thoughts." He shakes his head. "As much as I want to carry you back to the water, I can't."

"Why not?" The question surprises even me. It's like the ocean hypnotizes me, trying to trick me to return. If Carter wasn't in better control than me, I'm sure I'd remain a mermaid forever.

He inhales another deep breath. "I might regret this later, but you belong on land. You belong with your friends and your family."

"And you?" I ask.

"Right now, I belong where you are."

His words hang in the air. My attraction to him is crazy intense, but it makes me wonder if this is all because of the spark we share. Would I still like him as much if I were still human? Would he like me? Does it even matter? I don't even know what's going to happen after this dreamy vacation is over, and I have to return to my normal life back in Azure Waters.

"What about when we return home?"

He pulls me closer. "If you're worried about what happens to us, don't. We'll make this work, okay?"

A sliver of doubt creeps into my mind, but I push it away. I can't think about what happens next when I'm still trying to figure out what's happening now. All I know is that if I survived today in the water, I can survive anything.

I'm going to be okay.

❦**9**❧

DREAM ABOUT THE LAND

"OH, MY GOD, AVS! WHAT the hell happened?" Giselle jogs in our direction from her spot on the dock while everyone waits for our ride back to the Ocean Jewel.

I'm a mess. My half wet hair hangs limply around my shoulders, my ballerina bun nonexistent since I first hit the water. My damp sundress clings to me around my thighs, and she'd have a million more questions if she saw the rip on the side of my bikini bottoms. My slight limp doesn't help any. My ankle feels a lot better than it did, but it's still annoying to put too much weight on it.

I lean into Carter. "You know me. I'm accident prone."

Her eyes widen. "You fell in the ocean *again*? Seriously, maybe you shouldn't even be standing on the dock. Are you okay?"

Pouting my lip slightly, I try to appear frazzled even though I'm calmer than I've ever been. "Yeah, I'm okay now. My sandal got caught when we were walking down the beach, and then with my stupid luck, I got knocked over by a wave. I thought I was far enough away, but the ocean just snuck up on me." I turn to glance at Carter who holds a straight face through my flat-out lies. "I warned Carter I don't do well with water. He believes me now."

He smirks. "Hey, I've always believed you."

Giselle tugs me away, hooking her arm through mine. "Don't you know you don't have to impress that boy? He's madly in-like with you."

My shoulders shake from my laugh. "In-like, Gi?"

"Duh. I read it in *Teen Romance Weekly*. It's like this instant attraction you have for someone. I could tell from the moment he brought your bag into our room—total in-like." Giselle smiles over her shoulder. "Right, Carter?"

"Right, Giselle," Carter says, clearly unfazed by Giselle talking about him like he's not listening from two feet behind us. He's more amused than anything.

"See, Aves. Now no more falling into the ocean. Saving your ass is going to get boring." She laughs at her own joke, which makes me laugh. If I had actually fallen in the water, she'd have a point.

"You always have the best advice," I remark, a hint of sarcasm in my voice.

It only makes her smile wider. "I know."

When the inflatable motorboat arrives to pick us up, Matty, Sapphire, Logan, and Daisy ride to the yacht first before it turns around to get the rest of us. An ounce of fear prickles in my mind as ocean water sprays across my face. Carter wraps his arms around me, squeezing my arm slightly. I have no idea if sea mist could trigger my transformation, but I'm deathly afraid of finding out.

"Relax. Don't think about it," Carter whispers.

I bury my face into his damp shirt without responding.

My fears prove to be unwarranted. We reach the hydraulic platform, and a crew member, who Carter greets as Brooks, helps me onto the yacht. Everyone heads back to the main deck to our staterooms. Carter heads to the lower deck to grab a few things while I head to my own room to shower and change into dry clothes.

Carter sits on the edge of my bed when I stroll into my room after my shower, a towel wrapped around my undergarments. His eyes trail up my body before he smiles the smile he saves just for me. A dimple peeks on his cheek, and he motions me to sit next to him.

The way he watches me excites me so much that I can't stop myself as I unwrap my towel and head to my built-in dresser to grab a pair of pajama bottoms and tank top. Even though Carter has glimpsed me naked, being alone in the room and in clothes that aren't meant for swimming seems to change something between us. I'm not standing here because I'm about to transform. I'm standing here because I want him to see me as more than the girl he has given his spark of life to. I want him to see me as who I've been all my life without the allure and magic of the sea.

I pull my tank top over my head and meet his gaze. He sits utterly still on the bed, his hands gripping his knees. His chest rises and falls with every breath, and it's easy to forget all the complicated emotions swirling through me—my fears of revealing our secret, the fear of what happens next, the confusion of what to expect from my future—none of that seems to matter.

Getting caught up in the moment, I cross the small distance until I'm standing in front of him, sliding my arms around him. Pushing him back, I lie on top of him, pressing against him.

He leans up and kisses me. As his tongue caresses mine, a tiny shock erupts through me, traveling from my lips and down my neck to stop at my heart. Even while we're both dry in this room, in our human forms, he still reminds me of the ocean. The slight saltiness to his kisses, how he smells of the crisp air, how his muscles remind me of all the times he guided me through the water...

"Ava," he whispers. "We should stop."

His voice brings me back from our private underwater world. I sigh, rolling off him, and snuggle next to him, my heart still racing.

"Your thoughts are making it difficult to remember why I chose land over the sea in the first place. They might trigger your transformation."

I twist my lips into a half-smile. "I can't help myself."

"Then let me help you."

He bends down, pressing his lips to mine. A million images flash through my mind—his memories. He shows me what I looked like the moment he saw me, staring into the distance with scrunched brows, my bag dangling from my fingertips. The image transforms to the first night on the dining terrace, me laughing with Giselle and Sapphire, and then to the image of me watching my friends on jet skis on the sundeck. The final memory he projects of me is when we sat on the lower deck moments before I fell. How I smiled and walked beside him, wearing his sweatshirt. How I closed my eyes when I ate a cookie. All of the memories are of me standing on my own two legs.

As I envision the moments of me in my human form, it reminds me of the me before all this happened. I remember all the times Giselle and I danced in her bedroom, how I'd spend my mornings running the paths along the beach without ever looking at the water. I'm even reminded of my favorite pair of jeans—all the little things I enjoy that I can't enjoy in the water.

The memories travel from my mind to Carter's, and he kisses me harder, deeper, until the only thing left on my mind is him as he is right now. The way his leg rests between mine, the way the fabric of his shirt pulls tight against his chest, though I can still see his heart glowing with every beat. How his dry hair falls over, longer on top than on the sides. The way his warm breath tickles my bottom lip when he hovers an inch away, pressing his forehead against mine. It's something I can't feel in the water. All that he is on land is completely different than who he is in the sea, but it's him all the same.

I pull away breathlessly and stare into his oceanic eyes, sparkling brightly against his deeply tanned skin that holds the warmth of the sun. It takes everything in me to not lose myself in their depths. I trail my gaze to his lips instead but then turn it to our hands, afraid I'll lose myself in his kisses next. His presence is all consuming in my small room.

"I think I understand now," I whisper. "I think I figured out how the transformation works for me." It's caused by a battle of wills between my heart and my mind, and I must disconnect them. I must sever the two and realign them. The land is where I need to be. It's where I need to stay. The ocean already stole so much from me. I refuse to allow it to take my future, too.

He smiles, pushing my hair behind my ear. "Want to test it out?"

I think about it for a moment. "No, not right now. I think I've had enough of the water for today. I just want to dream about the land."

With those words, he kisses me again, showing me everything he loves about the human world through his eyes.

Sunlight trickles through the window, warming my skin even

more than Carter does. My hand rests on his chest, my stomach and chest cuddling against his side. I've been awake for a while, just lying here on the bed that should be too small for the both of us, but we somehow make it work.

I tried to sleep more, but my mind wouldn't let me. All I could think about was how unreal this feels, like at any second I'll awake from a strange dream. I've been through a lot the last few days, and it's hard to think about anything else. It gives me a major case of anxiety comparable to what I used to feel just looking at the ocean, but my anxiety now falls onto the fact that I'm afraid I rely too heavily on Carter. He just makes it so easy to like him and trust him. But my anxiety doesn't stop me from wanting to stay by his side. It doesn't stop me from believing in his words, about how we'll somehow make it work. At least, until it doesn't.

You liked him before you were a mermaid. It'll be fine. I push the thoughts away because I'm not so sure. And that's what really bothers me most. How can I be certain about anything when we're bound by this secret? Should I even care? The old me might've. The old me would think I was crazy for feeling like I don't want to be without him. I can't say that what I feel is love, because even that thought is definitely insane, but what I feel is more like a deep-seated need. Our heartbeats share the same rhythm for a reason. But Carter doesn't talk about that. He skips around anything that involves him saving my life.

Shifting, I look at the ceiling instead of Carter. The aches in my bones no longer bother me, and my ankle feels as good as new, no signs of bruising from when Carter ripped me free from the pod of dolphins.

Carter moves when I sit up. He stretches his arms over his head, arching his back, and my eyes linger at the tightening of his muscular stomach as his shirt lifts up on his torso. Reaching out my hand, I run my fingers along the curve of his sharp hips and up his side. He sucks in a breath under my touch, and I slide into his arms, my messy hair veiling our faces, and he kisses me softly.

A knock sounds on the door, drawing my attention away from him. Giselle calls my name through the wood. I groan, getting to my feet, and cross the room. I crack the door open, meeting Giselle's overly ecstatic grin. She presses her face into the opening to peer past me at Carter rubbing the sleep from his face.

"You have to get ready, stat. While you two were busy *sleeping*, we docked in the bay, and we have until tonight to see the city." Giselle pushes the door open and saunters past me into the room.

Carter lifts the curtain to reveal the Golden Gate Bridge hazed in the distance. I almost wish it wasn't there, because it means our vacation is halfway over and in just a few days, I'll have to figure out how to deal with my new life at home.

"So no ocean activities?" I ask.

She grins. "Nope. Just shopping, dining, and exploring."

I turn my eyes to Carter. "You don't have to come if it doesn't sound like fun." Unlike Matty and Logan, Carter has a pass from being subjected to the hours we're bound to spend checking out every store we pass.

"And miss showing you around?" The faint memories of San Francisco trickle through my mind, hints from Carter's life growing up.

A warm apartment, decorated in blues and whites, in a square complex with a pool in the center near the water springs to my mind. The flash of a green sign hanging from a restaurant in an old machine shop with an amazing view of the water comes next. People walking along a string of shops in a packed downtown area, sprawling hills of eclectic houses, the same bridge I stare at through the window, but glowing against the dark night—all the memories he's shared through our kisses are enough to make it feel like I've known him all his life.

"You grew up here?" Giselle asks. "That's so cool. You definitely can't bail on us then. Don't worry, Matty and Logan don't get a pass so you won't be forced to hold our shopping bags alone."

Carter's eyes dart to mine for a second, and I laugh, nudging Giselle to the door. If he can survive a day with my friends on land, I'm pretty sure things just might work out between us.

Giselle laughs when I close the door on her so she doesn't scare Carter off. He leans back on his elbows, a smile playing on his lips.

I relax my shoulders and puff a breath of air out of my lungs. "There's still time to change your mind."

He pulls me forward, and I sink into his lap. "Nope. I've

showed you my world, Ava. You can't keep me from yours."

I kiss him. "If you can handle it, it'll be your world too, you know."

His eyes darken with something I can't decipher, but as quickly as it came, it disappears. "I'd like that. More than you'll ever understand."

After spending the morning shopping in Union Square, we head to Fisherman's Wharf by cable car for lunch. As Carter put it, it's the most touristy thing we could do to see San Francisco.

"Why didn't I pick a university here?" Sapphire says.

We stand in front of a giant, dull-yellow sign with a crab in the center introducing Fisherman's Wharf of San Francisco. The circular sign is shaped like an old boat steering wheel, matching the nautical décor of the lively, crowded wharf.

Matty kisses her cheek. "Because you're going to UCLA with me." As an heir to her grandmother's beauty and fashion empire fortune, Sapphire can do whatever she wants. If she changes her mind about moving into the penthouse apartment in downtown LA that she already signed a lease for with Matty, she could easily do so.

She giggles. "Oh, yeah."

He laughs, tugging her away from us. Chloe, Daisy, and Logan trail behind them, but I don't move. Giselle spins around, taking in the view, before smiling at me. In the corner of my eye, I watch Carter watch me.

"Are you two going to college?" Carter asks, drawing my

attention away from my best friend.

"Yup. UCSD," Giselle says for me. "We're going house hunting when we get back. I want a place on the beach like I have now, but away from my parents. I know it'll take Ava some convincing. She already told me we better be somewhere she can no longer hear the ocean."

I suck in my bottom lip. "Actually, I think I might be okay with that idea now."

She tilts her head to the side like I've said the strangest thing in the world—which it probably is coming from me. I haven't thought much about college in the fall, but I'm really thankful we decided to stay close to home—my mom guilted me into throwing away all the brochures for the schools in the dead center of the country away from all bodies of water because she wanted me to stay near home.

Giselle turns and pokes her finger into my chest. "Who are you and what have you done with my best friend?"

I laugh, flicking her hand away. "You're going to argue now that I agreed to move on the beach with you?"

She smiles. "You're right. You better not change your mind, though."

I don't even think that's possible. "I won't."

Hooking her arm through mine, she drags me in the direction where our friends wait for us. Carter strolls silently behind us, and I wish I could hear what's on his mind. After a moment, he slides up next to me and laces his fingers through mine. He squeezes my fingers, his eyes unusually serious, and if Giselle wasn't pulling me along, I'd stop to turn to him.

All through lunch, the others laugh and talk, making it a competition to tell the most embarrassing stories about each other. I recount a story about Giselle and I stumbling upon Matty hiding naked under Sapphire's bed because they thought we were her parents coming home early from one of their fund-raising galas.

Matty rubs his reddening face. "What about you, dude?" he asks. "I can't be the only one caught naked somewhere."

"Somewhere?" Sapphire says. "Did you forget the time you and Logan thought it'd be funny to streak through the middle of my beach party last year? Remember how you left your clothes too close to the water and ended up having to leave in a towel."

Carter laughs. "That's happened to you, too?" While I doubt Carter would streak through a party, he's probably lost his clothes a few times over the years during his transformation.

The two boys bump fists across the table, and I lean back and enjoy how nice everything is in this moment. Carter fits in so well with my friends; I almost can't imagine him ever being born in the water.

After everyone finishes lunch, we split up to wander Fisherman's Wharf separately. Carter holds my hand, guiding me to a pier where dozens of tourists watch a ton of sea lions bask in the sunshine while some swim through the rippling water.

The melodic sounds of the sea lions hum in my ears like they're singing a song just for me, definitely different from the cacophonous noise I'm used to when I've encountered the animals in a time before we shared an underwater world.

A sea lion circles the water under the pier below us and jumps up, opening its mouth in what I can only describe as a smile. Carter tugs me back instinctively like this playful creature will somehow share our secret.

Carter waves his hand, and the sea lion swims away and slides back onto its wooden dock with the rest of his colony.

"He was just being friendly," I say, smirking. A few more of the sea lions dive into the water.

"Exactly," Carter says. "So were the dolphins."

I roll my eyes. "I'm not going to jump off the pier to join them."

"Until you start feeling the pull."

"I told you I think I get how it works for me," I argue. "Want me to prove it?"

He shakes his head, his brown hair flying around with the motion. Sliding his hands around my waist, he pulls me from the guardrail of the pier. We stroll a few feet through the crowd, maneuvering around people taking pictures. An idea suddenly strikes me, and I pull my cell phone from my bag and hold it up to take one of me and Carter. Giselle and Daisy have been taking the most pictures, but if I only remember to take one, I want it to be of me and Carter.

Leaning down, he brushes his lips against mine, drawing my attention away from my phone. The sea lions chatter from next to us, trying their best to entice me to join them in the sea.

It's enough to make me hide my face in Carter's shirt to block out the rest of the world for a second.

"Carter?" a feminine voice says from behind me.

Carter visibly stiffens under my touch and holds my chin to stop me from peering around when I jerk my head up. The sudden reaction sends fear trickling to my heart. My hands shake, dropping to my sides so Carter doesn't feel them. His stare jets from mine to the woman I can't see standing behind me.

"Who is it?" I whisper.

Pressing his lips to my ear, he says, "Why don't you go find Giselle? I'll meet you back at the yacht later, okay? And please, stay away from the water for now."

He kisses my forehead before pulling away, leaving me standing on the pier in confusion. I touch my fingers to the warm spot where he kissed my forehead. Spinning around, I search the crowd for Carter, but all I glimpse is his back as he strolls away with his arm around the shoulders of a woman.

Before anger and rejection can sneak up on me, the woman glances over her shoulder, her blue-green eyes sparkling in the sunlight. She's absolutely gorgeous with her smooth, tanned skin, waves of dark hair the same color as Carter's, and a perfectly white smile. The resemblance is uncanny.

Carter's mom waves her fingers at me from over her shoulder, and I can't help sighing a breath of relief that he abandoned me on the spot. Because for some reason, I'm terrified to meet his mom. I don't know if it's because she's a mermaid or because she's the mom of the boy who used his one chance to transform someone into a mermaid on me. Or maybe, because meeting her makes things between us completely real.

10

MERPEOPLE TRADITIONS

CARTER BOARDS THE OCEAN JEWEL minutes after Ruby announced we're going to cruise the bay during sunset. I almost thought he wouldn't make it and was about to leave to wait for him on the dock.

When he enters the saloon, I gaze up from the unread book resting on my lap. Sitting with my legs curled under me, I've been hanging out alone for over an hour as the others chill on the sundeck. None of them complained about my absence, and I'm pretty sure Giselle knew I was worried about something though she never asked more after I told her Carter met up with his mom.

He slides onto the couch next to me, sinking against me. His head rests on my shoulder without saying anything for a long moment.

"Did you have a nice time with your mom?" I ask when I don't think he's going to say anything at all.

"I'm sorry for ditching you like that, but I—" His words cut off as he thinks about what to say.

"Your mom doesn't know about me. I get it," I say.

He shakes his head. "Yes and no."

"What is that supposed to mean?"

"I told her that I was seeing you." He rubs his hands over his knees.

"But not about..." I wave my hand over me to show what I can't risk saying out loud in case someone is listening.

"She'll find out soon enough," he says quietly.

I frown. "We're leaving later tonight. Are you going back out? Staying?" The thought of having to make the trip back down the coast to Azure Waters alone scares me.

"We'll be okay if they leave without us. I can catch us up."

I swallow. "Us? You mean..." Oh, God. If he means what I think he means, I'm pretty sure I'm going to pass out from nerves.

He turns to me, taking my hands in his. "If I could get us out of it, I would, but it has to do with merpeople tradition, and she saw us. But it'll be okay, Ava. They're going to love you."

Whoa. Holy crap. Merpeople tradition? I want to ask him

more about it, but I can't stop thinking that this is next level relationship stuff. *He turned you into a mermaid. Now that's next level stuff.*

"And if they don't?"

A smile dances in his eyes. "They will. I have to warn you, though. What I did was kind of a big deal."

Obviously. "You think?" My voice rises higher than I expect it to. "You can't just call them and tell them? God, Carter. What if I can't even—" I wave my hand over my legs again to silently finish my sentence.

He grins, leaning closer, his breath tickling my ear. "What happened to the girl who wanted to prove to me she could?"

Damn him. My heart drops into my stomach. "She ran away."

He laughs while pulling me to my feet. "I guess I'll have to chase after her, huh?" He slides his arm over my shoulders, guiding me toward the elevator. "Now, come on. You need to pack a bag. Dinner is at nine."

We sneak away from the others when they settle down for a movie marathon after dinner. No one noticed that all I did was push food around my plate, because I'm pretty sure if I eat anything now, I'll throw up from nervousness.

The swim deck is empty when we reach it, only a small wall light illuminating the area before us. The yacht moves slowly through the water of the bay before heading back out to sea. By morning, we'll be on the way home with plans to anchor for the day for water activities tomorrow as we travel along the coast.

Rubbing my bare arms, I gaze down at my now least favorite torn bikini. I hope it doesn't take all night to catch up. Carter swears it won't. He swears he's taken this trip several times, and Captain Briggs never strays from his itinerary.

"You should undress here," Carter says, handing me the waterproof bag with a towel and our clothes.

Sighing, I don't argue. He unties his board shorts and tugs them off before handing them to me to put in the bag. I don't even realize I'm staring right at his night shadowed body until he strolls closer to take the bag from my hands so I can slide my bottoms off.

I stand in front of him, half naked, but his eyes never leave mine. I toss him my bottoms to put in the bag and then move to stand next to him on the swimming platform. He secures the bag across his chest before taking my hand. It's a lot easier to jump from here than the sundeck, and it's dark enough that even if someone were to be staring at the ocean from above, they wouldn't see us.

"Ready?" Carter asks.

I'm not. But I don't tell him. Instead, I nod my head and jump with him into the glowing water.

My mind races as I hold my breath, orienting myself. Carter tugs me deeper and away from the yacht. He's already transformed by the time my lungs burn, needing to breathe. But I haven't changed yet.

DIVING UNDER

You can do this, Ava. As the thought comes to me, I remember how good it feels to glide through the water, to explore the ocean's depth, how easy and uncomplicated the sea is compared to my human life. How mesmerizing Carter is swimming alongside me. How perfect things are.

Cramps seize my toes, traveling up my legs to my thighs. I arch my body, the muscles in my back tightening as my dorsal fin rises from my spine. My skin tingles, and scales grow over my legs in a beautiful, glimmering cerulean blue. I inhale a deep breath of the ocean, letting it fill my lungs and push out through my gills.

"That was much faster," Carter says, his voice swirling through my mind. "I knew you could do it."

His fingers link through mine, and he pulls me to swim forward, not giving me a moment to peer around the glowing water as my eyes adjust to the salty ocean. Navigating the water I'm unfamiliar with, Carter dives us deeper. I match his pace, staying right by his side. I'm not sure I'll ever be familiar with the ocean like Carter is. It makes me wonder how much he's seen and explored. I wonder what it would be like to keep swimming and never stop.

As we pass over seaweed, I trail my free hand over it, feeling the slimy plant against my fingers. Fish dart away from us, and we rush through the water too fast to even take much in. We reach the shallows, and Carter slows. It's as close as we can get to the shore in our merpeople forms without having to worry about stumbling upon someone.

"Think you can transform here and swim the rest of the way with me?" Carter asks, projecting his voice into my mind.

I nod even though I won't be sure until the process already starts. I hover below the surface, closing my eyes, imagining what it would be like to walk on the land, to dance with Giselle in my bedroom, to feel the air on my skin...

Nothing happens.

Not because I can't, but because I don't want it to. If I don't transform, I won't have to meet Carter's parents. Staying in the sea, exploring its vastness, is a lot more appealing at the moment.

"Ava?" Carter questions.

I turn to meet his gaze without answering.

"Please, try. For me."

Closing my eyes again, I wait for the muscle spasms to travel through my body. It takes longer than I expect, because even though my head wants to return to the land, my heart is still having trouble. Being a mermaid is the most amazing feeling, and I don't want to give it up so soon. I feel like I just changed minutes ago.

When my legs split apart, I kick to the surface and spit out the ocean water before sucking in a deep breath of cold air. Carter bobs up next to me, splashing me with a small wave. He slides his hand around my waist and pulls me with him, swimming with one arm. I can swim just fine without the help, but I like the feeling of our bodies next to each other in the water.

Up ahead, city lights glow brightly across the land. The

moon sparkles its silver beams over the rippling water, like a dancing pathway that leads to the sandy shore. Carter tugs me through the waves, and we emerge on the beach. As much as I want to fall down and lie in the sand, I don't because I don't want to show up at Carter's parents' door covered in sand.

Carter shakes his wet hair, pelting me with cold water. Removing our bag from across his chest, he pulls out the towel and wraps it around my shoulders as I shiver. Goosebumps prickle over my skin. He rubs his strong hands down my arms, pushing the cold away.

His warm breath tickles my skin when he kisses my bare shoulder while sliding the towel down my back, stopping at my waist. His hands fall away, and he takes the towel to dry off. A moment later, he hands me the teal sundress I had picked out to wear. Keeping my back to him, I pull the strings on my bikini top and let it fall to the sand before pulling my dress over my head. Carter helps me tie the halter strings, his body close enough that I can feel his body heat.

I slide on my bikini bottoms under my dress before shaking the sand from my top to put it back in the bag. When I turn around, Carter's already dressed. He rubs the towel over his hair, letting it stick up in every direction.

He grins, tossing the towel back to me, and I wring out my hair the best I can before running the brush I brought through it. I wish I had a mirror to apply some makeup, but if I'm going to end up back in the water in a few hours, it'd be pointless.

My wet hair drapes down my back, clinging to my still-damp skin, but this is as good as it's going to get. Carter looks me up and down for a second, his eyes intently staring at me, his approval lingering in his dazzling smile.

When we reach a cement walking path, I slide into my flip flops while Carter remains barefooted. It takes less than twenty minutes to walk to his parents' apartment, the one I saw in his memories.

The three story building is just a few blocks away from the ocean. Green lawns and flowerbeds decorate the outside of the small complex. The U-shaped layout surrounds a swimming pool, every door facing the courtyard of the property.

A man smokes a cigarette on a small balcony across the way. He raises his hand to Carter and waves.

"Hello, Mr. Mooney. How's it going?" he asks the old man as we meander around the pool in his direction.

"Good, boy. You haven't visited in a while. Your mom says you're working on a boat? Fishing?"

Carter shakes his head. "No, sir. Luxury cruises."

The man stomps out his cigarette, laughing. "Whatever pays the bills." He doesn't ask about me, and all I do is smile and say goodbye when he returns to his apartment.

Slowing down, Carter grips my hand in his. He guides me to the ground level apartment below the man. Light shines through the opened window, and I catch sight of Carter's mom dancing around a small dining room table while she sets down silverware.

His Adam's apple bobs in his throat as he swallows, and

I'm starting to think he's as nervous as I am.

"What if they don't like me?" I whisper, running my hand along his lower back to half hug him, and so he can stop me if my body decides to turn and run.

"They will," he whispers back.

"Then why are you nervous?"

"Because I've never introduced anyone to them. Merpeople are different. I'm worried they'll scare you away."

I laugh. "Not like I'm going far."

Carter's mom lifts her gaze to the window when she hears our voices. I puff air through my lips, forcing my mouth to smile through my anxiety. Carter doesn't let go of me, and I watch the woman dance across the room to whatever music she's imagining.

"Mateo, they're here," Carter's mom says, calling over her shoulder.

She opens the door for us and lets us inside. A man more chiseled than Carter strolls from a hallway. His skin is darker than Carter's, and his eyes match the deep brown, almost black of his hair color. He strides across the room, standing next to his wife. I freeze under their curious gazes.

"Mom, Dad, this is Ava Adair. Ava, meet my parents, Mateo and Starla."

I don't even have time to brace myself before Mateo's strong arms pull me in for a hug. He rocks us back and forth, nearly knocking me over. I laugh against the man's broad chest, surprised by such an unexpected greeting.

The moment he releases me, Starla embraces me much more gently and says how good it is to meet me into my hair. She smells of tropical fruit—a blend of mango, coconut, and pineapple—and also the subtle scent of the ocean that clings to Carter.

"Mom, please," Carter says. "You're smothering her."

Starla laughs, but it sounds more like a giggle—a chiming of bells even. It's the kind of unforgettable laugh that makes you automatically smile.

"It's fine, Carter. I'll take a hug any day," I say, thinking how much better this is than I expected. I thought for sure they'd stare at me with suspicious eyes while thinking how I'm a terrible choice for their son.

"See," Starla says, pulling me with her into the quaint living room.

Large sea shells decorate a few shelves, and watercolor paintings fill most of the walls. It's like they've done their best to embody the ocean in their décor without having to be in the water. They chose the land long ago after Carter was born.

"I still can't believe you were passing through and weren't going to stop in to say hello," Mateo says. "Already forgetting your poor parents."

"Dad," Carter says, heaving a long sigh. "I didn't expect to even leave the yacht. Plans changed, though." Carter's gaze flicks to mine. *Yeah, they do.*

"Do you work on the Ocean Jewel, Ava?" Starla asks, walking to the kitchen to check whatever she's cooking in the oven.

I expect her to pull out some sort of seafood, but instead she pulls out a glass dish of lasagna.

"No, just a passenger." My heart hammers against my ribcage. Starla's eyebrows lower for a split second. I wonder if I should've just lied. "I live in Azure Waters with my parents, but I'm moving out with my best friend before college in the fall."

"Oh, you plan to attend college?" Mateo asks it like it's a silly question.

Carter slides up behind me and rests his arms around my neck, nudging me toward the round dining room table. "I've considered going myself."

"So, you two are pretty serious?" Starla sets the casserole dish in the middle of the table before dancing her way back to the fridge to pull out a bowl of salad.

The question hangs in the air, neither of us knowing how to respond. Carter and I look at each other, waiting for the other to answer. While Carter's parents aren't suspicious, it does feel like they're interrogating me. I almost want to excuse myself to the bathroom just to escape their curiosity.

"Mom," Carter says, "Can't you give us a moment to sit down before the interrogation?"

She giggles again. "Sorry, sweetheart. It's just we have so little time with you and Ava."

"And there will be plenty of time to get to know her," Carter says, pulling out my chair for me. "Maybe we can visit later in the summer and stay longer than a few hours."

"We'd love that, son," Mateo says, joining us.

Starla sits down, and Mateo dishes out the lasagna before passing the salad bowl around. Carter's parents keep the conversation light, talking about the good business at their shop at Fisherman's Wharf, where Starla caught Carter and me kissing in front of the sea lions.

Everything feels so normal, and no one mentions anything merpeople related, and that's probably because by the time we arrived, both of our hair was dry. Carter mentions that I'm still too new to be recognized by other mermaids, and apparently only I can see the spark in his chest that holds his essence.

An hour passes, and I help Starla carry the dishes to the sink when we're all through eating. I remain on edge, listening to Carter recount how we met on the dock as I contemplated whether or not I could gather the courage to get on the yacht.

"Obviously, she got on," Carter says, smiling at me.

Both his parents stare at me with the strangest expressions.

"You're afraid of the ocean?" Mateo finally says after a moment. It must be an absurd notion for a merman to wrap his mind around. The irony still makes me shake my head in disbelief. "But Carter loves the ocean."

"When I boarded the yacht, yes," I say, shifting uncomfortably under his gaze.

"Dad, please."

Yes, please. I wish his dad would change the subject. I know any minute Carter's going to have to tell them about my transformation. But now, I'm nearly shaking in my seat. They'll either be relieved or upset. Maybe even both. The anticipation's killing me.

Starla's heavy gaze remains on me, like she can somehow see into my head and figure me out. I brush my hair behind my ear and glance at Carter, begging him to end this so we can go. I rest my hand on his on top of the table, twining our fingers together.

His mom audibly gasps as she stares at us with wide eyes. The reaction to me holding her son's hand is loud enough to startle me. I pull my hand away and rest it under the table in my lap.

"Ava, your hand," his mom says.

I pull it up to stare at it, thinking something's wrong, but I don't see anything out of the ordinary.

"The ring."

Oh.

"You gave her your ring, Carter?" I expect his mom to yell, but instead she waves her hands in front of her face as tears rim her beautiful aqua eyes.

"It's not what you—"

"Oh, Ava. I'm so happy you've accepted my son's proposal," Mateo says, reaching across the table. He takes my hand in his and inspects the sea stone glittering in the light.

Proposal? What? *The ring was intended for his mate...*

"Um, I—"

"There's so much planning to do," Starla says, interrupting me. "Summer is the perfect time for the transformation ceremony."

Darkness edges my vision.

"Mom," Carter says.

"And it'll give you just enough time to say goodbye to your family," Starla continues, ignoring her son.

My throat tightens. "What? I'm not leaving my family."

"But—"

"Mom!" Carter yells, his voice echoing through the room. "Stop! You need to listen."

The world spins as dizziness washes over me. This wasn't anything like I expected. Whatever this ceremony she's talking about—saying goodbye to my family—it's not happening.

Falling over, I crash onto the floor, the need to escape washing over me. But instead of triggering the mermaid transformation, I pass out.

The last thing I see in the darkness is the spark in Carter's chest but even that goes out.

11

LIFE ON LAND

VOICES CUT THROUGH THE DARKNESS, but I don't open my eyes. I will the voices to disappear so I can stay in this quiet, peaceful world with nothing to worry about.

A cloth rests on my head, and I'm lying on something soft. A couch? Strong fingers hold onto mine, and Carter's sunscreen and ocean scent wafts over me, calming my nerves.

"I promised Ava she could go back home." Carter's voice is barely audible over the sound of my heartbeat. "I'm not going to take her away from her family because of some stupid tradition. She didn't agree to any of this."

His words resonate through me. I didn't even think about

other merpeople or their traditions. Carter told me about the colonies, but they still feel almost mythical to me, like Carter and I are the only merpeople in the sea. It's felt like that since the full moon, even with Mateo and Starla. I can't wrap my mind around the alternative to a life on land, one I'll fight to keep.

"Oh, son. You should've called us sooner." It's Mateo. He sounds more sorrowful than disappointed, the pity for his son, for me, clear in his voice.

"What difference would it have made? I stole away Ava's choice to decide. I'm not going to steal her decision of what happens to her future as well. I'm letting her make the choice if she wants to be with me, and I doubt she'd know for sure after a few days." Carter sounds just as sad, putting his thoughts out loud. It reminds me of the moment he told me what he did to save my life, like because he made that decision for me, it's my job to decide everything else, including what happens between us.

"For your sake, I hope so, son," Mateo says.

"I'm ready to accept whatever happens, even if it doesn't happen how I imagine," Carter says.

It breaks me apart and puts me together at once, knowing that Carter really does want to be with me. I know he likes me. I can feel it deep in my bones, but the fact that he's unsure of where I stand and thinking things could change leaves an ache in my heart that beats in sync with his, for him, and because of him. The last thing I want is to hurt him and make him regret his actions, though I'm kind of sure he does. It makes this all so much harder.

If I didn't think they'd stop discussing what happens to me, I'd sit up and throw my arms around Carter, telling him not to worry about my choice, because I do want to be with him. I want him to be included in my future. This isn't only about me.

Mateo sighs. "I think you really need to think things through. You can't just hope for the best."

Carter's thumb rubs over the side of my hand. "I'm not hoping, and I can handle this. We have things under control."

"But Carter, she's a liability," his mom says, cutting in. "She needs to be in the sea. She needs to be with our people until she adjusts. You can't just put the sea stone on her finger and expect her to master the transformation without really knowing what she's capable of. What happens if she loses control in the car? Or in the middle of a mall? She said she's going to college. Could you imagine what would happen if she changed in the middle of a lecture hall in front of hundreds of people? We've survived so long by remaining a secret. As her mate, it's your job to protect her. This isn't a game. It's her life."

With a heavy heart, I slowly open my eyes.

"I *am* protecting her. It's more than just the transformation and keeping our secret. It's about protecting her heart too, and you don't feel her like I do. I can't devastate her like that. You two should know this."

His parents fall silent. Carter bows his head, and a tear trickles from his closed eyes onto my cheek. Reaching up, I run my finger under his eye. He inhales a deep breath before opening his eyes to meet my gaze. The sorrow sweeping across his face is enough to bring tears to my eyes. It's how he looked after he had given me his spark after I drowned.

"Carter," I whisper. "Please, don't be sad."

"But I've ruined your life," he says, his voice cracking.

"How could you have ruined a life I wouldn't have had?"

Though I try my best to comfort Carter, holding his hand, letting him know he didn't ruin my life, his mom's words rest heavy on my soul. I can't imagine having to leave my life in Azure Waters behind to remain in the ocean. All the hope I had for my future drifts through my fingers like the powdery sands of the beach outside my house, sweeping away on the same waves that stole my sister. And now, my parents will have to live the rest of their lives knowing that the ocean stole me, too.

"See, son," Mateo says. "She understands. Ava's a reasonable person. She wouldn't want to put our people at risk."

I frown at his words. "Of course not, but you can't expect me to never see my family again, especially if I can live on land."

"But Ava—"

I hold my hand up, cutting Mateo off. Turning to Carter, I lean up and whisper, "Can we leave?" His parents will probably hate me for being rude, but I can't process everything with them sitting in front of me. I'm afraid if we stay any longer, they might not let me leave at all. And then what?

His jaw tightens, but he doesn't tell me no. Instead, he helps me get to my feet. Turning to his parents, he offers them a sad smile.

Starla closes her eyes while shaking her head. "Please, Carter. What you're doing...it's not right."

"It's right for Ava—and me." He leans over and kisses his mom on the cheek. "Please, respect our choice to live how we want."

He pulls me toward the door with him without looking back. Peering once over my shoulder, I watch Mateo take Starla into his arms. Neither follows us to try to stop us, but it's clear that to protect my heart, Carter broke both his parents'.

We walk in silence back to the beach we emerged from, Carter holding me like if he lets me go, I might float away on the wind. It's safe to say that dinner was a disaster, and I'm pretty sure we won't be visiting again anytime soon.

When we reach the beach, Carter pulls me into a hug in front of the water. He buries his face in the nook of my neck, breathing in and out a few long breaths. We just hold each other, listening to the waves crash on the shore under the soft moonlight.

"I'm sorry about tonight, Ava," he whispers into my hair. "I thought my parents would understand. They haven't lived in the ocean all my life. I thought they'd respect our decision not to as well."

"I don't blame them for worrying. They don't even know

me and were right about my lack of control." I hate admitting it, but the thought had crossed my mind. What would happen if I triggered the transformation in the middle of a college classroom? It'd take at least thirty minutes or longer to get to the beach, if I could even get there at all.

"You're getting better. We'll keep practicing. We'll swim every day so you never have a chance to miss it. We'll figure this out," he says.

His words are encouraging enough that the worry gripping my heart releases so I can take a deep breath without my chest tightening from the anxiety threatening to sink me to the bottom of the sea. He put a lot of thought into this. He's known the risk, yet he thinks I'm worth it. For that, I'm grateful.

Standing on my tiptoes, I kiss him, cupping his face in my hands. He embraces me, his hands sliding around my waist to my back where his fingers brush through the tips of my hair. His tongue slips in my mouth, caressing against mine, and I suck on his bottom lip.

"I'm so glad it was you who chose me as your mate," I whisper breathlessly against his lips, his words about protecting my heart flashing through my mind. The memory is vivid enough in my mind that I project it to him.

He grazes his lips against mine again, lifting me off my feet only to set me down in the soft sand. My fingers run down his sides until I find the hem of his shirt to pull it off his head. My dress hikes up around my waist, and he trails his fingers over my thighs and along the waistband of my bikini bottoms, sending tingles through me.

He pulls away, gazing into my eyes before he tugs my dress over my head. The moonlight bathes my skin in a soft glow, and he licks his lips, drinking in the sight of my body for what feels like the first time—a time where it wasn't out of necessity but because I want him to see me. His warm chest presses against me when he lies on top of me, resting his arms in the sand while I rub my fingers across his shoulders.

"You're so amazing," he whispers through kisses.

Ocean water sprays across us, sending a chill over my warm skin. I hug Carter tighter, remembering how hot he looks in the water, how his muscles flex when he swims, how his eyes sparkle like the sun on the sea.

Tingles flourish from my toes to my torso, but Carter isn't responsible for the electrifying sensation now coursing through me. The sensation overtakes my desire like I've jumped from the hot tub into the cool pool, clearing my thoughts enough to realize what's happening.

I could scream if I wasn't so worried about someone hearing us. Just when I thought I had a handle on my transformation, here my body goes, ruining another next-level moment between me and Carter, a moment that I want so badly.

I quiver through the ache that runs deep in my bones as Carter rests on top of me. He freezes mid kiss and snaps his eyes open to look at me. To my horror, my pectoral fins jut from my forearms, and glittering scales emerge from my skin.

I don't even have time to tug my bikini bottoms off before

they rip away. My legs fuse together faster than ever, leaving me on the sand in my mermaid form where anyone with a flashlight could see. My lungs burn with every gasp of briny air I inhale into my lungs. Oxygen isn't what I need in this moment. I need water to finish my transformation. I need the ocean before I drown on dry land.

I open and close my mouth, trying to push words through my lips. Carter's already to his feet, panic lining his eyes. It's enough to send a wave of fear over me.

"Hold on, Ava," Carter says, scooping me up into his arms. If he wasn't here, I'd probably die in the sand, because there's no way I'm strong enough to pull myself the twenty feet it would take to even touch the water.

He jogs the short distance to the waves and runs into them with me in his arms. Water splashes our faces, and he sinks deeper into the cresting waves. My tail flops against the surface, setting me off. My body takes control, and I fight away from him, forcing him to let me go so I can dive under. I submerge into the water, inhaling a deep breath of the sea. My chest relaxes in relief as I adjust to the transformation. The speed in which I transformed into a mermaid ignites a hopelessness within me I haven't felt before. How on earth can I go home now? What will I do?

My tail smacks the shallow bottom of the shore, and I bob my head out of the water. Carter is back on the beach collecting our clothes before undressing and entering the waves. He doesn't even have to search for me. He just swims in my direction in his human form.

"That was close," he whispers, handing me my bikini top.

It *was* close. Unsettlingly close. How could I ruin such a perfect moment?

Carter helps tie my bikini top around my neck and back after a few failed attempts on my part. My hands won't stop shaking, adrenaline still coursing through me. Taking my hand, he pulls me farther into the sea. It's not until my tail no longer smacks the ground that he dives down to transform into a merman.

"I'm sorry, Carter," I say, projecting my voice into his mind while sliding my hands around his taut shoulders. "I really suck at this."

"You don't have to apologize. It's okay. It was probably for the best anyway." A smirk crosses his face, tiny bubbles clinging to his cheeks.

But I feel like I do have to apologize. I wanted Carter so badly but just thinking about him reminds me of what we are. It was enough to make my body want to be in the water with him instead of the land where my mind really, really wanted to be. The disconnection between my heart and mind is more prominent than ever, and it feels like they're at war within me.

"I shouldn't have rushed things like that. Your emotions are connected to your transformation, and you clearly enjoy me in both my forms," he continues. He grins, sending heat crawling up my chest to my neck and cheeks.

"You have no idea." Covering my face with my hands, I try

to calm my racing heart.

"I think I do."

He doesn't let me hide my face for long, because a moment later, he's tugging my hands away to kiss me again. I cling to him while he flicks his tail, shooting us deeper into the water.

Even after everything that happened at his parents' home and after learning what was supposed to be my fate, I can't bring myself to even think about those things. In this moment, it's just me and Carter and the ocean that has quickly become our own private world.

But thoughts of the land sneak up. No matter how much I enjoy this, I can't lose myself to the sea forever. I have a life to return to. I have family.

And now, I have Carter. Because he chooses the land, too.

No one can take that from us.

The moon hangs high in the sky when we catch up to the yacht, heading south on the Pacific, following the California coastline. At the speed Carter swims, we could probably make it home by the afternoon, leaving the yacht behind in our wake if we wanted to.

The yacht glides over the water, a bubbly trail cutting through the surface behind it. Even at the slow speed it's traveling, there's no way I'm going to be able to catch up to it to climb back on board in my human form. All the other times we've snuck back on have been when it was anchored.

"I don't think I can make it back on the swimming platform after transforming," I say, my voice traveling into Carter's mind.

He presses his lips together and thinks, "If you transform now, I can push you up."

Tugging the strap of our bag over his head, I remove it before sliding it across my chest. There's no way I'm going to end up naked on the swimming platform alone if someone spots us. Luckily, only part of the crew is awake and most likely in the cockpit where we won't even appear on their radar.

"Whenever you're ready, Ava," Carter says, wrapping his arm around my waist to pull me along to stay with the yacht.

The moment I close my eyes, the transformation rushes over me in a wave of dull pain and shock as I start to feel the cold water in my human form. Carter was right about my transformation speeding up. What took minutes before took less than a minute now. If only I could get a handle on changing back and forth effortlessly. It'd make my life easier. My house is on a private beach. It'd take seconds to rush to the ocean to transform, and if I could change back immediately, it'd be fine. The water isn't crystalline, so people wouldn't even see me in the waves. Maybe I'll just not leave my house for the next three months unless I get better control. And if I move in with Giselle on the beach, it could be just as manageable. I'll make it work. I have to.

Carter breaks the surface with me so I can clear the water from my lungs. His pearlescent bronzed skin shines in the soft moonlight. He turns his attention from me to the yacht, studying it in his intense gaze.

"Get ready to hold your breath," he says, cutting through the water, closing the distance between us and the swimming platform.

I inhale a quick breath of salty ocean air before Carter pulls me under. My eyes blur in the saltwater, and the usual glow of the water seems darker as my human eyes try to orient to the direction we're heading, my sense of direction lost on the current.

Before I have a chance to prepare myself, Carter launches me out of the water, and I spin through the air, hitting my hip hard on the platform. The sandpaper-like lining scrapes against my naked skin, sending pain through me. I slam into the wall of the small garage that holds the jet skis, the majority of my pain now radiating from my back. Gasping a few sharp breaths, I slap my hand over my mouth to stop from crying out.

My chest heaves, and I push through the pain. I don't have time to sit here and cry like I want to. I need to grab my dress from the bag before I'm discovered. The last thing I want is to be added to the list of embarrassing naked-in-weird-situations stories my friends just love to share.

A small wave of water splashes over my legs. Carter pulls himself onto the deck without using the ladder. I can't even wrap my mind around how fit he is. I, on the other hand, need to seriously work on my strength and stamina in the water. Ocean swimming is a lot harder than wading in a pool.

Carter groans, stretching his arms over his head. His eyes

meet mine, and he scrambles toward me. He silently brushes his fingers outside the scrape on my thigh. Nudging his hand away, I stop him from trying to get a look at my naked back. I just want to get dressed and hide in my stateroom the rest of the night.

With a shaking hand, I pull my sandy, half wet dress from the bag and shimmy it on over my aching body. I hand the bag over to Carter, and he slides on his shorts, leaning his back against the garage door next to me. He tilts his head back and stares up at the clear sky with an expression I can't decipher. Now that we're out of the water and away from his parents in San Francisco, I'm sure everything he's doing is starting to really sink in.

"Ava?" The loud whisper cuts through the air over the sound of the waves. "Ava, are you there?"

My eyes widen, and I grip Carter's hand. He rolls over to gently lie on top of me and rests on one arm. He kisses me, blocking the both of us as a figure emerges from the pathway that surrounds the deck.

"Oh! Whoa!" Giselle says, her voice cutting through the air.

Carter presses his lips together to hide his smile and pulls away from me. His bare chest gleams with the water that drips from the both of us. We're still sopping wet, and Giselle's surprise is obvious. We have a lot of lying to do, and even if I told the truth I doubt she'd believe me.

"Hey," I say, baring my teeth in an awkward smile. "You

found us."

"What're you doing out here?" she asks, glancing between us.

"What does it look like?" Heat crawls up my neck.

"You're wet. You cannot tell me you fell into the ocean again." She places her hands on her hips.

I laugh. "Of course not."

"We came from the pool," Carter says. *Please, don't say you were just at the pool, Gi.*

She opens her mouth to respond, but I cut her off by adding, "And got distracted on our stroll. The room was feeling small."

Narrowing her eyes, she tries to decide whether or not she believes us. It's not like there is a better explanation, so she doesn't argue.

After a moment of awkward silence, she says, "You should really make sure not to accidentally lock your door. I knocked forever like an idiot before getting the spare key to open it only to see you weren't there. I was starting to get worried since I hadn't seen you since dinner. I don't want to sound lame, but I want to hang out with my BFF, too."

I pout my bottom lip. "Sorry, Gi. You were all watching a movie, and we just felt like going for a swim."

"Well, do you want to go again?" She glances between me and Carter, including him in her suggested plans.

I think about the fact that I'm only wearing half a bathing suit under my dress, but the look on my best friend's face says that I can't back out of it. This is our vacation after all. Carter was never a part of our plans. She's not the jealous type, but in our group of friends, it's an unspoken rule that we always include everyone in all our plans. I've been the third wheel the last time Giselle had a boyfriend, and we've all been third wheels to both Sapphire and Matty or Daisy and Logan, but it's not uncomfortable like most think. We're all friends. It's just how it is.

Giselle taps her foot, waiting for my answer. I'm taking too long. A million different responses flit through my mind, nothing sounding like a good reason not to. And I'll definitely never hear the end of it from any of my friends if I suddenly pull away from them for Carter.

"Sure," Carter says, answering for me because I'm clearly incapable of responding under pressure. If he wasn't so sweet, totally understanding the situation without me having to spell it out, I'd pummel him for putting me in this awkward position. Of course, if I did, it would draw suspicion from Giselle.

"Um, actually," I say, clearing my throat. I shift my legs, fiddling with the hem of my dress.

Giselle tilts her head to the side. "What?"

Carter's brows furrow, a silent question crossing his face. Flicking my gaze down to my hands, I tug on my dress. My predicament dawns on him a moment later, and he has the nerve to laugh.

I flush, elbowing him in the side, but I still don't respond to Giselle. Carter might think it's funny, but I'm pretty mortified that I can't just explain how sprouting a tail caused my bottoms to rip right off me.

Giselle fake glares while pointing her finger at us. "I don't like this. I'm supposed to be included on inside jokes." She smiles as she says it.

"You have to swear not to say anything to Sapphire. Matty wouldn't let me live this down," I say.

Her smile widens. "Okay, spill. What is going on?"

With a sigh, I grip my knees. "I seem to have misplaced my bikini bottoms."

Her mouth drops open as she laughs, tilting her head toward the clear sky. If it was anyone else, I'd be even more embarrassed about what my words could possibly imply, but I'm sure my friends probably already assume that I've slept with Carter, considering we haven't even left each other's sides for more than a few hours. There won't be a question about it now, and maybe if it actually happened, I wouldn't feel this way.

"This is so hilarious, Aves. I'll help you find them," she says.

Carter clears his throat. "No point. They're gone."

"What?" Giselle is eating this up. I almost believe it, my sudden transformation happening while I was about to give myself to Carter a distant memory. This is how it should've ended anyway. *Stupid surprise transformation ruining my already bad night.* I just hope she doesn't ask for the details.

"Yeah, it's fine," I say. "I'll go grab another bikini."

"Oh, my God. You guys!" She cracks up, clapping her hands. "How do you expect me to keep something so funny a secret?"

I laugh. "Gi, come on!"

She waves her hands in front of her face. "Okay, okay. Only because I can't be the only one without a hilarious, awkward naked story."

Carter helps me to my feet, sneaking the waterproof bag behind his back so Giselle doesn't question it. I move ahead and stroll next to Giselle. A flicker of guilt squeezes my heart, knowing that our friendship is never going to be the same again, because I can't share with her my deepest secret. And she'll never have any idea. Not to mention how close she came to catching us emerge from the ocean. A life on land, remaining as I was before the transformation, is looking more impossible than ever.

How can my life just slip through my fingers like this?

I'm afraid I'm already too far gone from my human self to make it out of this unscathed.

12

BELONG TO THE WATER

I TRAIL NEXT TO GISELLE, following the others off the yacht and onto the long dock of the Santa Barbara Harbor. The picturesque view of the cream-colored sands and blue ocean was enough to draw me from the yacht instead of following through with my plan to hide in my stateroom all day.

"You sure I can't convince you to surf? Chloe's an excellent instructor, way better than Matty. I was able to pop up on the board after only a few hours. And I was twelve." Giselle swings her arms at her sides, knocking her hand into mine.

"Hey, I'm a master," Matty says. "I could have you riding the waves in an hour."

I roll my eyes at Matty. I doubt he has anything on Chloe. Her brother is sponsored by a major surf company, and she's been surfing since before I was afraid of the water. "Are you seriously asking me this, Giselle?"

"Yeah, I am. Because look—" She waves her hand to me and then to the ocean of the harbor surrounding us. "You're not sweating or shaking or crying when all I'd have to do is swing my arm to knock you in. I think this trip might be wearing you down."

That's one way to put it. The fear I felt before isn't even a faint memory. It feels surreal to think I was ever afraid to begin with. She's right, I'm not panicking like I would've last week. I don't even think I could pretend.

I sigh. "Maybe it is, but there's no way I'm willingly getting into the ocean."

"Then why don't you build sandcastles and watch us for a bit? You might change your mind."

I turn to glance at Carter over my shoulder, who talks to Chloe and Logan about surfing. It's all any of them have been talking about like they don't do it often enough at home. I guess being at a new beach is exciting. The swells are supposed to be pretty decent too, but I wouldn't know anything about that.

Carter catches my eyes and smiles but continues with his story, leaving me struggling for an excuse.

"Okay, I'll watch for a bit, but then you can't complain about my dread of the ocean."

Giselle claps her hands. "Yay! Did you guys hear that? Aves is gonna watch us."

"And you can take pictures," Sapphire says, waving her phone. "I don't have enough to show off."

"Well, if you're going to watch, then Carter can surf, too. There's nothing this dude can't do on the water," Logan says, slapping Carter's shoulder.

He blinks a few times, studying me for a moment like he's trying to come up with an excuse against going in the water to stay with me. He can't think of one, and I'm not going to seem like a needy girlfriend, but damn. Watching my friends in the water is one thing. Watching Carter? The temptation is real. Oh so drool-worthy real.

"I don't know," Carter says.

"You deserve a little fun. You saved Ava-babe from drowning at sea because of Matty's dumbass. How often do you get a vacation with awesome people like us, anyway?" Logan shakes Carter by the shoulders.

"It's fine, Carter," I say. "He's right. You should have fun."

"Yeah, my mom would be sad if you don't enjoy what she arranged for you," Sapphire says.

Carter smiles though his eyes don't. He looks even more uncomfortable than I felt last night standing outside his parents' apartment. He chose the land to be around humans. He enjoys everything about our lives, but I don't think he's been this immersed in our world. Working on the Ocean Jewel allows him to socialize with passengers and other crew members, but according to him, he's never made the effort to connect and form relationships with anyone. It was a means to living on land.

And here I am, taking it away because I can't be trusted not to blow our secret. I can see the nervousness in his eyes, though I can tell he wants to join in the fun with my friends. I wish I could, too. After staying out of it for so long, I can finally enjoy the water with them—but my state of uncertainty leaves me out once again. This blows.

"It's set," Giselle says. "You two aren't ditching us."

"I guess not," I say quietly.

Carter falls in step next to me, sliding his arm around my waist. "Don't stop thinking about the land," he whispers.

But it's already too late. Because my heart belongs to the water.

So far, so good. I've managed to find the perfect place under a palm tree away from any beachgoers. Luckily, it's a brisk day— not quite summer warm—so most of the people on the beach are wearing wetsuits as they surf the equally cool water.

I sit back in the chair I rented from the same surf shop the others picked up their boards and dig my feet into the sun-warmed sand. With my earbuds firmly in place, I can't hear the lull of the waves over my music. I almost forgot what it was like to relax and do nothing but lose myself in my favorite songs.

From this distance, I can't really see the faces of my friends. They float on the water, straddling their boards, waiting for the swells good enough to surf. I refuse to glance at Carter at all. I bet he looks so hot on the water all glistening and wet and... *Stop it!*

Shaking my head, I send my blond hair sweeping across my face, so I'm not tempted to draw my gaze to my incredibly hot merman in disguise. When Sapphire sees the few photos I took, she's probably going to be disappointed because I didn't even look at the screen as I took them. At least she'll have the posed ones on the beach.

A shadow falls over me, and I remove my headphones.

"Don't look so bored," Giselle says, plopping down on the sand next to me.

I shrug. "I'm not."

"You look like you're going to die of boredom. You should see your face." She wrings out her wet hair before flicking me with the seawater.

I quickly swipe it off my bare arm like it burns. "Sorry, I'm just thinking."

"About Carter?"

"He looks amazing out there," I say without answering her question specifically—Carter's only part of what's on my mind.

"It's like he's part fish but without the gross scales," Giselle says with a laugh.

My mouth drops open for a second before I catch myself gaping. There's nothing gross about his glittering scales. Or his fins. There's nothing gross about him at all. Of course, she doesn't know that.

"Jeez, you look like I've offended you," Giselle adds after a moment.

I force myself to smile. "What? Oh, no. Sorry. I was think-ing about something else."

She laughs. "Obviously."

"Sorry."

She flicks more water at me from her hair. "Well, this is enough of you sitting here looking bored. Why don't you come closer to the water? Put your feet in."

"Not happening," I say.

"Come on. You've fallen in and lived to tell the tale. I've never pressured you before because I knew how afraid you were. You'd pale at just the mention of the ocean, but something's changed. You can't tell me it hasn't. I want my BFF to have as much fun as I am," she says.

So, she has noticed something different in my behavior. Before, there was no possible way I could get over my phobia or anxiety. Some days, I'd even be physically ill over them, espe-cially right after Bailey died. My parents forced me to see a therapist until I refused to go. I just readjusted my life and kept living. But now? It's like my transformation reset everything in me. I'm still Ava, but I'm a new version of myself. Ava 2.0.

"I *am* having fun," I say. "Right here on shore." Apart from my new fear of sudden mermaid transformation, I don't want my friends or parents looking too much into things, not that they can guess that mermaid magic cured me. It's just easier to stick to my old habits the best I can. I won't be under their scrutiny forever. I just have to survive these next few months.

Carter's certain that time and practice is the key, and I'm depending on it.

"O-o-okay, Aves. I think you should try sometime, though. Carter looks miserable out there with you here on the beach. It can't always be about you."

Her words sting but not because Carter's out there and I'm not. It's because, in a way, they're true. Everything in my and Carter's relationship so far has been about me and what I want. I'd give anything to run into the water, to swim to him. Play human. Be normal—at least, as normal as I could be now. But it's just not possible. I couldn't imagine what the consequences would be for me if someone were to ever find out. Horrifying, probably.

"Ouch, Gi." I clutch my knees.

"You know I'm not saying it to be mean, but I see how you and Carter are around each other. You're getting serious pretty fast, and I don't want you to get hurt."

"We're fine. He understands."

"For now."

It takes everything in me not to snap at her and tell her she has no clue what she's talking about. I have no idea where this conversation's coming from. I didn't think she was jealous about all the time Carter and I spent together, but maybe she is. And she might have good intentions, but she doesn't know anything. The thought is enough to stir sadness within me. It's a reminder that she never will.

Pushing to my feet, I stand and turn away from Giselle.

She struck a painful nerve within me, and I'm afraid I'll say or do something I'll regret, all because I can't tell her the truth. "Thanks for the advice, Gi. I'm going for a walk alone if you don't mind."

"Aves, wait," she calls.

But I don't look back. I can't. I need to get away before she realizes this isn't even about Carter or what she thinks about our relationship but has everything to do with our friendship with each other and how I'm grieving the loss I know is inevitable.

I rush through the sand to the bicycle path. My flip flops slap against the concrete as I run from the truth I'm going to have to eventually face. And it sucks. This was supposed to be the best summer ever. *Calm down. You'll figure it out. It's not over.*

Tears stream down my face, my breathing heavy, but I don't stop. I keep running until the pathway ends, and I enter a secluded area with only a hill behind me with a road that over-looks the ocean. From here, unless someone comes down the beach, no one can see me.

Standing at the edge of the surf, I allow the waves to crash into my legs. I tug my sundress over my head and wrap it around my phone before I toss them both behind me far enough that the waves won't wash them away. And then, I jog forward, allowing the water to splash over me.

I swim farther and farther from shore until my feet no longer hit the sandy bottom. Closing my eyes, I let the ocean carry me along, dragging me away from the land. Here, among the waves, I can think. My head is free from all the worry that comes with living on the land.

After a few minutes, I tug off my bikini bottoms and wind them around my wrist so they don't float away. It's the first time I'm in the water without Carter. I need to prove to myself that I can do this on my own. I need to prove to myself that no matter what happens, I'll be okay. That I can do this.

Peering around the blue waters once more, I take a deep breath and dive, kicking my legs to propel myself under. Bubbles erupt from my mouth, and I exhale the air from my lungs. I sink lower into the ocean with nothing but my thoughts to hold onto.

And then the cramps rush over me, sending my back arching and tightening the muscles in my legs. I don't open my eyes until the pain stops, and I inhale the cool ocean water.

I did it. I transformed alone without having something trigger it. It feels better than I ever imagined, so freeing, so perfect, knowing that I'm in control for once. Flipping my tail, I surge forward, dipping down to the ocean floor to trail my fingers over the sea grass. Silver fish swim around me, darting away as I spin in a circle, swirling the sand up around me.

I follow the ocean floor as it descends. The light filtering from the surface fades the farther I swim. I only stop when my heart stops racing. Smiling, I peer around and take in the vastness of the blue water so full of life. I twirl my arms at my side, resting ten feet above the sandy bottom. A squad of squids dances through the current at a leisurely pace nearby, bobbing sideways. Swimming through them with deadly precision is a handful of hammerhead sharks as they stalk their prey. Their majestic beauty and grace tempts me to move forward, but I only get close enough to watch the start of the feeding frenzy.

A huge silhouette crosses overhead, blocking the pale light above. Fear sneaks into my heart as I watch the boat drop a net into the water, scooping up a school of unlucky fish.

I flick my tail, propelling up another ten feet, but I don't do anything. The fish push against the net, fighting the inevitable. It reminds me of an old mermaid movie I saw when I was a child, where the mermaid ripped the net, saving whatever trapped animals. I consider doing it myself, since my nails are sharp enough to impale a fish, but the shadow of the boat freezes me in place.

"Ava!" Carter's voice echoes through my mind, drawing my attention away from the boat. It passes over my head completely while retrieving the net.

Before I have a chance to see him, I flick my tail and jet away, swimming from him instead of toward him. I can't bear to face him. He'll hug and kiss me, tell me everything will be okay, that everything will work out, but I don't want to hear any of that. I want to hear how as much as I love my family and friends, I can never have the life I once had. I can't even share my secrets with Giselle. The tear in my heart is far too great to be mended with comforting words and affection.

How will I face my best friend after all this? She wanted to save my heart, but who will save hers? Who will protect her from the hurt I'm surely going to cause her? Cause everyone in my life, maybe even Carter. None of this was supposed to happen. My plan was to go to college, get a job, travel the world, not find myself immersed in a world I have no business really being a part of.

I swim as fast as I possibly can. Maybe I'll make my way to Hawaii where I can live offshore in the warm, tropical waters. Maybe I'll figure out how to get to Australia. I imagine being anywhere other than here where my human life waits for me to screw up.

Gliding faster in the water, I navigate through the ocean life, nearly missing kissing the tail of an enormous gray whale as it swims with its pod.

As I dodge past another, something strong hooks around my waist, startling me. I automatically dive deeper into the ocean. Carter swims above me, holding me against him, but he doesn't force me to slow down or stop. Instead, he lets me lead as I swim into the vast blue. His chin rests on my shoulder, his warm, taut chest pressing against my back, and I enjoy the feeling of him with me.

We swim together without a word until my body begs me to slow down and rest. And even then, Carter propels us forward with the strength of his magnificent tail.

"Carter," I say, my voice barely a whisper in my own head. "What are we doing?"

"Swimming."

His answer makes me laugh. I shift in his arms, and he

loosens his hold on me enough that I can twist to face him, pressing my chest against his. His spark glows in the same blinking rhythm as mine, and I swear I can see pulses of energy connecting us.

Resting my face in the crook of his neck, I close my eyes, relaxing against him. It isn't until we're miles and miles from shore that he slows down to finally stop swimming to search my face. We stare at one another, his hair floating around in the current and mine veiling the space between us. He's not doing any of the things I imagined him doing. All he does is wait for me to make the next move.

"How did you find me?" I finally ask when the intensity of his gaze threatens to unveil all the thoughts I hold in my soul.

He presses two fingers to the glowing spot in my chest. "I followed you."

"I didn't know you could do that."

"You can do it, too."

He doesn't ask the questions clearly written on his face. His lips tilt downward, probably matching my own expression, and his eyebrows hang low on his forehead. I wish he'd smile. His smile can change my world. It did.

"Oh." It's all I can say. It'd be a lot easier spilling my guts to him if he'd just ask the questions on his mind, if he would pry. "I don't know how to do it."

"All it takes is you wanting to find me, Ava. If you want me, you'll find me. You might not feel it like I do, but we're connected."

His words burrow inside me. He found me because he wanted me. This isn't about doing the right thing or trying to make it up to me. As much as I tell him I'm glad to be alive, he still blames himself for bestowing me with this priceless gift.

"Giselle thinks that I'm being selfish," I finally say. "She thinks everything between us revolves around me. And she's right."

He raises his eyebrows, shaking his head while he laughs, surprising me. "Ava, Giselle doesn't know what she's talking about."

"That's what I thought, but it really got to me. She'll never know. I lost the person I told everything to. It's just—" I close my eyes for a second. "This is really hard."

He lifts his hand to my face, caressing my cheek with his fingers. "That's why you ran."

I nod. "I want so badly to slip back into my old life like none of this ever happened. If I could just shut off my heart and turn my back on the ocean, I could make it work. I know I could. But then I—I'd be miserable. It'd be so much easier if I could tell my family."

His lips disappear as he presses them in a thin line, his expression matching the thoughts he projects to me. "Ava..."

I avert my eyes away from him. "I know, Carter. I can't. I won't. It's just—maybe I'm better off not going back."

"You really think so?"

I shrug. "Maybe."

"Okay then. We won't go back."

I guess I shouldn't expect him to fight for my old normalcy. If I could cry underwater, I would. The idea of never returning to land, while sounding like a good idea in my head, doesn't sit right in my heart. All I can think about is how much my family and friends would miss me—how much I'd miss them, too.

"No," I finally say.

He leans closer, forcing me to look into his alluring eyes. "Ava, what is it you want?"

"That's the problem. I don't even know anymore. But this isn't just about me, Carter. You said it yourself. It's about us. Your feelings matter to me, too."

He smiles before he kisses me. It isn't until now that I've said those words out loud. Since the night he asked me to meet him out on the deck, before I fell overboard, I knew I had liked Carter. I liked his confidence, how he made me feel like I wasn't crazy because of my fear of the ocean. I wanted to get to know him—I knew he was someone I would think was amazing—and I do. Then after the fall, the transformation, all I thought about was how I was going to manage this, because Carter shouldn't be bound to me by his guilt for saving my life. But this isn't about him or me. It's about us together and what works to make us both happy.

"I'd like to go back," he finally says. "I love living on land. The beds are much more comfortable and the food is better. If you think it's too hard to be with your family. If that's what this is all about, we can move anywhere, Ava. It doesn't have to be your family or the sea. We have a choice."

Choices. It hasn't felt like I had many until now. "I don't want to say goodbye to my family forever. I want to stay with them for a while before we figure things out."

He nods. "We'll make this work."

It wasn't until now—until I actually settled on a plan that felt good in my heart—that I believed things could work. I could have the land in my mind and the sea in my heart.

13

ONE HEART IN TWO BODIES

PACKING MY STUFF IS A lot harder than I expected it to be. The last day has flown by, and by sunset, we'll be anchoring back in the harbor of Azure Waters. Carter lies on the bed behind me as I lay my clothes across the other bed. He hasn't left my side since we returned to the yacht in Santa Barbara. Even when Giselle and I fell all over each other with apologies, Carter quietly observed us like he was lending me his strength.

"I can't believe I'm actually going home. I wasn't sure I was ever going to make it," I say, folding my sundresses to fit in my small bag. "How am I going to sleep knowing you're not nearby?" The reality of my situation sinks in the more I think about it. Carter won't be by my side all day and night when I leave this yacht. Vacation is over. I thought returning to the Ocean Jewel the morning after my transformation was hard. This seems impossible.

He smiles with sad eyes, and it hurts my heart. "I'll be around so much you won't even have a chance to miss me."

But that's not entirely true. Carter works on the Ocean Jewel. They leave again tomorrow afternoon for a short trip to Orange County. I'll be stuck at home, forced to gaze out my door at the sea. That is, if I can even make it through the whole day without triggering a transformation. *You've made it until now. You have to stay in control. It's the only way.*

"I already miss you," I complain. It sounds completely cheesy, but it's true. The anticipation of returning weighs heavy on me.

He pushes off the bed and stands behind me. Brushing my hair from my neck, he kisses just below my ear. I give up folding my clothes and just start shoving the rest of my belongings into the bag so I can give him my full attention.

His hands slide down my shoulders and collarbone until he rests them on my chest over my heart, just feeling each beat against his fingers, thrumming in sync with his, beating for him, because of him. Standing utterly still, I relish the scent of his skin, the sunscreen and ocean fragrance that radiates from him. His chest presses into my back, and his presence consumes my attention until I can't think about anything but him. About my attraction to him, my need to be with him.

Turning my head, he meets me for a kiss without moving his hands from my heart. A flash of myself appears in my mind as he shows me a glimpse of how he sees me. How much I consume his thoughts, too.

Ever so gently, he hooks his fingers to the fabric of my dress, tugging my straps from my shoulders. I catch his eyes flicking to my reflection in the door mirror, and his breathing quickens seeing me in my bra. He's seen me in a bikini nearly this whole trip, but this feels different. It's more intimate. We're alone in my stateroom without the allure of the sea or my out-of-control emotions trying to replace one feeling with another. This is all him and me and us wanting to be together before reality threatens to change everything.

My dress slips to my feet, and his lips trail down my neck to my shoulder, sending chills over my body as it reacts to his touch. The brush of his fingers drives me crazy, and I spin in his arms to face him and kiss him fervently, almost frantically, like his kisses alone can somehow guarantee we'll both be okay, that even if everything changes around us, we'll remain the same.

Pushing him back, we fall together on the bed with me on top of him. My hair veils our faces, and I suck his bottom lip between mine. He moans, rolling me over and trails his gaze across my bare skin. I tug his shirt off and run my fingers along the sharp curve of his hips along his muscular stomach and then up to his neck to pull him down.

His hands travel down my sides, sending my heart racing. I can't see his spark, but I know his heart matches mine beat for beat like we are one heart in two bodies. I never thought to ask, but in this moment, that's exactly what it feels like.

Carter explores every inch of me with his hands, from the curve of my hips to my stomach, trailing them up until they run through my hair. He holds himself over me, his eyes meeting mine, searching for something within them.

His sudden hesitation speaks volumes, and I suck my bottom lip between my teeth, knowing what he's looking for. He's trying to see how my body reacts to him—whether or not I'll be able to maintain my human form. It's a thought I pushed into the dark recesses of my mind. I'm not ruining this moment again. I want nothing to do with the ocean and everything to do with him. It's all I can think about. How much I want him in this form, on this bed, in the air and not the sea.

I kiss him, sending him an image of us in this very second, showing him exactly where my mind is—in the here and now.

"Ava, are you sure you want to?" he asks quietly.

Leaning over, I grab a small box from my suitcase that Giselle had left for me on the night of my first transformation when she thought I wanted to spend the night with Carter to be alone with him. It still has the note on it saying that Matty had over-prepared with a winking smiley.

"I do more than anything," I say, placing the box in his hands.

He smiles as he whispers, "You're the best thing to ever happen to me."

I answer him with another long, desperate kiss, showing

him exactly how much he means to me to.

Carter stands with me outside of my house, staring up at the grand, newly remodeled Victorian-styled home my grandfather bought in the eighties. The sea green paint stands brightly against the white trim. Palm trees line the circular driveway while hydrangeas bloom in giant, pink bouquets under the windows.

The ever-present hum of the ocean echoes through the air of the beachfront property, though I haven't been on the beach behind my house in eight years, not since Bailey was lost to the waves. That's about to change, though I have no idea how I'll explain my sudden change of heart to my parents. They've spent thousands of dollars on therapy over the years to try to help me with my fear, but when I turned fifteen, I refused to visit Dr. Hari again. I didn't need to be fixed or changed. I didn't need the reminder that I was the only person in all of Azure Waters who couldn't even look at the water outside my own bedroom window, which now faces the street since my parents allowed me to switch with the guest room when I was twelve.

My legs tremble the longer we stand in my front yard. "This is home for me." Carter doesn't leave again until tomorrow so I invited him back to my house because it felt weird just leaving him behind on the Ocean Jewel. "Are you sure you want to come in? You can say no."

"It's only fair for me to meet your parents after the fiasco with mine," he answers, smiling. "It can't be any worse than that, right?"

"Right," I say, "and you won't have to worry about an interrogation. My dad will be leaving for the hospital at any second, and my mom will soon lock herself in her office like every night."

My dad's an emergency surgeon at the Betty Green hospital in Sunset Terrace, a town over from Azure Waters. If he hasn't been called in already, he'll be leaving for his once a week overnight soon. As for my mom, she splits her time as chief editor for the Azure Waters Gazette or planning one of the dozens of fundraisers alongside Ruby and Giselle's mom, Anaya. Over the last ten years, they've raised millions for different organizations.

After a minute, we still remain just outside my house. The moment we decide to enter, everything will change. I'm not sure if I'm ready. I'm not sure if I can handle returning to my old life. Returning to the me before Carter.

I gaze up at the purple clouds scattering across the darkening sky. The scent of the ocean wafts through the air, blowing long tresses of my hair behind me. Streetlamps illuminate a deep orange glow across my quiet street, the lamps dark enough that I can still see the stars speckled across the night through the breaks in the clouds.

Inhaling deeply, I lock my fingers with Carter's and pull him toward the red brick steps that lead to the double doors with window cutouts that sparkle with the light on within my house. I open the door, swinging it wide to peer into my spacious living room. The floor gleams under the lights of the fan. Unlike Carter's parents' apartment of blues and white, my house is warm with tans and dark woods. The only things that pop with color are the framed abstract sea and sunset paintings my mom bought from a local artist.

"Mom? Dad? I'm home," I call out as I tug Carter along into my living room. We pass the stiff tan couches that border an empty coffee table, facing a wall entertainment center.

To the right is a formal dining room with a long, sturdy table with seating for ten. The brass chandelier dangles in the dark though the light from the living room gleams off the metal.

My parents sit at the small dining table in the kitchen with the curtain drawn open to show off the side deck and pool that sits on the side of the house. Cups of coffee rest on the table in front of them, and they share a piece of the chocolate cake I had baked and put in the freezer the night before the yacht trip.

"Oh, Ava. You've brought a friend home," Mom says, putting down her fork.

"I've never seen you before. Did you wash aboard the Ocean Jewel? I didn't think Ava would take me serious about the whole plenty of fish in the sea spiel."

"Dad, seriously?" If only he knew. "Carter works on the yacht." *He saved me from the ocean, turned me into a mermaid, and we'll be leaving Azure Waters soon to make it easier to hide my new life from you,* I imagine saying.

Instead, Carter steps forward and holds out his hand. "It's nice to meet you Dr. Adair, Mrs. Adair."

"It's a pleasure, Carter. Please, call me Beatrice," my mom says, shaking his hand next. "Are you two hungry? We have some leftover Chinese food or cake."

"We ate already," I say.

"But cake sounds great," Carter adds, grinning at me. He sets my bag down at his feet when my mom motions for us to sit down. Neither of them questions why I brought him home, which is a relief to me. They've treated me like an adult even before I turned eighteen. It helps that I'm not a troublemaker...or at least I've never been caught doing something I shouldn't have.

I don't sit down when my dad pats the back of the chair next to him. I shift my weight between my feet. "Is it okay if we take it on the back patio?"

My mom tilts her head to the side, not because she's confused about why I don't want to eat in the kitchen, but because I haven't been on the back patio in forever. She's going to realize how different I am soon enough.

"Uh, yeah. Sure, sweetheart." She shoots a quizzical look at my dad, who smiles widely at Carter.

My dad rises to his feet. "You feeling okay, Avie? You hate the beach." He says it in a way that wouldn't embarrass me if Carter didn't already know about my previous fear of the ocean.

"I feel great, Dad. A week on the water has given me a new perspective on things." I close the distance, giving my dad a hug. I didn't realize how much I missed my parents until now.

My dad hugs me tightly, pulling away only to grin. "Really?"

"Yeah," I say.

I stand awkwardly through a minute of silent smiling, like they're speaking through their gazes. My parents excuse themselves, but before my dad leaves, he tells Carter to come back anytime. It's probably the best introduction I could've asked for. I'm sure they'll save all their questions for later when Carter isn't here.

Taking both our plates, Carter follows behind me as I cut through the game room to the decorative glass doors that'll take us to our fenced in patio that faces the ocean. The white caps shine under the moon on the water, and Carter stares into the dark distance.

"I haven't stepped foot on this patio since I was a kid," I say, hugging myself, staring at our small patio table and chairs, the original palm frond pattered cushions now replaced by simple green ones.

He doesn't ask why. He doesn't need to. I'm sure my face says it all. Even when we're not kissing, Carter seems to know what I'm thinking. I wear my feelings splattered across my face with him instead of the unbreakable mask I'm hidden behind with everyone else.

I set my plate on the table instead of taking a bite. Carter holds his while he stands next to me, scooping a piece into his mouth. I grin, watching him close his eyes to savor the sweet flavor.

"Like it? It's my grams' recipe. She's the one who taught me how to bake and comes to stay with us during the winter to get away from the cold of the East Coast."

Carter bobs his head. "So good."

He devours the piece in a matter of minutes. I love how something so simple can make him so happy. After setting his plate next to mine, he takes my hands in his and then leans down to press his sweet lips to mine. Sliding my hands around his neck, I hold onto him for a moment, resting my cheek against his chest. His heartbeat drums in my ear, seeming to beat just for me, reminding me of our afternoon together.

My cheeks warm at the memory, and I can't stop from kissing him, reminding him exactly how much I don't want him to go. Tomorrow he'll be on the ocean for a night in the OC, and I'll be here, dreaming about a life after I can leave. A life where I don't have to worry about the consequences that come with my lack of stability. The dangers I'm putting every-one in just by being here. Dangers I know Carter wants to keep me from.

"You really are going to make it hard for me to leave," he whispers into my lips.

I flick my tongue across his bottom lip once before smiling. "Is it working?"

He moans, kissing me instead of responding. I break away and twine my fingers with his, tugging him toward the back gate that leads to the beach. I leave my flip flops in the sand,

and we trail away from my house. The crisp night air blows my dress around my thighs, and I release his hand to dance around him with a smile on my face. I twirl in front of him, wiggling my fingers for him to follow me toward the water. It's all I could think about since the moment I got home. My last transformation in Santa Barbara feels so long ago, and I can't wait to just give in to my heart's need to be with the sea.

My dress clings to my legs in the breeze, and I pull the fabric up and over my head, stripping into my bikini far enough away from my neighborhood that without a flashlight, I won't be seen. Without saying a word, Carter removes his shirt and jogs to catch up to me as I saunter into the waves.

His strong arms embrace me, tugging me deeper into the surf. It doesn't take long for him to hook his fingers along the sides of my bikini bottoms to pull me to him, pressing his hips against mine. Under the soft moonlight, in the crashing waves, I allow him to undress me before our transformation.

Carter picks me up, carrying me deeper. The cold water flows around and lifts us off our feet with every wave. Sea spray splashes our faces, specks of water drops sparkling on his cheeks and hair. His eyes shine like jewels, glowing like the sun penetrating through the blue-green waters of the ocean, shining from within.

The cramps don't even bother me as the ocean calls me into its depths. I break away, surging under before Carter. Inhaling a breath of sea water, I dive away from him, spinning through the bubbling current. It doesn't take more than seconds for Carter to swim up next to me. He slips his hands around my waist until his chest presses into my back and guides us through the surf until we reach some black rocks not far from the shore.

We break the surface together, and Carter helps me slide out of the water. The waves collide on the rocks, splashing over our glittering tails and pearlescent skin. From this spot, I have a view of my beachfront community, and it reminds me of how separated I am from it now.

Leaning over, Carter kisses me sweetly. "I can see why you love it here." He gazes in the direction of my house, the splatter of lights from the mansions lighting the shore like man-made stars.

"It doesn't feel the same as it did when I left," I say, puckering my bottom lip.

He runs the pad of his thumb over my lips before cupping my chin in his hand, forcing me to turn toward him instead of the shore. "Maybe that's a good thing."

He's right. It doesn't feel the same because I'm not the same. It helps ease the sadness clinging to my heart. "Maybe it is. Either way, I don't want to think about it anymore."

Carter propels from the rocks and back into the water. Popping back up, he holds his arms out to catch me. "Then come on. Let me help you forget."

14

LIFE GOES ON

SUNLIGHT TRICKLES THROUGH MY CURTAIN, warming my face. I stir in Carter's arms, feeling the heat of his body as he curls against me under my blankets. His breath tickles my shoulders, and he releases a soft sigh before brushing his lips across my skin.

After our swim last night, it was easy enough to sneak Carter into my room since my mom never left her office. My parents have been pretty relaxed the last year and even lifted my curfew after graduation a few weeks ago. They'd never admit it, but I'm pretty sure they're just as excited as I am—was—about me moving in with Giselle closer to the university.

Dad wants me to be able to enjoy college because he never really got to, since he struggled financially all through it and at one point slept on a couch of a friend's before he met Mom. The deal is that I have to actually go to classes and get good grades. I also have to keep volunteering when the time allows, all of which I never minded until now.

"I wish you didn't have to leave," I mumble, rolling over to face him. His arms circle around me, and I rest my forehead on his muscular chest.

"I know what you mean, but working is now more important than ever," he whispers. "Living on land costs money, and you probably don't want me to live on the Ocean Jewel forever, right?"

I definitely don't. "Of course not."

"And while I have a pretty good savings already, I need to be ready to take care of—" He snaps his mouth shut, probably noticing the fear suddenly sweeping over me at his words. It's that tiny bit of doubt in his voice that makes me question what we're doing. What I'm doing.

Despite what his parents insinuated, I'm not his responsibility. All of this shouldn't be on him, and the last thing I want is for him to feel that way.

"Carter..." My voice trails off. We shouldn't have to be discussing something like this yet in our relationship. It's as crazy as his parents thinking he proposed to me and I said yes because I was wearing his ring. "I hope you don't think that I expect you to take care of me, because I don't."

"I know you don't, Ava," he says, brushing his lips against my forehead. "It was just a thought."

"Okay, but to be clear, I'm capable of helping out. This isn't all on you," I say. "I'm not your respons—"

He cuts off my words with a kiss, purposely interrupting me. "You have enough to worry about. I don't want you worrying about something I was just thinking about," he says against my lips. "Let's just enjoy the morning before I have to leave, okay?"

Pulling back, I gaze into his eyes. "Fine, but only because I like you rudely interrupting me like that." I smile despite the sinking feeling settling in my stomach.

He kisses me again, combing his fingers through my blond hair. We stay in bed for a few more minutes before Carter slides to his feet and shrugs his T-shirt on. If I don't take my eyes off him, it's easy to forget I'll be without him for the first time since we met what feels like forever ago.

He holds out his hands to me, smiling the smile he saves just for me, and helps me out of bed even though I'd rather just bury myself in my covers for the rest of the day. Carter watches me get ready like I'm the most fascinating person in the world. I change into shorts and a shirt, and he can't resist trailing his fingers over my bare neck when I pull my blond hair up into a ponytail.

Reluctantly leaving him upstairs, I rush down the steps to see where my mom is. A sticky note hangs from the fridge, reminding me about dress shopping later today for the King's

Scholarship Foundation Gala that I'm to attend on Friday night. At the bottom of the note, she tells me to invite Carter as my date.

I guess life really didn't stop even when I grew a tail. I had completely forgotten about the gala. We usually don't shop so late, but with finals, graduation, and vacation, I never made time. It didn't help that Giselle and I didn't want to go. The galas are always so stuffy and dreadful, totally not our thing.

"Carter, we're alone," I call up the stairs. "You can come down."

His soft footsteps sound on the stairs, and when he enters the kitchen, I hold out a plate of muffins my mom left out. He takes one, peels off the wrapper, and consumes it in a few bites. His eyes crinkle in the corners as he grins at me before wiping the crumbs off his chin with a paper towel.

Dangling the sticky note from my fingers, I hold it in front of Carter's face until he takes it and reads it.

"You busy on Friday? I know it's last minute, and you probably have to work..."

"I—"

"They're really boring anyway," I say, interrupting him before he can finish.

"Then we'll be bored together, because we return to port Friday afternoon and don't leave again until Saturday," he says.

A smile creeps over my face. "You have to wear a tux."

"I look good in a tux."

I grin, because he looks good in anything. "Then it's a

date."

"I like the sound of that."

Thirty minutes later, I pull my silver BMW into the parking lot of the harbor to drop Carter off. He lingers in the passenger's seat, not wanting to get out as much as I want him to stay. But he can't. He still has his own life like I have mine.

"It's just until tomorrow night," he says quietly, staring out the window at the docks filled with all types of boats, from fishing boats to yachts like the Ocean Jewel. He plans to sneak away to swim to me when everyone's sleeping.

"I know," I say, squeezing his hand.

He chuckles. "I was reminding myself." With a strong hug and a soft kiss, he pulls away and opens the door. "Call me if you need me, Ava. I'll figure out a way back if I have to."

I nod. "I'll try to think of a good reason."

He smiles, flashing his dimples, and then exits, closing the door gently. He looks over his shoulder a dozen times, making his way down the dock until he disappears in the maze of boats.

I consider staying here to watch the Ocean Jewel leave, but it won't be for another hour or so. Like the universe knows how pathetic I'm being, my cell phone rings from my center console. It's the first time it's rung in over a week, since I've been with everyone who calls me.

Giselle's smiling face pops up on my screen, and I answer it after the third ring. "Hey, what's up?"

"You better not bail on me today. You know how crazy my aunt is about these things," she responds. "She's shocked we waited this long. I threatened to wear my prom dress."

I laugh. "Want me to pick you up now? I just dropped Carter off at the harbor so I'm close." Hanging out with Giselle sounds a million times better than moping in the parking lot as my merman heads off to sea without me.

Giselle puffs air through the phone. "Totally. Come save me so I don't have to go with my mom. She mentioned something about matching colors, and I do *not* want to end up in another salmon pink dress. If we beat her, I can already have something picked out."

I cringe at the thought of her last fundraiser's dress. "Oh, God. I hope my mom hasn't talked to yours."

"She's already here, Aves," Giselle says, giggling.

"Okay, I'll save you soon. Meet me on the corner of Surf and Sunset. If they see me, we might get stuck riding together with them."

"I'm running out the door now."

It takes less than ten minutes to reach Giselle's street. She waves her arms over her head on the corner of the street exactly where I told her to meet me. Fake panic crosses her face, like she's signaling me to rescue her from a school of hungry piranhas.

I hit the button to open my window and yell, "Get in!"

Hopping in, she buckles her seatbelt, releasing a loud laugh. She smacks her hands on the dashboard, bouncing in her seat. I fly around the corner and head onto Ocean Boulevard. Her bronze hair blows in the wind coming in through the window, and salty air wafts around us.

"You're a lifesaver, Aves," she says. "I for sure thought I was going to drown in pink satin."

"I'm glad you called when you did. I was about to sit in my car with a pouty face until Carter left."

I expect her to roll her eyes or remark about how ridiculous I'm being, but instead, she says, "I'm sorry he had to go. If only our vacation never ended. You two could've been married by next week, and I'd have made the best maid of honor."

"Whoa, Gi. There will be no weddings anytime soon."

"You sure about that?" she says, pointing at my left hand. "That ring on your finger says otherwise." She's clearly joking, but I can't stop the dozens of explanations flying through my mind.

A deep blush blossoms across my cheeks. This is the first time she's noticed it since Carter gave it to me and probably only because I'm the one gripping the steering wheel.

"It's not what you think," I say.

"I'm not thinking anything...except that my BFF is wearing a ring that she would never pick out in a million years."

I playfully slap her arm. "If you must know, this is just a token from vacation. It doesn't mean anything other than I thought it was pretty, and Carter wanted to impress me."

She hums as she sighs. "That boy is perfect. Too perfect, Aves. Just be careful."

"I thought you were all for it?"

"I *am* but he better not mess up our house hunting plans.

My mom scheduled an appointment with a realtor to check out what's for lease in La Tortuga Point. It's the perfect place between here and school."

I can't control the frown crossing my face. Luckily, my dark sunglasses hide my expression, and Giselle is too busy trying to get a better glimpse at the sea stone.

"It's pretty there," I say, navigating downtown Azure Waters in the direction of the dress boutique our moms had made appointments at.

"I know. I'm super excited you're actually on board for a beachfront place. My mom said they're almost done with some new condos. They'll be ready by the end of the month, and they still have vacancies."

I pull to the curb in front of Tatiana's Bridal and Gowns. "I figured we'd wait until right before school to move."

"Why? We started off the summer with a bang, might as well keep it up. And think about it. Carter can stay whenever he's in town. I'll allow it if he promises to clean up after himself and not leave dirty towels all over the bathroom." She tilts her head against the seat, smiling at her own would-be-awesome plan if it didn't mean that I'd have to eventually hurt her by moving out.

"That sounds amazing, but—"

She holds up her hand. "But nothing, Ava. Our parents are on board. It's set."

I force myself to smile at her though my heart sinks into my stomach. The old Ava would be bouncing in her seat, excited and ready to pack up her bags and leave home. Part of me is still really excited but guilt holds me back. Maybe this is a sign. Maybe this means I can maintain my normal life after all. I just wish Carter was here so I could get his opinion.

Giselle pushes her door open and hops out, waiting for me on the sidewalk. When I join her, she nearly drags me into the boutique. She hums her version of the wedding march the second we pass a few mannequins in wedding gowns, and I snort a laugh. My mermaid transformation might have rushed things between me and Carter, but I'm pretty sure he'd agree there won't be a wedding in the near future. I want to at least make it to college first.

Tatiana, the owner and a friend of my mom's, greets us with a smile halfway toward the back of the store where the dressing area is. I keep my eyes trained on the prom dresses and formal gowns, far, far away from anything in the color white so Giselle will quit joking about it.

"I hope you don't mind if we're here early," Giselle says to Tatiana, greeting her with a hug. "But we had to get here to try on dresses before our moms add in their two cents."

"I take it you don't want complementary gowns this time?" Tatiana asks, laughing.

"Definitely not," Giselle says.

"I think I can arrange that. I have a few new pieces I think will look stunning on the both of you already picked out."

Tatiana leads the way to the back of the store where several private dressing areas take up the back wall. Upholstered chairs line the walls and surround a platform outside of the rooms for bridal gown viewing. Mirrors hang on every available wall including inside the changing rooms with curtains to give us privacy from the other shoppers.

Tatiana already has several dresses waiting for us on rolling racks. She pushes the rack intended for our moms against the wall and focuses on the one meant for us. Giselle quickly looks through, eyeing each dress before pulling out a floor-length, midnight blue gown with pearlescent black beads sewn in an intricate swirling pattern along the sheer top fabric. The deep V-cut guarantees she'll be taping her boobs in place, but none of that matters to her. She's picking something unlike anything her mom would ever wear.

"That's super sexy," I say. "Try it on."

She takes it behind the dressing partition while I run my fingers along the flouncy fabric of a deep red number. We spend over an hour and a half twirling and spinning, trying on and taking off before trying on again, several different styles. If we don't pick something soon, our moms will show up to give the final approval.

"Why don't you try this one on? I think it's a better fit for you than the others, Ava," Tatiana says. "It'll match your pretty eyes." She holds up the dress I've been purposely avoiding. A cerulean, mermaid-cut silhouette dress made of the lightest fabric I've ever felt sparkles in the light. Tiny pearls swirl along the rounded, strapless neckline, trailing down the front and around the skirt of the gown.

Surprise keeps me frozen in place. If she'd have suggested this dress a few weeks ago, I'd have never even given it a second thought before trying it on, but it's like I'd be tempting fate if I do.

"Oh, yes! Try on that one, Aves. You'll rock the mermaid look. Imagine how Carter will drool. It's perfect and will accentuate all the right places." Giselle holds up her dark gray gown to keep the hem from dragging on the floor.

"I don't know," I say.

"Well, I do. Try it on."

With a sigh, I dangle the hanger from my finger and head behind my own partition. It only takes a moment for me to strip off my clothes and shimmy my way into the gown. It's a tiny bit long, but with heels, it won't graze the ground.

I step into the viewing area and spin around once before meeting Giselle's gaze. Her smile lights up her entire face, forcing her eyes to squint. She claps her hands, in true Giselle excitement, and rushes to snap a picture with her phone.

"Don't even bother trying on any more. That dress is yours. It's so gorgeous." She rushes closer and waves her hand over the dress without touching it. Grabbing my hand, she says, "And look! Your ring even matches it." Before I have a chance to stop her, she slides the ring off my finger to hold the sea stone against the fabric.

My mouth falls open, fear seizing my heart. I stare at the one thing keeping me out of my mermaid form in the hand of my best friend. Snatching it back, I slide it on my finger, praying I don't start the transformation in the middle of the dress shop.

Without hesitating, I rush to get out of the dress, leaving it crumpled on the floor and throw on my shorts and shirt. I'm not sticking around here to find out. This is different than all the times I triggered it before, and luckily, I don't just suddenly change. If that were to happen, I'd probably die since I wouldn't be able to complete my transformation without a breath of the sea. *Oh, God. Please, let me make it.*

"What's wrong, Aves?" Giselle asks as I fly from the partition.

"I have to go! I'm sorry, Gi. Take my stuff and my car, and please cover for me. Tell my mom I want the gown." I run toward the front door without stopping.

Giselle stays on my heels before reaching out to grab my shoulder. "Ava, wait!"

I tug from her. "I'll explain later. Please, just do what I asked and don't follow me. You have to trust me, okay?"

Without looking back, I dash through the door, running barefooted toward the end of the block where a set of stairs leads to the beach below. *Please, don't let me transform. Please, let me be okay. It was ten seconds.*

My feet sink into the sand, and I run as fast as I can down the beach and toward the water. A few beachgoers lie in the sun, and a few surfers wait for a good swell, so I keep running toward the cliffs where the beach remains empty. The rocks are too sharp and slippery and the tide will rise too high.

Cramps travel up my legs before I even reach the water. The transformation is definitely happening, and there's nothing I can do to stop it. I bolt into the ocean near the rocks, swimming through the tightening muscles on my back. I barely manage to remove my shorts before scales sprout on my legs. It's already too late for my T-shirt. The tight fit pulls against my dorsal fin and rips through on the sharpness along the lower back. At least my bra was tough enough to survive.

Inhaling a deep breath of ocean water, I dive deeper, traveling along the bottom, scraping my stomach against the rocks. I swim past the waves until the ground drops out from under me, and I can descend away from the surface.

If anyone saw me dive in and not come up, it might cause some serious trouble. At least I didn't recognize anyone, so while they might put the effort in to find a missing person, my name wouldn't be attached to it. It's the only thing that stops me from erupting into full blown panic.

I just hope I can figure out what to tell Giselle about my sudden fleeing. While fear nudges at me, the rest of me feels complete relief. This could've ended horribly. I never in a million years dreamed that someone—especially Giselle—would remove the ring from my finger and leave me vulnerable. I'm just thankful I had the chance to get to the water. I don't know what I'd have done if my mom decided she wanted to go to one of the department stores more inland.

And now, here I am, clutching my wet clothes against my chest as I drift along the current in my mermaid form without

Carter nearby. *Why did this have to happen now when he is already somewhere on the sea so far away...*

His face pops into my mind, and a need unlike anything I've ever felt consumes me. I want nothing more than to find him. It's all I can think about. The thought is so powerful I can't even manage to transform back into my human form.

I close my eyes and concentrate but nothing happens. A sudden tingling sensation crosses my chest, tugging at my heart. If I don't follow it, my heart might escape my ribcage and leave me behind. Instead of trying to force myself to change back into a human to find Giselle to try to fix things, I dart away from the shore and let my heart lead the way.

15

ON LAND OR IN THE SEA

THE OCEAN JEWEL FLOATS AHEAD off the coast in what I can only guess is Orange County. I'm not even sure how to find my way back home except for going south, and even then, it'll be hard to find my town among the dozens of beach communities along the way.

I circle the water below the yacht, weaving in and out of the sunbeams cutting through from above. I can't break the surface in fear of being seen, so the only thing I can do is wait for night to come and pray Carter walks the deck so I can call out to him.

At least he's here. I know it. I can feel him as he caters to the guests aboard.

After a few minutes, I swim around the yacht a few times. The wait is torture. I'm already too far from home to turn back, but I'm not risking going to shore either. I don't know these beaches. A random girl rising from the waves will surely attract attention if someone sees me.

I stare up at the bottom of the yacht, watching as whomever the guests are launch the jet skis from the hydraulic platform. Leaving behind a glittering trail of bubbles in their wake, the jet skis take off away from the Ocean Jewel. I follow along behind them out of boredom. Anxiety crosses my mind—not because I'm afraid of the riders but because I'm worried about their safety as one of the jet skis cuts through the water in a drunken-like pattern.

The jet ski flies along the top, bouncing across the surface before spinning and tipping over. A man flies from the craft, splashing into the water, though his lifejacket prevents me from seeing his face. He treads the water, kicking his legs to swim back to his jet ski. As I watch him, he struggles to climb back on. Every time he tries, it pushes the jet ski farther and farther away. He's quite a ways away from the Ocean Jewel, and after a few minutes, he gives up.

His muted voice sounds through the water as he calls for help. I glance around at the few fish darting away, afraid of the commotion he's creating. And he's sure making a lot of it. If I couldn't see under the surface myself, I'd think hungry sharks in the mood for something obnoxious were heading in his direction. But then I notice something strange floating through the water. Clear, orb-like jellyfish drift on the current. They float right near the surface, and in the clear water, he'd be able to see at least the one that floats two feet away from him.

He swims away from the jet ski in the direction of the yacht. He's too slow to get away from the jellyfish, and one brushes against his leg. His yells penetrate through the water to me, and I can't stop myself from swimming closer. If I get too close, he might think I'm some ocean monster, but I'm pretty sure his focus remains on the pain caused by the sting of the pesky jellyfish.

Getting as close as I can, I flick my tail, sending a current toward the jellyfish, shooing them away from the man. I fan my tail a few more times until he's free from the small school.

Another jet ski glides across the water, stopping near the man. A familiar figure jumps into the sea, helping the man up onto the craft here to help him. My heart nearly explodes in relief when I see Carter duck under the water to swim toward the abandoned jet ski to retrieve it.

I propel up to him, swimming just beneath him, and he freezes next to the jet ski before sinking under a foot to peer around. The surprise on his face is priceless, and he unexpectedly inhales a gulp of ocean water. In his human form, it causes him to choke, and he kicks back to the surface.

Staying on the side away from the yacht, I pop my head from the water where he treads. His eyes widen when he sees me, but he doesn't yell at me to dive back under. He only reaches out and rubs his fingers under my chin before he pulls himself onto the jet ski.

He peers down at me with sad eyes. "Ava, what are you doing here?"

"Giselle took my ring right off my finger in a moment of excitement while we were dress shopping," I blurt.

The horror that crosses his face mirrors what mine surely looked like at the time. "You transfor—"

"I made it to the water in time," I say, cutting him off. Holding up my hand, I show him the ring he gave me back on my finger. "But she knows something was wrong. I was so upset by the whole incident that I couldn't force myself to change back and somehow, I ended up here."

"Because you really wanted to find me."

A tear trickles on my cheek, mixing with the saltwater on my face. Carter glances around, turning his gaze to the Ocean Jewel.

"I don't know how to get home," I say, drawing his attention back to me. "What do I do?"

"Give me a few minutes. I'm going to take the next group on the water, and I want you to follow me. There are some caves along the cliffs where you can wait for me until tonight, okay? I don't want to risk leaving you out here in case you trigger the transformation back."

Without waiting for me to respond, he propels forward on the jet ski toward the Ocean Jewel, and I sink underwater to wait.

Ten minutes later, I watch all three jet skis take off together, cutting through the water. The glittering trail they leave behind guides me down the shore. One of the jet skis breaks off from the other two, navigating in a wide circle. Carter dives in the water, pretending to lose control. He smiles at me, pointing his hand behind him, and then he kicks to the surface and climbs on his jet ski before taking off with the others behind him.

My heart aches with every passing second, the trail of bubbles left in Carter's wake now popped along the surface. I wish he could come with me now, but it'd be impossible for him to escape without drawing attention to himself or causing people to panic, thinking he fell overboard. He'd never be able to show his face again, which means that I probably wouldn't be able to either, not if I can't handle this on my own. Obviously after today, I know I can't. I don't want to even if I could.

With one more longing look in the direction Carter left, I swim toward the cliffs. Waves pulverize the scattered rocks leading up to them, and even with my underwater vision, I can barely see past the stirred up sand and bubbles.

It's like a maze navigating the shallow water, and my tail skims the rough surfaces of the rocks as I fight the current to make my way to the caves only the brave would ever attempt to explore. It'd be humanly impossible to make it to them by sea without getting injured. No boat could fit through the spaces between the rocks, the waves threatening to send even me back deeper into the sea. To safely get to them, a person would have to rappel down the cliff and still fight off the angry, rising tide that protects them.

Remaining in my mermaid form, I pull myself from the water and drag my tail into the narrow cave. Water splashes me, knocking me deeper within. Darkness sends a chill to my bones though it fades as my eyes adjust to the dark waters.

Another wave crashes against me, flipping me backward, and I fall into a glowing pool of water that laps gently around me, rising and falling with the waves. It's the size of a small swimming pool and just deep enough that I can float upright without breaking the surface or hitting my tail against the bottom.

Sparkling jewel-like rocks form the walls, the gems flickering in imaginary light. It takes me a moment to realize that their power source isn't coming from within them, but they're catching the light emanating from the spark in my chest. Their soft glow quiets the stress and anxiety in my heart, and after a few minutes, I drift in and out of sleep, wrapped in the safety of this beautiful place with only a sliver of dread tickling my mind about what's to come and how my life might soon be changed forever once again.

"Ava?" Carter's voice enters my mind, tugging me from sleep.

Snapping my eyes open, I peer around the jewel-encrusted pool, trying to orient myself to my surroundings. Without seeing the sun, time escaped me, sending fear rushing through me again. I should be used to the constant state of panic, but being with Carter has been such a relief.

"Ava, I'm here." He slides into the pool, stirring up the sand along the bottom.

I close the distance between us and embrace him. A mixture of emotions courses through me—from excitement and joy to trepidation and uncertainty, but most of all just sweet relief. I pepper him with kisses, so glad that he's here. Laughing underwater, he pushes bubbles from his mouth, a smile lighting his entire face. He brushes his fingers through my floating hair, brushing it from my face before meeting my lips with his for a long, passionate kiss.

When he pulls away, he studies my eyes, a seriousness now narrowing his lips and lowering his brows on his forehead. "You okay?" His soft voice trickles through my mind like a whisper.

Pouting, I say, "I don't even know if I am or not. What time is it anyway? I'm sure my mom's put out a search party by now."

He glides his hands down my sides, hooking them around my hips to keep me floating in front of him. "It's almost nine."

It's been hours. So long so that I don't even know what kind of excuse I can make up. If Giselle took my car for me, it'd be less to explain to my parents, but I have no idea what to even say to her. I don't know what I would do in her situation, but I hope that she trusted me enough to hold off before going to the police or something.

I groan. "We need to go."

"Okay." He pulls me closer. "But I want you to be prepared. If your family has already put out a search party, we're not going to be able to stay. It'll draw too much attention and unwanted questions."

If my heart wasn't anchored in my chest, I think it'd slide out of me and splatter on the sandy floor. I squeeze my eyes closed, tears burning but never falling because they blend with the sea. I was afraid this might happen, but the fact that Carter says the words to me makes it worse. It was always a what-if possibility, but it's turning into a what-must-happen situation.

Carter pulls me close, resting his chin on my shoulder, pressing against me. He rubs soothing circles on my back, but it does nothing to ease the pain of knowing I might have to say goodbye to my friends and family forever.

"Carter." I hide in his neck. A million thoughts rush through my head as I try to think of something—anything—that I can use as an excuse to explain my disappearance to make anything bad that might've happened go away. Nothing sounds believable, though. Maybe I can just not say anything at all. Fake amnesia.

He kisses my temple. "Please, Ava. Don't panic just yet. Everything might be okay. We might not have anything to worry about. I just need you to be prepared in case."

"Okay." The words barely sound in my mind. I'm not even sure if I projected them to Carter.

Hugging me to him, he guides me to the edge of the glowing pool. The water churns with his sudden movement as he propels himself onto the slippery floor first and then helps me up, pulling me along through the darkness until we reach the cave entrance that drops back into the ocean.

He exits first, jumping into the shallows with enough precision not to hurt himself like he's done this dozens of times. I sit on the ledge, my tail smacking the water. It takes him opening his arms for me to fall into before I launch from the cave and back into the sea.

Even with the glowing night water, it's hard to see a few feet in front of us because of the white foam and sand. Rocks skim against my tail as Carter swims us back to the open water, me locked under him in his arms so tightly that it's like I'm just carried on the waves.

The ocean floor steepens, Carter diving us deeper in the open water a good distance from shore. His grip loosens, and he lets me go but only so I can move to ride on his broad back. Without looking around, I press my cheek between his shoulder blades, just feeling his body against mine as we jet through the current.

After what feels like no time at all, Carter slows down. He swims us into shallow water near the same rocks I recognize to be the ones not far from my neighborhood. We break the surface, and I peer around. The beach is empty this time of night, and I sigh a breath of relief when I don't see anything out of the ordinary at my house. If my parents thought I'd gone missing, there'd have been dozens of people around like after Bailey disappeared. The whole community would be on alert.

"Can you transform?" Carter asks softly, his breath blowing

against my hair. He holds me to him so I don't drift away.

I close my eyes, imagining the land, but after a few minutes, nothing happens. No cramps or tightening muscles. Only thoughts of dread and despair.

"I can't," I finally say after a long moment.

"Try harder." Carter dips under the water before popping up to spit water away from me. His legs slide against my tail as he waits for me to follow his lead. The fear and anxiety of leaving the water proves to be too much, because even after another ten minutes of trying, I just can't get myself to return to my human form.

"Carter, I don't think I'm going to have to explain myself. I can't change. Something's wrong with me." I brush my wet hair from my face before bobbing under.

He pulls me back to the surface. "What do you want to do? We can wait it out, or we can head back to the Ocean Jewel, and I can quit tomorrow. We'll head up to San Francisco to see if my parents will help, but you know what they'll say."

I cover my face with my hands. "I just want to change b—"

Carter's words, the idea of going back to San Francisco to prove his parents right, is enough to trigger the transformation. Muscle spasms seize my legs, and tingles rush through my body. Carter holds my hand as I thrash underwater, the pain of the transformation burning through me like fire while the icy water licks over my skin. It takes a lot longer than usual, but after another minute, I spit out water, clearing my lungs.

"It's a lot harder to come back when it's the lack of the sea stone that sets you off," Carter says, forcing me to swim next to him even though I just want to sink back under the waves.

I don't respond. I can't. Exhaustion takes hold of me, and the only reason I manage to make it to the shore at all is because Carter carries me. We lie together on the sand without moving, the waves crashing over our bodies. Carter turns his head to look at me and offers a small smile, not the one he usually saves for me. Under this one lies pity and sorrow. Things I don't want or need right now. I don't call him out on it, though. This is bad enough as it is.

After another minute of rest, he helps me unwind my clothes from my arm. They leave a deep indent in my skin, but there was no way I was going to lose them and end up naked somewhere. When I'm dressed in my ripped shirt and sandy shorts, Carter pulls his own board shorts and shirt from the bag across his chest.

"I'm not leaving until we make sure everything's okay," he says, dusting the sand from my arms. "And if it's not, we'll stay around long enough for you to pack a few things."

I swallow, a lump in my throat making it hard to even speak. "Okay."

Carter leads the way up the beach to my house. The back porch light shines over our patio, but I don't see any other lights on. Sneaking around to the front, I peer into the window near the door, but I can't see anything in the darkness.

I head to the side stairs that lead to the balcony of the guest apartment over the garage and pull the key from the combination locked box on the wall. Cool air drifts out as Carter follows me inside. I enter the hallway and pad my way across the carpet to my parents' bedroom. It's empty.

"It's not unlike my parents to have drinks at the vodka bar near the marina with their friends on my dad's night off," I say, hoping I'm right and they're not searching the area for me.

Carter follows me downstairs where I find the sticky note on the fridge from my mom saying she left money on the counter so Giselle and I could have a nice dinner somewhere and that she really loved the dress I picked out.

I puff a breath of air through my lips. "Everything's fine with my parents. Giselle covered for me."

His brows scrunch together. "But what about Giselle? She's going to expect an explanation, Ava. You can't tell her."

I crumble the sticky note in my hand. "I know that!" I can't stop the anger from entering my voice. "Give me some credit. I know how important our secret is."

He blinks a few times, probably because I've never directed my anger at him before. It's just the day's events have my emotions all over the place. I was expecting the worst possible outcome, and Carter reminding me doesn't help the situation.

"I'm sorry. I just know how close you are," he says softly.

Relaxing my shoulders, I turn to face him. "And it kills me not telling her, but it is what it is. I get it, Carter. Don't ever doubt me."

"I don't." He leans over and brushes his lips against my forehead.

As I gaze into his eyes, I can see that even though he says he doesn't doubt me, a part of him still does. It's enough to make me step away and turn my back on him. It's hard for me to meet his eyes and face this reality. Not because I'm hurt by his lack of faith, but because I might doubt myself as well. It would be so much easier to tell Giselle, to trust her with my secret. I have a million reasons to do so. She'd never betray me. We have the kind of relationship that could survive something even as absurd as this. But it's the secrets that might be our undoing.

After a minute of silence, I turn back to him and say, "I'm going to call Giselle and then hop in the shower. Want me to walk you back to the beach? I can handle my best friend without you."

The concern that crosses his face disappears with a small shake of his head. "You don't look so sure."

I force myself to smile. "I am, promise."

He doesn't question me or argue though the doubt still lingers in his eyes. This is his way of letting me figure this out on my own, letting me make my own mistakes. I can't blame him for not putting up a fight. I wouldn't if I were him. But even so, his trust in me emanates from him stronger than the spark of doubt, and it's enough to calm my nerves, to make me feel like I won't screw this up. That everything will be okay no matter what happens in the end.

I slide my hands around his neck, standing on my tiptoes to kiss him. He relaxes under my touch, kissing me back like our kiss is all that he needs from me, like it's more important than where we find ourselves in the world, whether it's on land or deep within the sea.

When he pulls away, he grins, flashing his dimples in the smile he saves just for me. "You know, my life has gotten so much more exciting with you in it."

"It's safe to say I feel the same," I say with a laugh.

I stroll next to him to my back door, and we step onto the patio together. The moon shines above us, casting soft light on the water, and my heart aches a tiny bit as he kisses me once more.

"I'll come back tomorrow night, okay?" he says as he pulls away.

All I can do is nod. Gazing after him, I watch him undress and head into the ocean. He looks back once to wave, and then his tail cuts through the water as he dives, leaving me alone, damp, and cold on the beach.

Hugging myself, I turn and head back inside to face what's to come. I hope I can figure it out to save everything Carter's worked hard for to stay on land. I hope I can figure things out to save me as well. I don't want to be responsible for forcing us into the sea.

16

DEVASTATING SECRET

THE HEADLIGHTS OF MY BMW illuminate my front door. Giselle pulls my car into my driveway, keeping the car running. I dash down the steps and climb into the passenger's seat, a whirlwind of emotions leaving my hands shaking in my lap.

She doesn't say anything, driving my car back onto the street and in the direction of her house. The tension between us is suffocating, nearly unbearable, because I know what's on her mind, but she's waiting for me to say something first. If only I could find the words to make this better.

I inhale a slow breath through my nose. "Gi, I—"

"You don't know how damn worried I was about you!" she yells, smacking her hands on the steering wheel, jerking the car in the lane. "What the hell happened?"

My words stay locked in my throat as her anger sizzles between us. This is worse than the time I ditched her during a party last summer when someone suggested they move things to the beach. I can feel her emotions ten times more than I can feel my own with the way she directs her worry, fear, and fury at me.

Instead of answering, I stare out the window. Nothing I could come up with excuses my erratic behavior and sudden disappearance today. The only plausible thing I can think of is the truth, and there's no way I can let Carter down like that. I know there would be consequences if someone were to find out, and they're bad enough that Carter won't even tell me besides the fact that we'd have to disappear.

Giselle's anger fizzles out the longer I don't say anything. "Aves? Are you okay? Did something bad happen?"

I still don't respond, because whatever I say won't be able to answer her questions.

She reaches out and grabs my hand. "Please, say something."

I blink away tears. "I'm okay, Gi. I just—I can't answer your questions. You have to trust me that everything is fine. I rushed out today because—because—" I take a deep breath. "I can't explain."

Giselle side-glances me in her vision before pulling over to park next to the curb. She cuts off the engine and shifts in her seat to look at me. Her amber eyes, dark in the orange glow of the streetlight above us, study me. I focus on the shadow cutting across her face instead of her eyes, because I'm afraid she'll somehow read the truth in my mind if I let her see the emotions lingering on my soul through my eyes.

"If you're in trouble, I want to help you," she finally says. "Does this have to do with—" She snaps her mouth shut before saying Carter's name. I know it's him she's thinking about.

I shake my head. "Carter's not even here, Gi. And you can't tell him either, okay?"

Her twisted lips and furrowed brows tell me she's going to reach out to him the moment she can. Carrying the kind of worry she has for me is enough to make her confide in someone close to me, and at this time, it happens to be Carter.

"I'm serious, Giselle. Please, just trust me when I say I'm fine."

"If our places were switched, would you trust me? Wouldn't you do everything you could to make sure I was okay?"

She's right. I would. "But I *am* okay. I swear, if I wasn't I'd tell you. I just—I can't tell you or anyone what happened."

"Why not, Ava?"

I sigh. "Because if I do, it'll ruin my life."

She's quiet for a moment, processing my words. Then she surprises me by saying, "Please, tell me you didn't murder someone or something."

I laugh. I can't help it. "Do you honestly think I would murder someone?"

She frowns. "This isn't funny. What am I supposed to think if whatever you can't tell me is capable of ruining your life?"

"Just trust me. It's nothing illegal."

"I do trust you, but it's not going to stop me from being hurt and angry with you because I want you to trust me as well. I'm your BFF. That's best friends *forever*, you know." She brushes her hair behind her ears with her fingers.

My heart aches with every passing beat knowing how this one devastating secret is enough to tear my friendship apart. But what would be worse? Damaging my friendship with Giselle or losing it altogether?

"Gi, please. You have to understand."

"I can't, Ava. I'm trying, but I can't."

I sigh, tears of frustration splashing onto my cheeks. "Okay, here's the deal. Something happened to me on vacation. It does involve Carter, but he's not the bad guy. This secret I'm keeping—it's his, too. If anyone were to find out, we'd have to run—disappear—and I'd never see you again. So, I'm sorry if you're hurt and angry. But I don't want to give up my life to make you feel better. I'm willing to piss you off so I don't lose my BFF, because I want it to be *forever* more than anything."

Her mouth falls open, and she sobs hysterically, crying into her hands. It sets me off, and together we bawl our eyes out on the side of the road overlooking the dark ocean. She sniffles, wrapping her arms around me, and I embrace my best friend like I'll lose her if I let her go.

"A-Ava," she says, hiccupping. "I-I'm so scared f-for y-you."

I nod my head, tears blurring my eyes. "Don't be. I'm not in danger. I—I just have to keep this secret."

Taking a deep breath, Giselle composes herself enough to wipe the tears from her face with the back of her hands. "Okay," she finally says. "But if you do decide to tell anyone, I better be the first to know."

"Deal."

We hug each other for a long while, just sitting in the car with the soft sound of the radio to drown out our sniffles. It isn't until the dashboard clock blinks midnight that Giselle starts the car again and pulls from the curb.

"Want to spend the night?" I ask as we head onto Surf Way. "We didn't get much time on vacation."

The corners of her glassy, red eyes crinkle as she smiles. "I'd like that. I'm really missing my BFF."

"Well, don't. 'Cause I'm right here."

For now... I push the thoughts away. I can't bear to even think them.

"Ava-babe, you decided to come!" Logan yells from his spot next to Daisy on the sand.

I kick sand up, strolling next to Giselle. We head down the beach toward the massive fire pit glowing on the shore. Sapphire and Chloe sit next to each other while Matty stands, holding a wire hanger with a marshmallow stuck to it into the flames.

"Gi, how did you convince her?" Sapphire asks, smiling.

"She didn't have to," I say. "I'm here by my own freewill and desire to hang out with my friends. Besides, half of us aren't going to be here for much longer."

Chloe groans. "Don't remind me. I'm going to be the third wheel with these two." She points at Logan and Daisy who both laugh.

"We won't be far," Giselle says, plopping on the sand next to Sapphire.

I take the empty spot next to Chloe with my back to the ocean. While staring at the fire, I can almost pretend I'm not on the beach. I really wanted to bail on Giselle, but I still feel really bad about our confrontation last night. She hasn't asked me more about what I'm hiding, but I know it's constantly on her mind.

"LA's not that far either," Sapphire chimes in. "We'll have a spare bedroom so you all can visit anytime."

"Which we will," Daisy says.

"Definitely," Logan adds.

As my friends talk about what's ahead in our futures, I can't help thinking about what's next for me. I was accepted into the same school as Giselle—we have plans to live together—but it's starting to feel impossible. I know it'll only last a short while, but even so, how will I explain staying out all night every full moon? Or why I come home soaking wet when I'm supposed to be terrified of the ocean?

"Ava-babe?" Matty's voice cuts through my train of thought. He snaps his fingers in front of my face. "Aves, hello?"

I jerk my head up. "Huh?"

"Jeez, zone much?" Sapphire asks, laughing.

"Sorry, I was just thinking. What's up?"

"I asked about Carter. When's he coming back? We're supposed to make plans to go surfing," Matty says.

"Oh, tomorrow. He'll be going to the gala with me," I say.

Giselle listens quietly while watching me, but she doesn't say anything. I know she probably thinks badly of Carter now. Why wouldn't she? I wish I could say something to make sure she really knows that none of this is his fault. He saved me.

"Cool, we can all ride together. The limo picks us up for a little pre-gala partying. You know how those things are," he says.

I smirk. The obligatory pre-party is the only way any of us has ever made it through one of these boring fundraisers people pay a fortune to attend to sit around and make small talk with people they gossip about behind their backs. I've been gossiped about along with the rest of my friends for one thing or another.

Last year it was because Chloe's brother gave up his full scholarship to Stanford for a surf sponsorship. The year before that, it was because Logan was arrested for trespassing. This year will surely involve either people speculating how quickly Sapphire will blow through her trust fund, how Daisy's taking a gap year and probably won't even go to college, or even me, because I'm bringing a boy none of the elite in our community has ever met. They'll probably talk about all three. I'll have to smile my brightest for the photo that'll appear in the Azure Waters Gazette.

"Matty, it's your year to be the center of attention," Sapphire says. "I already told a dozen people you pushed Ava off the yacht."

Heat blooms in my cheeks. "You didn't!"

She laughs with a shrug.

Giselle rolls her eyes. "She didn't, Aves."

"Should we take bets?" Logan asks.

I toss a marshmallow at him. "You always lose."

My friends laugh, retelling their version of how I flipped over the guardrail, and how Carter flew off the yacht moments after me. Now that we're all still alive and sitting in the sand, the horrors of that night are just one of the adventures we've all shared. That night feels like a blur to me as well. I only remember Carter apologizing and the spark. Everything else came from Carter's memory.

When the topic shifts to what dresses us girls are wearing, I hop to my feet and stroll around to face the waves. Giselle shows Sapphire pictures of our gowns, and I wonder which one Giselle ended up picking out. She never once mentions my erratic behavior.

As I stare at the ocean, a glimmer of light within the water catches my attention. It cuts through the waves, like a small beacon of light, luring me to follow it down the shore away from my friends.

"Ava? What's up?" Giselle calls from behind me.

I'm already strolling away through the sand. "I'll be right back," I call before I start to jog.

"You're not going to jump in the ocean are you?" Matty calls out.

I shake my head, whipping my blond hair back and forth. "I'm going to the bathroom if you're that interested."

Thankfully, no one gets up to follow me. The public restrooms are visible behind the empty lifeguard tower, so my friends can watch me walk, but probably only Giselle stares at me. No one else has reason to be suspicious. Though going to the bathroom is the least thing for her to be suspicious about.

I round the corner of the bathroom where the women's restroom is, but I don't go inside. I keep jogging down the beach, using the building to block my friends' view of me. Turning my gaze back to the ocean, I study the light moving closer to the beach, and then I see him.

Carter emerges from the waves, his dark silhouette contrasting with the whitecaps shining under the moon. He pauses to slide on his swim trunks and then jogs through the sand to me. Smiling, I close the distance, wrapping my arms around his wet body not even caring that water soaks through my shirt. He promised he'd come to me tonight, but I thought it'd be much later and where I could swim with him amid the waves.

"I expected you later," I say, pushing his wet hair from his forehead. "I'm not alone."

He licks the saltwater from his lips. "I couldn't wait. I've been anxious all day."

"I told you I'd handle it, and I did..." My words trail off.

"But?"

I exhale a long breath. "Giselle kinda thinks we're involved in something awful. She asked me if I murdered someone."

He laughs, having the same reaction I did to her question. "She's gonna hate me."

"She'll get over it. All that matters is that she won't ask any more questions."

"Good," he says, kissing me again.

His lips taste of the ocean and something sweeter, like he's just eaten dessert, and I sink into him, letting him pick me up off the ground a few inches. Even after how I left Carter last night, it's so easy to forget that he might've doubted me. And now, he won't ever doubt me again.

"Ava?" Giselle's voice rings out over the sounds of the surf and our beating hearts.

I cringe, pulling away from Carter. "You have to go!" I whisper-hiss, pushing him back.

"One more kiss," he says, tugging my arm. He pulls me to the back of the building, facing the water. Cupping my face, he kisses me deeply, teasing me with his tongue, until I consider following him back to the ocean.

"Ava? Where are you?" It only takes Giselle's voice to call

me back to the land before something happens that I'll regret.

Carter kisses my cheek once more before he charges toward the water and dives under. Turning away, I stroll around the building and watch as Giselle comes out from looking in the women's bathroom for me.

When she sees me, she tilts her head to the side in question. "Why are you wet?"

I brush my fingers over my damp shirt where I was pressed against Carter's dripping chest. The thought sends a shiver through me. Rubbing my hands over my arms, I play it off like I'm cold and not thinking about my hot merman boyfriend.

"The stupid hand dryer is broken again," I say, stepping up next to her.

"But why were you over there?" She points to the back of the building.

"The water fountain." The lie comes so easily that I almost believe it. But for some reason, doubt crosses her face though she doesn't admit it.

"We're all heading back to Sapphire's to use the spa. Wanna come?"

I consider it for a moment, but the thought of Carter sits in the back of my mind. "I have to decorate a few cakes for the gala. My mom's paying me. Want to come help me instead?" I only ask because I know baking is the last thing she likes to do.

She frowns. "It can't wait?"

"I can get up early," I say.

She shakes her head. "No, it's okay. I don't want you to

crash halfway through the gala. I can't survive it without you."

We kick our way back to the others through the sand. Daisy helps Logan put out the fire while the others pick up the blankets and trash.

"I can drop you off if you want," I say, glancing at the ocean every so often.

"Sapphire can drive me," she says, hugging me. "I'll come by tomorrow before our hair appointment with lunch to make up for not helping you with the cakes."

I laugh. "Thanks."

The others groan when Giselle tells them I'm bailing on them, but only Matty offers to help decorate the cakes I already finished this afternoon while Giselle was having lunch with her mom and grandma who came in from out of town.

"You can't eat them, though," I say, teasingly, knowing well enough that Matty doesn't actually intend to decorate anything.

"Damn, you're on your own then, Ava-babe," he says, climbing into the front seat of Sapphire's Tesla.

I climb behind the wheel of my car and start it up, but I don't leave. I wait for my friends to turn the corner before I shut off the engine and climb out.

After dropping my clothes in the sand under the lifeguard tower, I rush into the ocean before diving under.

Carter greets me with a smile, and we swim away from the shore.

17

IRREPARABLE DAMAGE

BRIGHT SUNSHINE WARMS MY SKIN as I lean against my silver BMW, eyeing the docks anxiously for signs of Carter. I only have tonight and tomorrow morning with him on land, and I want to enjoy every second of it.

The black bag of his tuxedo hangs on the back window of my car from where I picked it up from the rental place only an hour ago. He had picked one out in Laguna and had it sized and rush delivered to the local mall near my house just in time.

When Carter enters the parking lot, he's all smiles, striding to me. He stops in front of me, bringing his hand to my cheek and gazes into my eyes for a moment. He's never seen me wear this much makeup ever, but Giselle insisted on fake lashes and glittery eyeliner to match the shimmery pearls of my gown.

"I almost didn't recognize you," he says, running his fingers behind my ear to graze them over the curls of my low bun.

"It's a bit much, huh?"

He shakes his head. "You're still just as beautiful."

After a moment of admiring me, he kisses me softly before pulling away to stick his duffle bag behind my seat. He then opens the door for me, and I get behind the wheel and start the engine as he gets in the front seat beside me. Locking our fingers together, I drive from the harbor with one hand, glancing at Carter in my peripheral vision every so often.

Fifteen minutes later, I pull into my driveway, parking in front of the door instead of the garage. My mom greets Carter with a warm smile when we enter the house. She's already ready, wearing a floor-length, capped sleeved gown in a deep burgundy color that brings out the dark streaks of gold in her hair.

"I'm so happy you could make it, Carter," she says, offering him a hug instead of a handshake. "Ava told you that you could stay in the guest apartment, right?"

He nods, beaming a smile. "Yes, thank you for the offer, Beatrice."

"My pleasure. Now, if you two will excuse me, I have to find Ava's father so we can head out. Ruby wants to go over her speech once more before the gala starts." She turns to look at me. "Don't be late, Avie."

I sigh. "Can't promise that, Mom. Matty rented the limo. He's in charge."

She shakes her head. "I'll see you two later."

I guide Carter up to my room where Giselle sits at my vanity table taking pictures of herself in the mirror. Her bronze hair cascades in soft curls down her bare back. The backless, navy blue gown has a deep V neckline and small cutouts that run up the sides, starting at her hips, showing off tiny slivers of her smooth skin.

"Our date has arrived," she exclaims, grinning, but something in her eyes makes my steps falter.

"How did I get so lucky to have two of the prettiest girls of Azure Waters on my arms tonight?" he asks.

Giselle's eyes soften. She's a sucker for a compliment. "We're sure to be at the center of the gossip."

"Totally," I say. "Can you imagine Mrs. Goldberg's face?" Mrs. Goldberg sits on the scholarship board along with our moms. She once tried to ban people under the age of eighteen from attending the gala a few years ago, but it didn't stand well considering that the rest of the board members had children.

"She's going to be huffing about how inappropriate we're being at such a prestigious event," Giselle says, rolling her eyes.

"Do I have time to back out?" Carter asks with a teasing smile.

"No way. We might just send you in alone."

Carter laughs, adjusting his tuxedo bag on his arm.

"Let me show you to the guest apartment so you can get

ready," I say, pulling him away.

"Yeah, you can't see Ava again until after she's completely ready, so go downstairs when you're done," Giselle calls as I guide Carter from my room even though he knows the way.

After I get Carter settled in the small suite over the garage, I head back to my room to change into my gown, the one I've dreaded wearing since it nearly ruined everything. *That was you, not the dress.*

Giselle helps me zip up the side and hooks a pearl necklace my mom let me borrow around my neck. Matching pearl earrings shine from my ears, the perfect addition to my dress. I touch up my makeup, add a few jeweled bobby pins to my curled bun, and grab my clutch off my dresser before turning to Giselle.

"We're so hot," she says. "Like, I just want to stare at us in the mirror the rest of the night. Everyone will be looking at us. Who knows, maybe I'll actually meet someone tonight."

Nerves tighten my stomach at the thought of being under the microscope. "I just hope I don't fall on my face in these shoes," I say, lifting my dress to show my ivory strappy heels.

"Well, if you do, I promise to fall, too. You can do the same for me."

I smile and hug my best friend. "We'll take Carter down with us. Might as well make it a dramatic performance if it were to happen."

She giggles while pulling away to grab her own purse. "Speaking of Carter, everything okay with you two?"

"Yeah, it's great. Promise."

She nods. "Okay, let's go find him. I can't wait to see his reaction to you."

We head downstairs where we find Carter hovering by the back door, gazing out the window at the ocean. As he turns, my heart flutters at the sight of him in his slim-fit, dark gray tuxedo with a matching bowtie. His dark hair is styled back out of his face, and he's shaved, his dimples in clear view when he smiles his perfect smile as his gaze lingers over me.

"Wow," he says breathlessly. "Ava, you're—you look just like..." His voice trails off.

"So hot, right?" Giselle says, laughing.

"Beautiful, stunning, breathtaking," he says, leaning down to kiss me softly.

"Okay! Enough with the gushy stuff. We need pics. The limo will be here any minute." Giselle grabs my arm to pull me away from Carter.

Carter takes a gazillion photos of us on the back patio with the ocean as our backdrop. I manage to get her to take a few of me and Carter before we all squeeze together for Carter to get one of the three of us.

Giselle, now swept up with the excitement of the night, doesn't look at Carter with suspicious eyes anymore. She's all smiles and twirls, acting like she did while we were on vacation. It's such a relief considering how uncomfortable we all felt knowing that there is basically a whale-sized secret hanging out next to me.

Ten minutes later, the doorbell rings, and we rush out to join the others who yell and catcall from the limo. Logan helps me in, and I slide in on the opposite side of him, leaving room for Carter, who climbs in last. Giselle sits on the other side of Carter and forces Daisy to take another picture.

When the limo takes off, Sapphire pulls out a few glasses from the drink compartment, and Matty helps her pour champagne into the flutes to pass around. It's prom night all over again, except I actually have a date who can't stop looking over at me.

Carter clinks his flute with mine, taking a small sip. Giselle downs hers in two gulps and holds out her glass for Sapphire to refill. Matty laughs at Giselle, holding his glass up before gulping it down just as quickly.

"You might want to finish that," Logan says, tipping his glass toward Carter. "Because these things suck. If my mom wasn't on the board, I'd have bailed and left Daisy to fend for herself."

Daisy glares. "I guess you don't want to have fun at *my* after party."

Logan laughs. "You know I'm just playing, babe."

The two of them kiss, and I turn away to gaze out the tinted windows as we wind up the coastal highway toward the Grand Le Mer hotel, which sits atop a cliff overlooking the water. I finish my champagne, and Sapphire fills up my glass again before I have a chance to decline since Carter still babies his drink. I wonder if it's because alcohol and merpeople don't mix.

I can't exactly ask him, but he only smirks when I clink my glass with Giselle's as she downs her third.

If she continues at this pace, Carter will be dragging her into the ballroom, and we'll be forced into our dramatic falling on the floor entrance. Her cheeks flush even through her makeup, and she giggles, reaching across Carter's lap to grab my hand.

"You're my BFF, Avie," she says, using my childhood nickname that my mom uses. "And Carter, you're my BFF now because she's my BFF." Uh-oh. At least she's being a sweet drunk. That I can handle.

The others laugh, grinning at her need to be affectionate.

"I love you too, Gi," I say, squeezing her hand.

"You know you guys can tell me anything, right?" she continues. *Shit.*

Carter stiffens next to me, but I force my smile to remain. "Yes, Giselle. I know we can."

"Okay, because I hate secrets."

"Giselle," I say.

"No, Ava. I've been thinking about it a lot lately," she says, waving her empty glass through the air.

Silence falls around the limo as the others realize Giselle's getting serious. My heart pounds in my chest, though she doesn't know my secret to tell, only that I have one big enough to change my life.

"Giselle, please. Just stop," I say.

She sighs. "Fine, but only because I don't want you to run away with Carter."

I close my eyes to compose myself. When I open them, the others stare at me with expressions of surprise and curiosity. Carter just stares at his hands, folded in his lap. Things get awkward quickly, and we can't arrive at our destination fast enough.

Sapphire leans forward. "What the hell is she talking about? You two planning on eloping or something?"

I place my right hand over my left to hide my ring even though it's not an engagement ring in the sense they'd think. I can't exactly explain that it stops me from growing a tail. Like that'd go over well.

"Because that'd be crazy," Chloe says, speaking up for the first time from her corner of the limo.

"You two just met," Matty says.

"I think it'd be romantic," Daisy says, smiling. "I know you all think love at first sight is cheesy, but I think it's possible. Right, babe?" she asks Logan.

He shrugs. "Sure, babe."

I cover my face with my hands. "Okay, you all need to stop. You're embarrassing me. Carter and I are *not* getting married. And if we were, you'd all be invited."

"Then why would you run away?"

"Honestly?" I ask. "If I told you I'd have to kill you."

Everyone except for Giselle busts up laughing. As quickly as they were prying for answers, they drop the subject. Carter twines his fingers through mine, relaxing the best he can, and then he gulps the rest of his champagne. The limo pulls to a stop outside of the Grand Le Mer. A glittery blue carpet lines the entrance while a few photographers gather on the walkway to snap pictures of anyone they find newsworthy. There are always a few celebrities at the events held by the Kings, mostly the faces of their beauty brands.

Sapphire pours everyone one more glass, finishing off the third bottle of champagne, and we all clink our glasses together. I try to catch Giselle's gaze, but she refuses to look at me as she gulps down the last sip of her champagne.

Heat blossoms up my shoulders and neck, the alcohol settling through me, making me feel lightheaded. The chauffeur opens the door, and Giselle hops out without a word. Sapphire shrugs at me before exiting with Matty, followed by Logan, Daisy, and Chloe.

I turn to Carter. "I'm sorry. I'll fix this."

He scrunches his brows. "I'm not so sure you can. Suspicion makes people take a closer look. We can't have that. It's not safe."

"Will you please let me try?"

He nods as he steps out of the limo before me to help me out. "Yeah, of course, Ava. I just don't want you to get your hopes up. Secrets tear people apart."

That's what I'm afraid of.

An array of art pieces—from paintings to sculptures—decorates the ballroom, surrounding the perimeter. The sea of people, all adorned in their finest attire, moves and shifts through the ballroom like a wave of luxury and power. Azure Waters' finest gleam with glittering jewels and an air of wealth thick enough to suffocate me in.

Carter gazes around the room. Some spectators laugh and clink champagne flutes while others glare through the room looking for someone to talk about. A few eyes fall on me, following my every move. I weave through the crowd in search of my mom to make my mandatory round of greetings to all her friends. Once that's over, we'll be free to do whatever we want.

"Ava, dear, don't you look stunning," Mrs. Tenant says. Bright purple orchids cascade out of a cylindrical vase in the center of the table she sits at. "Your mother said you'd be here tonight."

"Thank you, Mrs. Tenant. I love the color of your dress," I say. Pulling Carter closer, I add, "This is my date Carter Stevens. Mrs. Tenant's husband is on the board of directors at the Betty Green Hospital where my dad works."

Carter kisses the back of the old lady's hand in the perfect gentleman fashion. "It's lovely to meet you, ma'am."

She chuckles. "What a charming young man you have, Ava." Turning to Carter, she says, "I'm afraid I don't know any of your family, dear. Are you new in town?"

"He's from San Francisco," I answer for him. I dart my eyes in search for an escape before she starts questioning his entire existence. "His parents own a business up there."

"How interesting."

I spot my mom across the room. "Oh, I hate to have to excuse ourselves, but I must check in with my mom. It was nice seeing you again, Mrs. Tenant."

Before she can respond, I drag Carter away through the crowd. Giselle stands at her mom's side, looking bored. An older man talks to her, waving his arms around as he tells her something he obviously thinks is fascinating but clearly she doesn't. She doesn't even try to pretend, yawning, wobbling slightly on her heels.

"Are you going to speak for me all night, Ava?" Carter asks, pulling me to slow down for a minute before we can approach my mom. His words surprise me even though he smiles while he says them.

"Only when it's someone nosey and gossipy like Mrs. Tenant," I say. "She has to know everything about everyone. It's better not to give her too much to go on."

He raises his eyebrows but doesn't question me.

When we reach my mom, she smiles at me and then kisses my cheek. "The dress looks gorgeous."

"It's a shame you didn't stay around to give us your opinion on our gowns," Anaya, Giselle's mom, says from next to her daughter.

"I think you did a fabulous job without us," I say instead of trying to explain my absence. "I love the bead work," I add, twirling my finger over the delicate beads sewn into the skirt.

"Thank you, darling." Her gaze turns to Carter. "This must be the boy who saved your life."

My mouth drops open, and I flick my gaze to Giselle.

"It wasn't me, I swear," she says. The heat in her voice she had in the limo is barely a whisper of warmth now that she's had a minute to cool off. Even after everything, she doesn't want to hurt me. Even after I hurt her by not telling her what's going on. I suck. This sucks. Everything just sucks.

Fear flashes in my mom's eyes before it quickly disappears. "It's okay, Avie. Ruby told us when I asked about Carter. I'm just thankful for what he's done. I don't know what I'd have done if I..." Her voice trails off as she loses herself in her memory.

"It was nothing," Carter says casually, like him jumping overboard is not a big deal when we both know it was a huge, life changing, world imploding deal. One I was lucky to sort of survive.

"It was everything," I whisper.

Carter wraps his hands around my waist from behind and then leans down to brush his lips against my cheek.

Anaya's gaze flickers between us for a moment. "It's a shame you don't have a brother for my daughter."

"Mom!" Giselle exclaims. "I can find my own boyfriend, thank you very much."

Carter laughs. "I have a few cousins, though I haven't seen them since I was a kid."

"I can't imagine why," Giselle says with a fake smile, clearly thinking that Carter is the worst person in the world, though she has no idea.

Ignoring her words, I tilt my head to the side, thinking

about his family outside of his parents for the first time. They must not have been part of his life because he didn't include anyone else in his memories when he shared his life with me.

Silence falls between us, and a moment later, Giselle excuses herself, leaving me and Carter shifting awkwardly in front of my mom and Anaya.

Anaya places her hands on her hips. "Don't let her get to you, Ava. She's been moody the last few days. It's hard when your friends start splitting their time with boys. Don't you remember how it was, Bea? We almost didn't talk for three months when I met Griffin."

My mom bobs her head but doesn't smile. "She's right."

But she's not. This has nothing to do with spending time with Carter and everything to do with the secret that threatens to tear me from my human life.

Instead of agreeing, I say, "I should go talk to her." I turn to Carter. "Why don't you find Logan and Matty?"

Without waiting for a response, I cut through the crowd. People part away from each other as I rush through them only nodding when they say hello. When I don't find Giselle in the bathroom, I head out of the ballroom to the only place that could provide the privacy she wants.

Pushing open the glass door to the empty balcony, I step out. The ocean breeze clings to my skin, blowing up from the sea below. Giselle rests her elbows on the stone partition on the balcony. The air is chilly enough and the night dark enough, that it stops anyone from wanting to stay out here long. All the fun's happening inside, anyway. Even the front entrance is closer for the old lady smokers who sit out most of the event, gossiping between each other about how scandalous some people are.

"Giselle," I call.

She doesn't turn around.

"Please, we need to talk."

Bowing her head, she rests her chin on her arms without looking at me. "Why? So you can make me feel like crap."

My brows scrunch together. "No, Gi. That's the last thing I want."

"Then why don't you just go find Carter. Apparently he's the only one worthy of your secret."

Anger and sadness wash through me. "I told you already. It's not only my secret."

"It doesn't matter. I don't care anymore!"

"You don't mean that. It's the alcohol talking," I say, closing the distance between us.

"I thought I was okay, Aves. I thought I could handle you not telling me whatever it is you're so afraid to, but I can't. Best friends don't make each other miserable like this. I just—I think it's better that you do your thing until you figure it out."

Tears spring from my eyes, sending a glittering haze across my vision. Hurt sweeps through my mind, and I consider telling her my secret this very second. Life would be more bearable to share it with someone I've been close to all my life. But I can't. I can't do anything to stop her from basically breaking up with me as my best friend.

"Giselle..."

"No, Ava."

Pain pounds against my ribcage, my heart shattering into a million pieces. The one person I used to always rely on, the person who saw me through the worst moments of my life, the person who I never thought I'd ever live without can't even look at me. She shifts away, putting distance between us, and sobs, her cries catching and disappearing on the wind.

This is what it felt like when I realized Bailey wasn't coming back. But this feels even worse. It wasn't the ocean who stole my best friend this time. It was me. It was who I've become. The damage is irreparable between us, and as much as I want to, need to, there's nothing I can think of to fix it.

Neither of us moves from the balcony, like the moment one of us leaves, it will truly be the death of our friendship. Despair settles through me, and I shift my gaze away from Giselle crying to stare off into the dark night. I drag my feet to the cement partition, resting my elbows on it not far from her. I can't go back inside like this. I'm sure my makeup's already a mess.

"You know what hurts me the most, Aves?" she asks after a minute of silence. The fact that she's even talking to me at all sends my heart racing.

I don't have it in me to list all the things that have hurt her. I feel bad enough that my new existence, the stupid secret, the ocean, all of it has turned me into someone I'm not used to having to be. Someone who would rather hurt my best friend than give up the life I have here in Azure Waters. But this isn't all about me either. I'm saving Giselle the hurt. She'd blame herself when she realized I wasn't lying about disappearing. I can't put her through that guilt no matter how easy it would be to just say the words and fix this.

Finally, I ask, "What, Gi?"

"That even after all this—after knowing how you're ruining our friendship—you just accept it like I'm not worth fighting for. I don't give a damn if you've done something unthinkable. Yeah, it would be super disturbing if you loved a boy who turns out to be a murderer, but I'd still love you. That's what friends do. That's why this hurts me so much. You've chosen a boy you've just met over me."

I close my eyes. "I didn't choose him. You have to believe me. I chose you, Giselle. It's why I'm here right now."

"You're here because you're afraid I'll make a scene."

I release an angry breath between my lips, closing the space between us. "Are you kidding me? You have no idea! I didn't mean I chose you because I'm standing on this balcony. I meant I chose you over everything. The only reason I'm standing in front of you is because I chose you."

Her brows knit together in confusion, but I don't know how else to explain it without revealing anything else. "Ava..."

"Let me finish," I snap, inhaling a deep breath of sea air, letting it sink to my core. The dull roar of the waves hums from below us, and I imagine what it would've been like just leaving with Carter in San Francisco so I didn't have to face Giselle's hurt eyes right now.

"Ava—your arm." As she says the words, a series of cramps rush through me, buckling my knees.

I stare at my arm in horror. My pectoral fins jut up from the skin of my forearms. I heave forward, spinning around for somewhere to run, but the only exit off the balcony leads back inside the hotel far from the front door.

Panic laces every quick breath I take, and I try to will the transformation to stop. I'm trapped high above the ocean with nowhere to run, about to reveal everything to Giselle. It's like my body purposely went against my mind to save me the trouble of holding onto a secret that leaves the two of us broken and devastated.

I lean against the partition, pain threatening to send me sprawling to the ground from my weakening knees. I won't be able to stand much longer, let alone get to the ocean if I don't act quickly. It doesn't help that I'm about to change into a mermaid in front of my best friend at the worst possible moment without warning. *This can't be happening!*

"Ava!" Giselle yells, her eyes widening. "What's wrong with you? What's happening? Oh, my God."

My heart tears apart at the sheer fear lining her words. "Gi, please don't freak out. I have to go, but I can't go back in there."

Confusion replaces the anger she held for me moments ago. "What? I don't understand."

"I can't explain now. But this is what I've been hiding." I cry out, another spasm shooting up my back, forcing me to bow forward. I turn away, blocking her view of the short fins on my arms, my now webbed fingers, and the gills burning for the sea on my neck.

"Ava..." Her voice trails off. She's stunned speechless.

My pearlescent skin shimmers in the soft lighting. "You have to promise not to tell anyone. No one can know. If my mom asks, I got sick, okay? And please, go find Carter."

I heave myself over the partition, feeling the tingling sensation of my scales sprouting over my legs. The ledge is barely wide enough to stop me from falling, but I'm afraid to jump just yet.

Giselle grabs my shoulders. "Ava, please. Don't do this. Don't jump. We can work through this."

I arch my back, my dorsal fin now pressing against the fabric of my dress, threatening to break through.

"You have to trust me. I'm begging you. Don't tell anyone."

She only nods, tears smearing her mascara. "Okay."

"Ava!" Carter's voice echoes through the night.

But it's too late. I have no choice. I have to let go.

18

PROMISES

CARTER WRAPS HIS ARMS AROUND Giselle, pulling her away from me. Both their eyes widen as I complete the transformation and dive from the balcony. I free fall into the glowing sea, inhaling a deep breath of saltwater to stop the burning in my chest.

I don't stay underwater long. Popping up to the surface, I float on the churning sea. Giselle screams once, and Carter covers her mouth with his hand to stop her from drawing attention from anyone who might be nearby. His attention shifts from her to me in the water. A strange expression crosses his face, but he doesn't look at me for long, not with Giselle freak-ing out in his arms.

He bends down, whispering something to her I can't hear from here, and then they run from the balcony together. Whatever he said was enough to get her to cooperate, but I wish he'd have just dived after me instead. Because now, I don't even know what to do.

My beautiful gown clings to me, half ripped and completely ruined by the water. My once perfect makeup is probably now a streaky mess. Swirling amid the waves, I unzip the side of my gown before I'm dragged anymore through the rough waters and slammed into the rocks that line the cliffs. If it weren't for the balcony extending over the water, I'd probably have died, turning into a splattered mess across the surf.

Once I shimmy from my gown, I roll it up and hold it to me. Part of me wants to let it wash away with the waves, but another part of me wants to cling onto the last part of my human life.

With one more glance at the empty balcony, I swim away, heading out to sea. From here, I can find my way back to my house. It rests only a few miles down the shore. I don't know what I'm going to do—Giselle saw me. She watched in horror as I changed before her eyes. It'd be different if it was some random person who didn't know me, a person who people would laugh at for claiming to have seen something so ridiculous. But with Giselle, there's no way to talk myself out of this. I jumped off a balcony into the brewing sea.

How can we even leave now? What will happen to Giselle?

The fear is enough to propel me faster through the water. I dart through the shallows, speeding along the shoreline as fast as I possibly can.

When I reach the rocks near my house, I slow down. I swim through the waves, getting close to the shore, because if I'm too far out, I'll never be able to swim with the gown, and I refuse to let it go.

Bobbing in the surf, I close my eyes and concentrate. My tail slaps against the sandy shore, and I drift back and forth in the current. Fear holds me back from changing immediately, but the thought of not being able to explain to Giselle is enough to push me forward. I have no idea what Carter's told her, but it should be me who fixes this mess. Not him. *There's nothing to fix, Ava. It's over.*

As the thought rolls through my mind, I spot two figures emerge from my house. They stand on the patio, watching the waves, and I duck under a few times to wash the tears from my face. Carter's spark glows in the center of his chest, unfazed by his tuxedo. I assume Giselle stands behind him, but the shadows of my deck hide her from view.

My muscles tighten, the transformation grabbing hold of me. This is the easiest it's ever been to change back, because the only place I want to be is with them on land, far away from the ocean. It's what ruined my friendship and now is about to ruin my life all over again like when it stole my sister from me.

The waves push me forward until my feet find the soft sand below. I drag my gown with me, using it to cover my naked body. Carter rushes through the sand, yanking off his tuxedo jacket. Waves crash against his legs when he closes the distance, wrapping the jacket around my shoulders.

I don't make it far before my knees give out, and I fall to the sand, lying on my gown. Carter doesn't give me a chance to lie with my cheek pressed into the beach for long. He scoops me into his arms, uncaring that my sandy, wet body is about to destroy his tux.

He doesn't say anything, quietly carrying me to the back patio. Giselle stares at me with startled eyes, but she doesn't say anything either. I don't even know what she could say. All of this is probably incredibly hard for her to wrap her mind around.

Carter sets me on one of the patio chairs, looking my body up and down. "Are you hurt?"

I shake my head. "No, I missed the rocks."

He releases a long breath, pulling me against him to embrace me in a long hug. His warm breath tickles the nape of my neck, hot in comparison to the chilly night. Goosebumps prickle over my arms, and I shiver.

He turns to Giselle. "Can you grab a few towels?"

Without hesitating, she dashes inside and returns with a stack of towels. Carter takes my destroyed gown from my fingers and lays it across the patio table. Giselle absently runs her hand across the torn fabric, grazing her fingers along the pearls—half of which are missing.

My eyes turn to Carter's hard gaze. He wraps the dry towel

around me before stripping from his own wet clothes. Giselle blushes and turns to look away until Carter wraps the towel around his waist. He gathers up our clothes and folds another towel around them, and Giselle offers to take them.

After a long moment, tears escape from my eyes again. "I'm so sorry," I say, my voice barely audible over the roaring white-caps behind us. I don't say it to either Carter or Giselle specifically, because I owe them both an apology. "I didn't mean for this to happen."

Carter helps me to my feet. "It could've been a lot worse."

"I'm sorry, too, Ava. I never imagined that this—" She waves her hand at the world in general. "This wasn't what I was expecting."

I can't stop the laughter bubbling from my throat, coming out almost like a sob. "At least you know we're not murderers."

"You're a mermaid," she says, like it's finally sinking in. "I don't understand. How?"

I glance at Carter. He only shrugs in response. It's already too late to try to make up another story when she saw me.

"When Matty knocked me off the boat..." My voice trails off. How do I tell my best friend that I drowned? "Carter saved me."

"He couldn't save you without turning you into—into a— a mermaid?" Her voice rises through the air, and she shoots a glance at Carter like he's given me some incurable disease.

Carter's shoulders slump. "I would've loved to have done that, Giselle. But in my human form, swimming that distance to get to her—the ocean already took her under. I tried, but it just wasn't possible. I was already too late by the time I transformed."

Her mouth opens and closes. "I don't think I understand. Are you saying…?"

"Giselle, I drowned," I finally say.

Tears burst from her eyes like I'm actually still dead. She rushes forward, wrapping her arms around my shoulders. Shaking, she cries into my wet hair, and I rub my cold hand along her back until she calms down.

"I wasn't even supposed to allow her to return to the Ocean Jewel. I defied tradition and broke a few mer-laws. The only thing protecting us was that no one knew our secret. But now you do."

She huffs. "I swear on my life I'm not going to tell anyone."

"The same way you promised Ava you wouldn't tell everyone we had a secret in the first place?" Carter asks. I can almost see a flash of fire in his eyes as he directs his sudden anger at my best friend.

She cringes. "You're right. That was messed up of me, but I was worried."

"You should've trusted Ava."

I pull myself together and cut between them. "Just stop it. It's happened, she knows, and there's nothing we can do to change it."

"So, what now?" Giselle asks the question I'm not ready to

face, because I already know the answer to it.

"Ava and I have to leave," Carter says.

"Why? I swear I won't tell. You can trust me. For real," Giselle says.

I see her point. "I agree with Gi. Now that she knows our secret, she won't be begging for answers. If anything, she can help. She can cover for me."

Carter rubs his neck. "Ava, it's not about Giselle knowing. It's you."

My heart slides into my stomach. "Because I'm the one who transformed?"

He nods. "You're too unpredictable. This is a small town where everyone knows you. It isn't safe. Bringing you home was a mistake. It's too risky to stay."

"But where will you go?" Giselle asks.

He shrugs. "I don't know. Living on land is expensive. It's not like I can continue to work on the Ocean Jewel. I'll be accused of hurting Ava if she disappears."

The thought sends fear up my spine. "Carter, I can't just disappear. You *promised.* You promised I could keep my ties to my family."

"You don't think they'll search for you if you run away?"

I place my hands on my hips. "I'm eighteen. I can legally do what I want, and there's nothing they can do. I'm not going to just dive into the water and disappear forever. When I get better control, I can come back."

"And how exactly are you going to explain your absence?"

he argues.

I cover my face in my hands. "Who cares? They'll just be happy I'm back."

"She makes a good point," Giselle says.

He shoots a glare at Giselle. "This is between me and Ava."

She throws her hands up. "I'm only trying to help. I can't lose my BFF."

I press my hands to Carter's chest, feeling his heartbeat thrum against my palms. "Why don't we just pack a few things and stay somewhere else tonight? It'll give us a chance to think and figure things out."

"My parents own an apartment in the city," Giselle says. "We can go there."

Carter's jaw twitches as he clenches his teeth. "Giselle, it might be better if you stay here. Make sure no one saw any-thing." His voice is a lot softer now.

She wrings her hands together. "No way."

"Giselle," I say softly. This isn't just my life we're talking about. It's Carter's, too.

"Don't *Giselle* me. I know what he's thinking." She waves her hand at Carter. "The moment you two are away from me, you'll be gone."

I flick my gaze to Carter, but he doesn't disagree with her.

I puff air through my lips. "Okay, you can come, Gi. But I do have to leave. You know this, right?"

"And I'm staying with you until then. Got it?"

I wrap my arms around my best friend. "Got it. I promise I

won't leave without telling you goodbye."

She swipes the back of her hand over her cheek. "I wish you didn't have to say goodbye at all."

19

A PLAN

DARKNESS SURROUNDS ME WHEN I open my eyes. Giselle sleeps on the bed next to me, but Carter is gone from the chaise lounge. Giselle refused to leave my side, so she won the spot next to me on the bed. I guess Carter didn't want to leave my side either because instead of taking the couch bed, he curled up on the lounge.

Sitting up on my elbows, I peer through the darkened bedroom. Through the opened curtain, I can see the lights of the building next to us but no sign of the moon in the light-polluted sky. An orange streak of light cuts across the wood floors, lighting my way as I head to the door.

Carter's soft voice trickles down the hallway, and I tiptoe across the warm floor runner to eavesdrop. Peeking around the corner of the hallway, I find him perched on a barstool with his phone glued to his ear. His shoulders slump forward, and he leans his elbows on the granite counter, facing the open kitchen.

My fingers curl on the corner of the wall as I steady myself so he doesn't notice I'm here. I should feel guilty about creeping up on him, but he obviously didn't want me to hear his conversation or else he would've done it while I was awake.

"Dad, please," he says softly into the phone. "Mom can't be reasoned with. I called you because I need your guidance. Ava slipped up. I need to know what to do."

I hold my breath, willing for his dad's voice to echo through the line, but all I can hear is Carter's own breathing while he listens.

"No, you don't have to worry about the human. It was a stranger. No one will ever believe such a story."

I cover my mouth as Carter lies to his dad. For whatever reason, he doesn't want his family to know that it was my best friend who saw me. He's protecting Giselle. For that, I owe him.

"There has to be something else we can do. She won't go for it," he says.

Tears line my eyes at his desperation. He's never sounded so defeated before. It breaks my heart that this all stems to me and what I want and don't want.

"No, Dad. I'm not going to make her." He listens into the

phone a moment. "That's not true. I'm taking her side because I love her, and I think what she wants is what's best for her. You out of everyone should understand. You chose the land over the sea. We chose it, too."

I slide my back down the wall to sit on the floor. He just admitted he loved me to his dad before he's even admitted it to me. I've known all along that Carter cares for me. We have a bond that I can't even explain, connected through our hearts. This whole time I believed he went along with what I wanted because he felt bad for putting me through this. Another part of me thought it was because he loved the land as much as I do. I don't know why it's so hard to think that maybe he truly does love me. Could I love him, too? If I didn't, I'd fight a lot harder to maintain my old life. I would have to be dragged away kicking and screaming. But in this moment, all I can think about is what this is doing to Carter and how much I want him to be happy as well.

"I don't know why I bothered calling you. You might've chosen the land, but you still think like you live in the sea. Goodbye, Dad." After hanging up the phone, he rests his head on his folded arms.

I push off the floor and cross the room. He turns to look at me before I can sneak up on him, like he knew I was already here. I hug him, wrapping my arms around his shoulders. He takes my hands in his and presses them to his cheek, closing his eyes like all he wants is to feel me near him.

"Your parents don't want to help us," I say, my voice

cracking.

"I asked if we could live there for a while until we got things situated, but my mom said no. She's too wrapped up in the mer traditions. My dad stands by her decision. He said if I loved you, I'd do the right thing, but they have no idea what that even is."

"You love me," I say the words quietly, because I'm afraid he might've just said them to his dad to prove a point.

He turns his gaze to mine. "More than I could've ever imagined." He brings his fingers to my chest, where my spark glows. "It's what happens when a merman gives his life to someone—he gives his heart, too. Have you ever noticed ours beat in an identical rhythm?"

"Oh," I whisper. No wonder there's a ceremony involved in the transformation. "But what if I never drowned?"

"Ava, are you questioning whether or not what I feel is real?" he asks, a smile playing on his lips.

"I'm just thinking about where we'd be if I didn't."

He brings my hands to his lips and kisses my knuckles. "We'd have a lot more dates away from the water."

I laugh but don't say anything.

"You want the real reason I saved you? It wasn't only because I didn't want you to die. I gave you my life because I felt like we could have something together. I saw a future with you, living on the land with the girl who loved it as much as I did. And then when you went overboard, I saw it all being ripped away from me. I've never met anyone like you, Ava. That's why

I did what I did. I had hoped that one day you could love me back."

"And if I didn't?"

"It was a risk I was willing to take. I don't blame you if you can't ever love me, especially after all this."

I lean over and kiss him sweetly, brushing my lips lightly against his. "Don't be ridiculous," I say before I kiss him again. "I wouldn't be standing here with you right now if I didn't feel something for you, Carter. You know, I think a lot about my life and my future but never once was it without you in it."

We sit together on the barstool for a long while, me cradled in his lap, my head resting on the crook of his neck. The world feels so simple when we can sit and just be together. No ocean, no worry, just the sound of our hearts beating.

When the sky lightens through the window, reality sets back in. Carter wants to leave, and as much as it hurts me, I know I must go...at least for now.

"Carter, I think I know what I'm going to do about my parents," I say, drumming my fingers against his chest. "But it involves me going home. Just for a few hours. I can't leave without saying goodbye."

"A clean break is better."

"Not for me. I had plans this summer. I was supposed to move in with Giselle. We were going to start college in the fall, and my parents were going to pay for it. I'm going to ask them to give me the money for the rent instead so I can travel until school. And then when school comes around, I'm going to tell them I'm postponing and taking a gap year instead. Hopefully we'll have jobs by then, because taking a gap year wasn't on the agenda, and I doubt they'll just give us money without me being in school." It's the perfect plan to get away from here without having to worry about money for now, but also to make sure my parents know I'm alive and safe. That I'm just living my life, which is exactly what I'll be doing. Just not in the way I imagined.

"And what about Giselle?"

"What about me?" Giselle asks, yawning in the hallway.

"I need you to stay in Azure Waters. At least until the fall," I say. She opens her mouth to argue, but I raise my hand. "Please, Gi. I'd feel a lot better about leaving if I knew you would be around. Plus, you're the only one I can visit if everyone else thinks I'm traveling the country."

"Or I could just go with you."

Carter shakes his head. "You can't exactly go everywhere we do."

She sighs. "If only I could sprout a tail."

"Are you willing to risk your life for the chance? It's not always successful. Plus, you'd be stuck with whoever transforms you like Ava's stuck with me." Carter says it like he'd be willing to find Giselle a mate to do it.

She frowns. "No thanks. I have commitment issues."

It's enough to gain a laugh from Carter, which lightens the depressing mood. I slide from his lap and hug my best friend. She sniffles into my hair, and I let my tears fall onto the T-shirt she borrowed from me.

"This summer's going to suck without you, Aves," she says into my hair. "I'm going to kill Matty for this, you know. He's the reason you're in this mess."

I laugh. Even after everything, I can't be mad at Matty. It was an accident. A really, stupid, terrible accident. And if Carter really thinks we'd be together regardless, it's easy to think we just took a shortcut and bypassed all the awkward stuff.

"It's not so bad. I got over my fear of the ocean," I say. "And when I can go in it without worrying about transforming, I'll take you up on your surf lessons with Chloe."

She squeezes me once more. "You better."

Making plans with Giselle makes my leaving feel less final. It helps me hold onto hope that one day I'll be able to come home, and Carter and I can have a normal life together, acting as humans.

I'll do anything to make that happen. If it means I have to say goodbye to my life for now, then so be it.

Both of my parents sit in the kitchen, sharing a piece of leftover cake from the gala. The simple act they always do together will change when I leave. This will be the last cake they'll share that I've baked for who knows how long. At least they look like they're enjoying it.

Carter and Giselle took my car to the harbor to give Carter a chance to put in his resignation and give them Giselle's address so they can mail him his last check. I needed them to be gone so I could do this alone. I need to share one more moment with my parents that I can hold onto for a while.

"Oh, Avie. You're home," Dad says, setting his fork on his plate with a clank.

"You must be feeling much better," Mom says, a smile on her lips. "You know, you didn't have to lie to leave. I would've understood. I know how boring those events can be, and I'm the one who helps throw them."

I cover my face with my hand. "I'm sorry about that."

She pats the seat next to her. "It's okay, Ava. Carter seems like a really nice boy."

Oh, great. And now she's going to think I'm crazy with what I'm about to ask next.

I swallow the lump in my throat. "I'm glad you say that."

The rest of my words fly out of my mouth as I tell my parents about my desire to travel, and to travel immediately. I give them a thousand excuses of why I need to go. I even guilt them, telling them that I've never traveled much outside of Azure Waters. When I'm through, they both sit there with surprised expressions.

"Ava, why didn't you ever tell us this was how you felt?" Mom asks.

I shrug. "I didn't know that it was how I felt until our trip up to San Francisco. I just don't want to sit around until school starts. I want to do something, you know."

"Well," Dad says. "You are eighteen. We technically can't stop you from going. But I do have some concerns about you taking off with Carter. We don't really know him all that well."

"You want to do a background check or something?" The hint of annoyance in my voice sends my dad's eyebrows peaking on his forehead. "I like him a lot, and this whole thing is my idea. If you don't want me to go with Carter, then I'll go on my own. I just thought knowing that I was with someone would make you feel better."

My mom raises her hands. "Whoa, Ava. We didn't say no. But what kind of parents would we be if we didn't worry?"

I take a breath. "I get it. I'm sorry. It's just I like Carter, and you two should as well. He jumped off a yacht to save my life, he's been respectful toward me, and I introduced you to him the moment I got back from vacation. You need to trust that I know how to pick a boyfriend."

"You have to promise to check in all the time, okay?" Dad says.

My heart flutters with excitement. "Promise."

"Then okay. We hope you have a great time," Mom says.

"You don't know how much this means to me. Thank you!" I jump from the table and hug both of my parents. "Carter's going to be so excited. We're going to leave tonight."

"Tonight?"

Uh oh. "Yeah, there's—" I rack my brain for something, anything, to tell them before I finally say, "There's a music festival up north. I don't want to miss it. We saw flyers when we were exploring San Francisco. Giselle wants to come as well if that makes you feel any better." Giselle's going to hate me for dragging her into this, especially when she can't really go.

My parents are quiet for a long while, looking at each other. My attention draws to the window that overlooks the pool, but something beyond the wrought iron fence catches my attention. A familiar woman stands along the waves from my narrow view of the beach.

It can't be.

"Wow, that sounds like it's going to be a great time. I guess we better transfer you some money now, huh?" Mom asks.

I turn my gaze back to my parents. "You two are the best! Seriously, the best."

I hug them again and head out of the kitchen. Instead of going to my bedroom, I race to the game room. Through the glass doors, I gaze at Carter's mom standing in the surf in a two-piece bikini and a sarong. A bag hangs from her arm, and I'm pretty sure she didn't drive down here. But how did she find me?

She glances in my direction, smiling at me from her spot on the beach. Everything in me tells me to turn around and run. To find Carter and to escape. But instead, I open the door and step out onto the patio.

"Starla? What are you doing here?" I ask.

She motions me to walk closer, but I hesitate. "Please, Ava. Just hear me out. We need to talk."

20

UNREASONABLE HOPE

HUGGING MYSELF, I STROLL DOWN the beach next to Starla, staying just out of the water. All I can think about is her turning against me and dragging me away against my will. If she's dead set against me living on the land, I wouldn't put it past her.

"You're afraid of me," she says after a long moment where neither of us talks.

I flick my gaze behind me, my house growing smaller the farther away we go. "Can you blame me?"

"I know it might not feel like it, and Carter seems to believe we don't, but my husband and I do have your best interest at heart. Neither of us can imagine what you're going through—what Carter did, well, he shouldn't have done such a thing to you."

"You mean save my life?"

She reaches out and grabs my hand, pulling me to a stop. "No, of course I wouldn't wish you dead. But Carter should've taken you to the sea immediately instead of giving you unreasonable hope like he has. It was cruel."

I can't imagine what I'd have thought had he taken me to sea as a mermaid instead of allowing us to be rescued. I'd have probably flipped out and held it against him despite that he saved my life. I know I would have.

My nose crinkles. "I think your idea of cruel differs from mine. What would've been cruel is if I'd never gotten a chance to say goodbye to my family. Stealing away my right to decide what to do with my future would be cruel. Forcing a human into the ocean is cruel, Starla."

"You're not human anymore. We follow different rules. This—" She waves her hand around the land. "Living on land comes with responsibility. You might have legs, but that doesn't mean you're still the girl you were before the transformation. She died. She's not you." Starla squeezes my fingers more tightly, forcing me to face the ocean. "You can't continue this half life as you are. You need to learn our ways."

"I *am* learning. Maybe if you didn't turn your back on your son and allow us to stay with you, I could learn more."

"That is our home as much as this is yours. We can't risk

your instability." Sadness hangs in her words. "If we could, I'd gladly take you in. You're my family now."

Dating her son does not qualify as family. If anything, I'm a burden. "We're not family. My family would never turn their backs on me no matter what. I bet if I went home right now and told them I was a mermaid, they'd still accept me."

Her eyes widen. "You cannot talk like that, Ava. Not to anyone. You understand? Not only for your safety, but for your family's sake. Hasn't Carter told you anything? Just like humans have laws, so do merpeople. Our king is a kind and understanding man to a point, but when it comes to the sake of his people, he will not hesitate to snuff out the risk. You're so fortunate your accident occurred in front of a stranger. That's forgivable. But for someone who knows you, they'd face a morbid fate."

I blink, surprise washing over me. Giselle saw me transform. If anyone were to ever find out, something terrible would happen to her. I couldn't live with myself if my mistake would hurt her in any way. Just the thought leaves me sick to my stomach.

"Your kind is as cruel as the ocean that stole my sister," I say, yanking my arm from her.

"Our kind," she corrects.

Crossing my arms over my chest, I stare at her, wind tossing my hair behind me. "Either way, you don't have to worry. Carter and I are leaving Azure Waters tonight. No one will have to worry about any mistakes I make."

"You should reconsider, Ava."

"Is that why you're here?"

She nods. "I want you to come with me. I'll take you somewhere safe where you can adjust."

"But Carter prefers the land as much as I do. How could I do that to him?"

Something changes in her expression—her eyes softening as she smiles for the first time since she showed up on my beach. "You care for my son."

I frown. She says it like she's surprised. Like I'm somehow incapable of giving Carter the love he gives me. The bond might be one-sided, but when you know someone on an entire new level, it's different. Carter has opened up to me so much so that I feel like I've known him forever. I've lived his life through the memories he's shared. My attraction for him goes soul deep.

"I do, and I know we'll both be happier on land. You know as well as I do that if I went with you to wherever it is you think I need to be, Carter will follow me." My gaze shifts to the waves, and I try to imagine some underwater colony of merpeople. It's hard to even imagine. The vast ocean makes it easy to believe it's just me and Carter.

"Of course he'll follow you. He should be the one taking you in the first place. You shouldn't have to stress about whether or not you can maintain your human form. You should be able to enjoy our world. You say you love the land, but I bet you could love the sea. The Pacific colony is breathtaking. You'd be near the palace."

I can't imagine the world she speaks of. Underwater cities,

palaces—it all sounds like a fairytale. *You're a mermaid, Ava. It is a fairytale.*

"I—I'm sorry, Starla. It all sounds fascinating, but I'm not going to just go with you without talking to Carter. We already have a plan and a means to do it. He'll be here any minute for me. Maybe if our plan fails, then I'll consider it. But until then, no." I turn my back on her. She's wasted enough of my precious time trying to convince me to do something I'm against. All I want to do is run back to my house and hug my parents.

"Ava, please," she calls. "Don't make this mistake."

I dash back to my house, the sand kicking up with every step. How can the choice that makes me the happiest be a mistake? Now more than ever I want to prove his parents wrong. I want to show them I can do this. It's enough of an incentive that maybe I won't accidentally ever change again. Like Carter said, we'll swim enough that my mind will never yearn for the sea. Without having to worry about my parents and friends all the time, it'll make things possible.

When I return home, I rest my back against the glass doors, my hands trembling at my sides just imagining how much Carter's parents will be disappointed in us. They probably think I'm the worst. I've always gotten along with people's parents, but I've also never been in a situation like this where I've downright disagreed with their wishes.

It takes everything in me to move away from the door. I don't have much time. I have to pack and get things ready to go. How do I even decide what to take and what to leave?

I head upstairs to my room and take a long moment to look around. I haven't even unpacked my bag from vacation yet. Dumping out its contents into my dirty laundry basket, I shuffle to my dresser and stare at the heaps of bikinis that lie in a mess in my top drawer along with my undergarments. I have at least a dozen pieces to choose from. Instead of deciding, I scoop them all up and tuck them in the bag. I ignore my jeans and head to my closet to slide all of my sundresses off their hangers. I'm not too worried about the colder weather just yet. I can always buy more clothes later. Right now, all that matters is choosing stuff that can survive an accidental transformation. *You won't. You'll stay in control...* But if I don't, I need to be prepared.

After I pack a few necessities and change into a bikini and sundress, I sit on the edge of my bed and stare at my corkboard full of pictures. I pick out a few of my favorites and stuff them into a Ziploc bag that had held some of my beauty products to stop them from spilling.

Even with a few items missing, the room still feels like mine. It gives me the hope I need to carry to know I'll be able to come back someday. I'll always have a home here in Azure Waters no matter what happens elsewhere.

A knock sounds on my door, and I pad across my room to open it. Carter hovers in the hallway, a smile on his face when he sees me.

"I came in through the guest apartment. I'm going to assume everything went okay with your parents?" he asks, glancing at my packed belongings.

"Surprisingly well. They were a little unsure when I told them we were leaving tonight, but I told them we wanted to go to some festival in San Francisco," I whisper in case my parents are around to listen.

He frowns. "I hope they're not expecting pictures because San Francisco is the last place we'll be. My parents would never let us hear the end of it."

I shift nervously when he brings up his family. "I don't think distance will stop them. Your mom showed up on the beach. She was trying to convince me to leave with her."

His aqua eyes darken for a moment. "Of course she did. She just won't let this go."

"Maybe we should head to the East Coast," I say. "It'd take her a lot longer to interrupt our lives."

He twists his lips to the side. "I don't know if you're ready for that kind of trip, Ava."

He's right. I couldn't possibly journey to the East Coast by car. What would happen if I transformed in the middle of the desert? That'd be a disaster. And a plane? That'd be worse. It'd cause hysteria, which could be deadly in the air.

"I liked Santa Barbara," I say. "We could just slowly make our way to every beach city."

"That sounds like a good plan to me." He leans down and kisses me. "We'll plan as we go. Who knows, maybe we can even go to Hawaii."

Thinking about all the places we'll go and explore makes

leaving my family seem more like a vacation than anything. It sounds a lot more exciting than staying in Azure Waters anyway. And Hawaii? I've only ever seen the islands in pictures. My parents have gone, but the idea of flying over the vast ocean and staying somewhere surrounded by the sea was never something I wanted to do since Bailey.

"I'd like that," I say, smiling.

"So, do you think you're ready to go then?"

I kiss him. "Yeah, I think so."

"Good, because I'm ready to start this new life with you."

The sun sets on the horizon, casting its fiery glow over the sandy shores of Azure Waters. I can't believe this is my last sunset in front of the home where I spent my entire life—the life I can never get back.

As I stare out at the vast ocean, a sense of relief washes over me. Carter laces his fingers through mine, standing next to me, and I rest my head on his shoulder. In just a few minutes, we'll be getting in my car and driving up the coast. And then tomorrow, who knows where. It'll be far enough from here that we won't have to risk being known.

The back door opens, and Giselle steps out. She wraps an arm over her chest, holding her other arm and glances between me and Carter. I know she's upset I have to go, but she's being optimistic for my sake.

Her lip quivers as she smiles. "Everything's set, Aves. My mom arranged a hotel in Santa Barbara for the night and one in

San Francisco for the weekend."

"You know I owe you," I say, hugging my friend.

She blinks away tears. "I know you'd do the same for me. Plus, a night in a hotel in Santa Barbara? Amazing. I just wish I could go up to San Francisco."

I purse my lips. "You have to stay far away from there."

She bobs her head. "I know. I expect that I'll get sick and have to go home tomorrow afternoon."

Though Carter protested against her leaving Azure Waters, he understood why I did it. I had to make sure my parents didn't put up too much of a protest. I kind of didn't want to have to sleep in the ocean if they didn't agree to pay for my "road trip."

Carter turns to Giselle. "And remember, if a stranger ever asks you about us, you don't know us. Understand?"

Her eyes line with fear for a second. "Definitely. I think I'll give up talking to strangers all together for a while."

I close my eyes, tears threatening to spill on my cheeks. Starla's words about the merpeople laws and how it doesn't end well for people who discover the truth sit heavy in my chest. I wish there was a way to turn back time, but I'm just going to have to trust that Giselle will be safe. She's smart. I have faith she can keep us all out of harm's way by protecting our secret.

"Good," Carter says. "Then we should probably head out."

With one last look around, I silently say goodbye to the shores that were supposed to be my home.

21

MERMAID LIFE

SAYING GOODBYE TO MY BEST friend turns out to be a million times harder than saying goodbye to my parents. It doesn't help that Giselle knows what I'm going through and what I'm giving up. She also fears that she'll never see me again.

We sit on the small couch of her beachfront hotel room with a view of the darkened Pacific Ocean though the blinds to her patio are tightly closed. It's like Giselle doesn't want to even glance at the sea we'll soon be diving into. Until I can get better control over my transformation, we'll be swimming nightly in hopes that it'll keep me human during the day. Getting in a routine will help, Carter thinks. I just hope so.

"I'm going to miss you so much, Aves. You know the others are going to freak when they find out you left without saying goodbye." She rubs her hands over her face.

"Tell them it was spontaneous, and I promise to call all of them in a couple of days, okay?"

She bobs her head. "Okay."

My eyes water with hot tears. "And I will come back to visit."

She sniffles, a tear splashing on her cheek. "You better."

"I'll call you whenever I have a chance. We can video chat," I say.

She beams a smile through her tears. "That reminds me." Pulling her cell phone from her pocket, she pops the case off. "I want you to have this. It's waterproof up to fifty feet. I expect a ton of awesome pictures."

I laugh. "I'm pretty sure that might be against the king's rules."

"The king?" Her eyes widen.

"Crazy, right? I wish I could tell you more, Gi. But just knowing about us puts you at risk." I take the phone case and pop it onto my cell.

She crinkles her nose. "Well, I don't care about those stupid rules that keep us apart."

Carter clears his throat. "Obviously we don't either, so don't worry. We'll send lots of pictures. Just not of us."

She bounces on the couch. "And to think I thought you were bad news."

Giselle gives Carter a quick hug before turning back to me. She flings her arms around me, rocking us back and forth. Her dark hair glows almost red in the soft lighting of the lamp, and her amber eyes remind me of the land unlike Carter's blue eyes that look just like the ocean.

Carter pulls me to my feet, encompassing me in his arms for a moment. "Ready?"

I nod. "I guess so."

Giselle jumps to her feet and gives me one more hug. "Stay safe. Call me if you need anything at all. If your parents ask if I've heard from you, I'll always say yes."

I smile. "Thanks, Gi."

"Best friends forever, remember?"

"And always."

Carter takes my hand, and we stroll to the back door. He slides the glass open and cool sea air wraps around us. A shiver trails down my back as I inhale the damp, salty air. It sinks deep into my soul, and excitement courses through me the closer we get to the waves.

In the darkness away from the hotel, Carter helps me take off my dress before he strips down and puts our clothes in our bag with my cell phone so I don't lose it on the bottom of the sea. In the morning, we'll come back for my car and the rest of our stuff.

Lacing my fingers with Carter's, I pull him with me into the water, allowing the waves to crash around us for a few minutes. My hands circle his neck, and I lean up to kiss him for a long while, tasting the salt on his lips. I want to cherish this moment forever. This is where my mermaid life will truly begin. Instead of falling into the waves like so many times before, I'll be diving in willingly. I'm ready to accept that I'm now a mermaid posing as a human. This is who I am.

Carter tilts his head back, smiling at me with the soft moonlight illuminating his face. He dives in before me, dipping under the water. I spin once more, taking in the dark beach, and then I dive in after him.

Cramps seize my legs as the transformation takes hold of me. I arch my back, floating along the current, feeling the dull ache from my fins popping up from my back and arms. The tingles consume my legs, and I flip my tail, propelling me deeper into the sea.

Carter greets me with a kiss the second after I inhale a deep breath of water. He circles around me, creating a small whirlpool, and I let it catch me, sending me into his arms. Through the glowing water, his eyes shine like two beautiful gemstones. It reminds me how much I now love the sea.

"What is it, Ava?" Carter asks, his voice traveling into my mind. "You okay?"

I smile before I kiss him, bubbles still clinging to both our faces. "It's almost easy to forget the land when we're together out here."

He cups my face. "I know what you mean."

Taking my hand, he launches us forward through the deep water. The sea grass looks magical this time of night with the way my eyes adjust to the darkness. It never ceases to amaze me how active and alive it all is while the world above sleeps quietly, unaware of what truly lies beneath the waves.

Schools of red, silver, and black spotted fish dart around us, and a few bat rays glide across the bottom of the sand. Tall kelp forests reach for the night sky, shifting and moving on the currents, and I tug away from Carter and weave in and out of the green ropes. He chases after me, always right on my tail, and every so often, he swims right above me, reaching out to hold me by my waist.

I flip over and swim with my back facing the ocean floor so I can wrap my fingers around Carter's shoulders, allowing him to pull me along. My back arches when he dives deeper, me still holding onto him. My hair floats in my face, creating a veil between us. He only stops when we're deep enough that the glow of the moon barely shines above us. My body adjusts to the cooler water and heat crawls over my skin.

He touches his fingers to my chin, guiding my head to peer up, and a white shark, longer than Carter is, swims with such precision and grace. I can't help but admire the beauty of the beast people fear.

"She's magnificent," I say, watching the shark push through the current to wherever she's heading. "You sure she won't bother us?"

He shakes his head. "You have to be more careful of the playful animals like the sea lions and dolphins. Some whales, too. They think they're guppies when their tails could knock us all the way to Hawaii."

I grin, remembering my terrifying swim with the dolphins who just wanted me to have as much fun as they were having.

"I'd like to go there someday," I say, my voice echoing through my mind. "Grand Cayman, Tahiti, Jamaica, too. I want to see the ocean from different shores."

He smirks. "One day I'd love to take you. We'll practice your long distance swimming. You'll have to be brave enough to try the fish, too. Can't exactly order a pizza down here."

I grimace, and Carter laughs. I'd stick to the land for the food alone. I haven't tried his version of sushi yet, and I'm not exactly interested in doing so. I can't help it that I think all the fish are so cute as they bolt around me. I feel like I'm visiting an underwater aquarium and not an all-you-can eat seafood buffet.

"It's not bad, I promise," he says, smiling. "It's no dessert, but I'm sure I can find something you like."

Ugh. "I'm not ready," I say. "Can we start with a sushi restaurant on land?"

He kisses me. "You're the only mermaid in the world who was afraid of the ocean and displeased by the meal options."

"I guess that means we can never leave the land," I say, smiling.

"And we won't."

He swims around me once, smiling, but then suddenly his smile fades. A strange shadow casts over us, and my heart nearly stops when I see the silhouette of another mermaid swimming above us.

And then I see another and another.

Carter's eyes widen as he charges toward me, sliding his arms around my waist and flies through the water faster than I've ever seen. His heartbeat races against my back. I half swim and he half drags me in the direction we came.

"What's wrong?" I cry, my voice echoing loudly through my mind.

"You don't hear them? They're calling us," Carter says, worry in his voice.

But I don't hear anything but my own panic screaming in my ears. Whoever is calling us has Carter fleeing through the ocean. I can't help but think we might be in trouble—or danger.

"Ava, listen to me," Carter says in my mind. "I need you to transform when we hit the kelp paddies. I'm going to propel you as far as I can through the waves, and then I need you to run, okay?"

What? From who? Doesn't running make us look like criminals if we're in trouble? I'm not even sure I could transform back as quickly as he wants me to. What happens if I can't? Fear grips at me, twisting knots in my stomach.

"What about you?" I ask, panic in my thoughts.

"I'll be right behind you, okay?"

"Okay." My voice barely whispers in my mind. I'm not so sure I even thought it.

The ocean blurs around us. Carter swims along the ocean floor, weaving in and out of any animals that get in our way. I blink through my blurry eyes, concentrating on keeping myself together when fear threatens to tear me apart. This was supposed to be our first night of freedom. The first night of our adventure learning how to find balance between life on land and the sea.

And now, I can hear the voices. They sneak through the water, slinking into my mind like invaders.

"Don't make this hard on yourself," a masculine voice says, louder than my own thoughts. I hate it. I despise the sound more than anything. Carter's voice is the only one I've ever heard in my head, and I want to push this stranger's voice from my mind.

"We're not going to hurt you, Ava," a feminine voice says, knowing my name.

"Be reasonable, Carter," another feminine voice says, one so familiar it sends a shiver down my spine. It's Carter's mom. She's come looking for us, and this time she has others with her.

Carter ignores the voices like I do and swims as fast as he can, practically dragging me like a rag doll. Every time I flick my tail, all it does is slow us down. So instead, I relax. The sea brightens the closer we get to shore, the moon's light shining through, making the tiny bubbles sparkle through the water.

"Get ready," Carter says into my mind. "The kelp forest is up ahead. You'll have only a minute."

Closing my eyes, I prepare for the transformation by clearing my mind. If I fail, the other merpeople will catch us. They won't allow me to return to land. I know it. As much as I thought I could accept my life as a mermaid, knowing they're going to try to steal my ability to live on land makes me want to enter the beach and never look at the ocean again. I can't let them catch me. I can't let that happen. I won't.

"Do it now, Ava!" Carter shouts in my mind.

I squeeze my eyes shut, willing my human form to take over to help me leave the water. My stomach tightens, and nerves rush over me when nothing happens. My own inability to consistently change will prove Starla right. If I fail, it'll be my own fault. And I'll end up dragging Carter into the deep with me. *Come on! Transform!*

The thought of failing Carter kicks my body into action and cramps pulse over me. My hair flies behind me as Carter propels us through the current, and then the comfortable water turns icy. He picks up speed without the weight of my tail slowing us down and ascends toward the surface so I can take a breath of air to clear my lungs of the ocean water.

My head breaks the surface, and Carter throws me as far as he can toward the shore. Flying through the air, I get a head start over Carter. The whitecaps swell up to catch me, and I hold my breath, landing in a cresting wave that pushes me forward to the shore.

I kick my legs, swimming as fast as I can through the night-rough waters. It feels like every time I get ahead, a wave gets pulled back to the sea, dragging me with it. Exhaustion slows me down but determination keeps my head above water.

"Hurry, Ava!" Carter calls from behind me. "Head toward

the hotel. They won't follow if it'll draw attention."

Another wave knocks me forward into water shallow enough that I can kick against the sand to push me forward. Saltwater stings my eyes, and my hair clumps to my cheeks. Seawater sprays my face as I fight through the waves, but the shore's so close that I'll be on land with the next wave.

A figure pops up next to me, startling me, and I scream out. When I see it's Carter, I take a heaving breath. He tugs me faster through the surf until we crash onto the shore together. I barely have time to find my footing before he jerks me forward.

I fall to my knees, tripping over my weak legs. Voices sound out over the waves, no longer in my head, and I turn to glimpse behind us to see a man only feet away. He launches forward, landing close enough to me to grab onto my ankle. I wail, thrashing to get out of his grip.

Carter yanks me by my wrists, sending pain through my arms, but it's enough to get the man to let go of me.

As I turn to show my relief to Carter, a woman charges him, knocking him right off his feet with a strength that seems impossible for her petite frame. He tumbles through the sand in front of me, landing on his stomach. I stand frozen, watching as she presses his face into the sand. If my heart wasn't threatening to escape me, I'd blush at the sight of these naked strangers. I'm sure it'd be an eyeful for anyone to see.

"Ava, run!" he yells, thrusting the woman off him and back into the surf.

But I never get the chance.

Strong hands wrap around my shoulders, pulling me toward the waves. I scream as loud as I can, the heat of a naked body pressing into my back. If we attract attention, they might leave. But my scream only goes so far. A swell engulfs me, hitting me in the face. I choke and spit on saltwater as the man shoves my face underwater. Twisting in his slippery arms, I elbow him in the ribs, taking the moment to jet forward, but then another hand grabs me by the wrist.

"Mom, don't!" Carter yells. "Please, don't do this."

I flick my gaze to Carter standing helplessly on the shore. Another wave drags me farther away from him, away from the life we were trying to manage together. With me in the grip of his mom, no one bothers him or tries to force him to come after me. Hopelessness settles on my soul.

From behind him, my eyes dart to Giselle's hotel room, the one I was hoping to reach, and the blinds shift as she peers at us from within her room. As much as I want to call out for my best friend to get help, I can't. All I can do is watch her watch me with horror in her eyes.

Seeing her gives me the strength to keep fighting, to do anything I possibly can to get away. Swinging my arm out, I smack Starla in the shoulder. Her nails dig deeper into the skin of my wrist, and someone else grabs me from behind, holding me in place.

"Just let me go," I cry, thrashing. But it's no use. I'm outnumbered.

"Ava, calm down before you hurt yourself. I'm not your

enemy," Starla says. "I'm saving you."

But she's not. She's destroying me, destroying my world. Digging her fingers into my palms, she pries at my hand. My knuckles crack, and I'm pretty sure she's willing to break my hand to force my fingers to open. The pain in my hand is enough that she doesn't have to. My fingers relent, automatically spreading open, and she slides the sea stone ring off my finger.

Everyone lets go of me, putting distance between us as I spin, screaming. They're already too far away for me to try to steal my ring back.

"No!" Carter yells, rushing closer to me.

But there's no point. It's too late. I've lost the one thing that offered me a second chance at living my human life. Without the ring, I'll be anchored to the ocean by my mermaid form. In a matter of minutes, my entire human world slips through my fingers like the sand slips through the waves to sink to the bottom of the ocean.

Covering my face, I sob into my hands, grief stealing my breath away from me.

A soft hand touches my shoulder. "You're going to be okay, Ava. You'll be happy, I promise," Starla says like she could possibly make this better with soft words after she basically broke me into pieces.

But I don't think I'll ever be happy again. Not unless I can have a piece of the human world.

My grief turns into pain, spasms pulsing through me because of the forced transformation. I groan, sinking deeper and deeper into the waves, my mermaid form pushing me into the sea against my will with nothing I can do to stop it.

Starla tries to touch me again, encouraging me to submit to the sea to take a breath. "Stop resisting. It's just making it worse. Let me help you."

"I hate you!" I scream.

Starla blocks my view of the others with her, including Carter. They're purposely keeping us apart. "I'm doing the right thing, Ava. One day, you'll understand," she says calmly, standing strong in her convictions.

"How is destroying my life the right thing?" I ask, my chest burning. The moment I go under completely, I'm afraid I'll never see the shore again.

"Ava, please," she pleads.

"Just get away! Don't touch me!"

I flail away from her, flicking my tail to propel me forward. She might've forced me to transform, but I refuse to let her control me. I'll stay on the shore near home. I'll stay anywhere that she isn't.

I don't get far before the merman flanks my side. His long brown hair floats around his face as he looks at me with pitiful dark eyes, like he feels sorry for what he's done. But his sympathy won't return my ring to me. It won't let me have a life on land. All it does is make me hate him, too.

When the merman relaxes, thinking I'll willingly go with him, I dive down and circle back toward shore, fleeing from him. I don't care if I don't have my ring. I'll figure out how to change. I'll will myself to do it. I can't just go away with these merpeople. I can't just give up.

I swim right into Carter's chest. His arms circle around me, and he buries his face into the nook of my neck.

"I'm so sorry, Ava," he whispers into my mind. "You can't go back."

My lip quivers as I stare into his ocean blue eyes. "My family. I can't leave them. They'll freak out."

He squeezes me tighter. "Please, forgive me. I swear we'll figure it all out, okay?"

"But—"

"Please, Aves. The more you fight, the more trapped you'll be. I have no influence where we're going. You have to try to be strong. We'll get through this."

But I'm not so sure. Even though I'm breathing in the water, I feel like I'm drowning. I'm drowning in all of the lost possibilities. I can't even force myself to feel an ounce of hope. The sea took my life like it took my sister's. The ocean won.

"I don't know if I can," I whisper in his mind.

"Please try."

I sink against him, feeling his heartbeat against mine. It takes everything in me not to break down and sink to the depths of the ocean—to disappear. I don't even bother to swim. Carter cradles me in his arms as he's forced to follow his mom by the other merman.

After a while, the water shifts around us, a magical light

cutting through the darkness of my closed lids. I don't look around though. I can't. If I open my eyes, this becomes real. And I can't have that.

"Welcome home, son," a masculine voice says, cutting through my mind though it's directed at Carter. A soft hand touches my shoulder, but I still refuse to look. "Welcome to Pearlestria, Ava," Mateo says to me. "Welcome to your new home."

I slowly lift my head and glare through my blurry eyes. "This is not my home. You dragged me away from my home. This—" I wave my hand at the water around me. "This is my prison within the sea."

❧EPILOGUE❧

ROUGH WATERS

THE CLEAR OCEAN WATER SPARKLES outside the look-out from my underwater room made from a mixture of stone and strange, colorful glass. The walls shine with a pearlescent glow like I'm inside a person-sized seashell.

The small city beyond, Pearlestria, bustles with the life I never could imagine. The merpeople colony, which surrounds a massive underwater castle made from the same magical stone that gives my room its pretty sheen, is protected by some unexplainable shield that prevents humans from ever discovering us.

The last few days have been pure torture. I can't go anywhere without being escorted, so I don't leave the small house—if that's what you can even call it. The enclosed space could fit in the guest apartment above my garage back home. *Home...*

Not a second passes that I don't think about the world

above me, the world just out of my reach. The world I can't be a part of because I broke the laws. I transformed in front of a human, and because of that, regardless if it was a mistake or not, has given Starla reason to steal my ring away. She claims it wasn't her decision, but King Attilonious', yet it doesn't stop me from placing blame on her. It's her fault I'm here. She could've left well enough alone. And for that, I won't even talk to her. I hate that she's decided to stay in Pearlestria with me at all, leaving her husband on the land.

Pulling myself away from the window, I sink down to the soft sand on the floor. The room is mostly bare apart from a small bed made of sea grass, a few empty shells I've piled in the corner, and a pesky little butterfly fish that has made its home in the reef along the wall under my lookout.

I lie flat on the ground, kicking up sand as I lift and drop my caudal fin. The ceiling above me sparkles with pretty blue and yellow rocks in a pattern that looks like the sun in the sky. If only I could break the surface, but it's not allowed yet. I'm not trustworthy enough.

"I've brought you something to eat," Starla says, swimming into my small room. She holds a netted bag with what looks like oysters above my head.

I turn my eyes away before shifting onto my side. I don't respond, and she settles down next to me and cracks open the shell with her sharp nail. Pieces of the innards float in my direction as she slurps down the meat. I flick my hand, waving the pieces away. I want to yell at her to get out, to stop ruining my sanctuary with things I refuse to eat.

"Come on, Ava. You should at least try them. I know this is hard, but your stubbornness is just making things harder. You can't be comfortable so hungry. It's been days." She touches my arm, and I pull away.

Luckily for me, as a mermaid I don't have to eat like I did as a human. I could go a few weeks without eating if I wanted to, though she's right about being uncomfortable from hunger.

"If you don't want to eat, let me take you somewhere. How can you learn to love Pearlestria if you've made this house into your prison? There are so many merpeople who'd love to meet you. It's not very often to have a human-born among us." Her voice drifts softly through my mind.

But I still refuse to talk to her. If I ignore her long enough, she'll give up. And if I were going to talk to her, I'd tell her to leave me alone and go enjoy the life she chose for herself on land—the place I'd give anything to be.

"They want to celebrate your life," she continues. "Remember the ceremony I told you about? The one to welcome you? I'd like to start planning it. It's important for Carter too, you know? He has the only mate in the ocean who refuses to make it official. Do you know how sad you're making him by acting like it's the end of the world?" Her voice grows angry in my head.

It takes me biting my tongue to stop myself from retorting.

"You're being so selfish and—"

"Mom," Carter says from the archway that leads to the just

as boring living area. "Leave Ava alone, please. You're not help-ing her any. Why don't you go visit Dad so I can have some privacy with her. You've been smothering us both."

"But—"

"You know we can't run away. Please, just give us some space."

Starla flips her beautiful pink tail, propelling away from me. She hugs her son once before disappearing without another word. My eyes linger on the archway, expecting her to change her mind and come back.

But she doesn't.

Carter swims forward and settles down next to me, sliding his arms around me until I'm nestled against him, my tail rest-ing across his. I press my cheek to his chest, trying to remember the scent of what he smelled like as a human—like sunscreen and the sea—but I smell nothing at all.

"I'm sorry about my mom, Ava. I know she can be over-bearing," he says, brushing the floating strands of hair from my face.

"She accused me of destroying your happiness because I'm depressed," I say.

His lips turn downward. "You know that's not true. I'm unhappy because of what they did to us."

"She thinks I'm embarrassing you."

"Are not. You never could. The only one embarrassing me is her."

He brushes his fingers along my quivering lip before he

kisses me. His soft lips taste of something familiar, something sweet, and I pull away and tilt my head to look at him. He grins as I study him, like he's hiding some exciting secret from me.

"You taste like home," I say.

He sucks in his bottom lip. "I surfaced."

I close my eyes, horribly grief-stricken that he got to feel the sun on his skin without me. Unlike me, Carter doesn't get to sit in a room and do nothing all day. He must help out in the colony doing whatever it is he does.

He frowns, rushing to tug the bag off his shoulder. "Wait, wait. I brought you some things."

The sadness gripping my heart slides away at his words. "You can do that?"

He nods. "I had to wait for the chance, but I finally got it today."

He unlocks his waterproof bag, and I realize all the contents within it are in plastic Ziplocs. He holds out a baggie of cut fruit and another with a lettuce wrap. I don't even care that the saltwater messes up the flavor of the apple slices. I didn't realize how hungry I was until I chewed and swallowed.

"I can't believe you brought these," I say, my voice projecting to Carter while I continue to shove the pieces of fruit into my mouth without slowing down.

"I couldn't let you starve, Ava."

I smirk. "You know I would've eventually eaten."

"That's what my mom said, but what kind of boyfriend would I be if I didn't try to make you as happy as I possibly could?" He pulls out another Ziploc from the bag. "I also picked up the pictures you took from home."

My heart soars when I see the stack of pictures within the Ziploc. In a separate baggie is a postcard in familiar handwriting. *Giselle...*

"You saw her?" I almost don't believe it.

"She found our bag with your phone on the beach by the room and has been pretending to be you to your parents. She'll keep the charade up as long as she can."

"So, there's still hope?" I ask. I almost don't believe it. "I can go home?"

"I'm going to do everything I can, but you're going to have to do some things as well."

My brows scrunch together. "Like what?"

"You're going to have to pretend you've come to terms with your mermaid life."

"Is that all? I think I can handle faking it."

"We'll get out of here, Ava. I promise."

I hug him again. I haven't been so hopeful since I left home. Carter hugs me for a long moment before I finally bring my gaze to the postcard from Giselle. It's a picture of the harbor of Azure Waters with the Ocean Jewel among the boats.

Ava,

The sea seems so cruel now that it's taken you. Be strong and fight the current. The waters might be rough now, but they're no match for the girl who survived the waves twice. I love you, Aves. I know we'll see each other again soon. I'll head to sea if I have to. I'll figure out a way. Be safe and don't get into any trouble. I'd like you back with your legs one day, because no one would believe me that my best friend's a mermaid. What would I tell my kids?

Until the sea washes you back to shore, I'll be waiting.

Love,

Gi

Tugging the postcard from its protective bag, I let the water erase the ink of my best friend's words. I can't risk anyone seeing this and hunting Giselle down to destroy another part of my life. But her words sit heavy in my heart. She has faith that I'll return to her.

I slide my fingers through Carter's. "Thank you. For everything."

He kisses me on the lips, sending a dozen memories and thoughts into my mind—of Azure Waters, of Giselle, of me strolling along the beach. He imagines kissing me on the sand, running his fingers along my human legs, the thought so vivid I can almost feel the heat of the sun on my skin. And he imagines a future that had felt lost to me.

But not all is lost.

The ocean can't imprison me forever. I won't let it.

TO BE CONTINUED...

ACKNOWLEDGMENTS

NONE OF THIS WOULD HAVE been possible if it weren't for my talented team and all their amazing skills and support they so awesomely share with me. Thanks to Jan Moran, Jamie Hall, Katie Harder-Schauer, Sarah Collier, and Amy Holliday. Without you, I'd be a mess.

A huge thanks to Nikki Godwin for helping me with my blurb, for always being a listening ear, and for letting me share with you all the things I find amusing on Snapchat.

Thanks to Jazmin Garcia, my BFF and one of my biggest fans, for the never-ending encouragement, for letting me send you tid-bits as I write, for investing in me, and especially for the mermaid blanket to inspire me along the way. Much love!

A heartfelt thanks to all the bloggers and readers who show such wonderful support to the indie book community. You've made this whole experience incredible.

As always, thanks to my family, who are too many to name, and a special thanks to my mom and stepdad, who were the first readers of this book. Your words of encouragement always get me through the tough times.

Lastly, I just want to give and shout out and thank all the remarkable professional mermaids in the world. You've really helped inspire this novel. You've also made my Instagram feed the most magical thing ever. XOXO!

ABOUT GINNA MORAN

GINNA MORAN IS a writer from sunny Southern California. She started writing poetry as a teenager in a spiral notebook that she still has tucked away on her desk today. Her love of writing grew after she graduated high school, and she completed her first unpublished manuscript at age eighteen.

When she realized her love of writing was her life's passion, she studied literature at Mira Costa College in Northern San Diego. Besides writing novels, she was senior editor, content manager, and image coordinator for Crescent House Publishing Inc. for four years.

Aside from Ginna's professional life, she enjoys binge watching television shows, playing pretend with her daughter, and cuddling with her dogs. Some of her favorite things include chocolate, anything that glitters, cheesy jokes, and organizing her bookshelf.

Ginna Moran loves to hear from her readers so visit her online at www.GinnaMoran.com. You can also find her on Facebook, Twitter, Instagram, and Snapchat (@GinnaMoran). To stay up-to-date on new releases, sign up to her newsletter. You'll not only get a FREE story, but you'll be able to participate in monthly giveaways!

Ginna Moran is currently hard at work on her next novel.

Other Young Adult Novels by Ginna Moran

PARANORMAL

Destined for Dreams Series
Demon Within Series
Finding Nate Series
Going Ghostly Series
Spark of Life Series
When Souls Collide Series
Demon Watcher Series

CONTEMPORARY

Falling into Fame Series

STANDALONES

Life After Lila

www.ingramcontent.com/pod-product-compliance
Lightning Source LLC
Chambersburg PA
CBHW051650180726
48284CB00006B/1940